THE
Savage
RAGE
OF
Fallen
GODS

NEW YORK TIMES BESTSELLING AUTHOR

JA HUSS WRITING AS

KC Cross

SAVAGE FALLS BOOK 1

ABOUT THE BOOK

Welcome to Savage Falls, where the men have horns, doors have agendas, and the God of Love will never fall in love. Hate is his soulmate. His soulmate is hate.

Love. When mutual, it's Heaven on Earth. When one-sided, it can tear you apart.

There is no greater weapon than the heartsick soul. That is the power I wield, for I am the God of Love. No one has power like me. No one can poison a heart and pollute a mind the way I can. That is why the gods kicked me out. That is why they made me fall.

But then a door appears on the side of my hill. The opportunity to ruin kings and destroy gods is mine once more. I can crush the whole wicked world if I can just get back the power I lost.

But this magic of mine requires sacrifice.

And now, I have to decide… am I willing to pay the price?

Savage Rage of Fallen Gods is a story of a broken man. It is a tale of regret, promises, and how revenge can darken a god's soul. It is a new start of a spinoff series by *New York Times* bestselling author, JA Huss, writing as KC Cross.

CHAPTER ONE - EROS

There is a point in a man's life where he just has to face facts. Reality check, if you will. When all the senseless self-reflection is over and it's no longer useful to deny the truth.

I'm at this point, standing on the roof of my bar and looking out at the sleepy little town of Savage Falls. My kingdom. The one space where I am allowed to live—if that's what I'm doing—and be in control.

In past times Savage Falls used to live in a sort of tandem with Granite Springs, Pennsylvania, which resides fully and completely in the human realm. At least it *did*. I could see through the veil of fog on occasion, and with some magiceutical effort, I could even travel across it every now and then. But for the most part Savage Falls existed in a state of in-between. A stasis, if you will. Or, in my opinion, a stagnation.

But things have changed over the weeks and months since the Saint Mark's Sanctuary curse ended. For one, Granite Springs and Savage Falls have merged. The straddling of worlds is over and now both places exist in the same stagnation.

Which does nothing for me, if I'm being completely honest. And that's the point here. Reality check.

It's early morning. The sunrise is probably a couple hours away but there are still a few monsters roaming the streets down below. Drunk, most likely, as monsters are wont to be if left to their own devices. I have no interest in reining them in, so their own devices will have to suffice. I like them here only because they fill the place up.

It is less lonely than it could be.

But the state of being alone is a funny thing. Because it doesn't actually require the absence of others. I've learned, over the course of thousands of years, that you can be completely singular while in the company of the masses.

I don't know exactly how long I've been here in Savage Falls because time runs a little funny on this side of things. This town was once a village. Was once a camp. Was once a forest and an ancient city. Savage Falls has been many things over the course of time, which goes faster, or slower, or something in between every now and then depending on outside influences.

But I can point out the event that started this current curse cycle that I am now in the middle of. It happened nearly twenty years ago on the day I stole a little gryphon chimera lion*ess* called Pie right out from under the noses of the succession gods and sent her to live a lie in the Realm of Pennsylvania as a human.

She was six years old and had been gifted magic that

day by the ancient god, Ptah. It was very big, powerful magic in the form of rings that could open doors to other worlds. And, see, doors are what I need. Doors go places and all you need is a *key*. You don't need to come up with elaborate spellings or procure rare magiceuticals that must be mixed just so in order to coax out transformative properties which can be then applied for life-altering change.

No. None of that is necessary. You just use your key to open the door and then you walk through to a brand-new life waiting on the other side.

Unfortunately, my plans were thwarted. Moves and countermoves, as they say. But the interesting part about this thwarting is that there is no way to pinpoint where it falls on the timeline. Twenty years ago is the recent past, in my opinion. But in other worlds—or specifically the world this thwarting took place in—it was the ancient past, not the recent.

Time. It's variable.

And so the plot thickens.

Empty promises.

Betrayals all around.

But isn't everything always about betrayal?

I could've found more magic in that girl, Pie, but it would've taken considerable effort, so I retreated.

Live to fight another day, as they say.

And here I am. Standing on my roof, looking out at my town, alone.

Singular. Solitary. Apart. Isolated. *Separate*.

And trying to come to terms with things. Doing my best, at least.

Reality check.

The wind passes over me, cooling the hot night and making the membranes on my giant bat wings shudder. They droop low now because they are so heavy, the tips almost dragging on the ground. They are not much good for flying, but they get the job done in a pinch. Mostly, they are attached to me as a reminder of what I've lost.

Which is much more than feathers.

I am the god of love.

I am immortal.

I wield the power of both obsession and indifference.

But I will never be anything more than alone.

Hate is my soulmate.

My soulmate is hate.

CALLISTINA IS ALREADY *in my bed* when I enter the bedroom of the little apartment above the bar. She's naked on top of the sheet and stretched out in a pose reminiscent of a cat, which makes sense because in her other life, before the cursed one she was thrust into here, she was a gryphon chimera. A lion*ess*. Pie's big sister, to be exact. A royal beast from the House of Fire. First Daughter, in her case. Not Second, like little Pie.

The birth order makes a difference. Second Daughters are much more desirable. But still, Callistina is a very important lion*ess*. She is the Queen of Vinca.

Or she was. Now she's just a has-been. A fadeaway, like the rest of us. Someone who was important once, but has been stripped of power for bad behavior.

She is human. A sad, pathetic race of magicless creatures that are as ordinary as ordinary comes.

She made it pretty far in her other life though. I mean, being Queen of Vinca is quite a thing.

Not as good as being the god of love, but ordinary or not, she is the highest-ranking monster in this town. It would've been nice to have access to the monster side of her. Fur on females can be quite attractive if properly groomed. Callistina's was a nice short velvet that covered her whole body. And just looking at it made you want to touch it with your fingertips.

I feel like I got a consolation prize with her in this form.

Still, she's a nice-enough-looking human. Tall and willowy in the arms, like a dancer, but curvy in the hips and breasts, like a stripper. She's got a sweet face— genetics, obviously, since she's a complete bitch—and the long, golden hair certainly doesn't hurt.

But Callistina, former Queen of Vinca, is insane.

That's not an exaggeration, nor am I being hyperbolic. It's just a fact.

At nearly all times of the day the former Queen of Vinca is wearing a giant rack of antlers on her head that have been badly spray-painted gold, a mangy leopard-skin coat, and blocks of wood on her feet to simulate hooves.

Which, as a gryphon chimera, she never had. So I haven't yet worked out just how the wooden blocks fit in.

She carries around a broken broom handle like it's a scepter and constantly bangs it on the floor demanding that people call her 'queen.'

That's only during the day though.

At night she takes all that shit off and goes naked, as she is right now. And I cannot deny that when I see her stripped of all her madness, I am turned on.

I, myself—or Himself, as they sometimes call me (because I am so full of myself)—am only wearing a pair of jeans and some boots. I like shirts as much as the next guy. And I *love* leather jackets. Especially mine. Especially these days, since I'm top dog here and I treat the whole gang of monsters like a motorcycle gang. I offer up patches to get shit done around the place. Like Boy Scout badges, but better. Because they often have titties on them.

This is how I motivate the monsters and eros chimera alike.

It's visually... *cool*, ya know? To wear the cuts and sew the patches on. One cannot dismiss the value of production quality. We even have a rocker for the back of the jackets and vests. And rankings and everything. We are called the Savage Springs chapter, a little homage to Savage Falls and Granite Springs combining in order to facilitate some kumbaya bullshit.

I, of course, am the founder and the president. Plus I

have a nickname—Himself—and my personal philosophy in the form of numbers. Eleven-eleven, written one-one-semi-colon-one-one. Which is actually a Bible verse. *Behold, I will bring evil upon them, which they shall not be able to escape; and though they shall cry unto me, I will not hearken unto them.*

Powerful shit, if you ask me. I like to let people know where they stand and 11:11 gets the job done. The evil I'm planning is inevitable and though they might beg, there will be no mercy.

But shirts and jackets are such a pain in the ass when you've got wings. More often than not, I just opt out.

All of the aforementioned is just a roundabout way of getting to the point. And the point is, I don't have much to take off to get naked and slip into bed next to Callistina.

Even though I do not like her, I do enjoy sleeping with her.

And by sleeping, I mean fucking.

One arm immediately slides around her waist and I tug her towards me. She's warm, and soft, and nice, actually. A 'ten,' as they say. I might be cursed, and unloved, and unable to love—but she doesn't care about any of that. She doesn't care about anything, actually. Aside from the insane idea that dressing up like a gryphon chimera will turn her back into one, she floats through her new, cursed life mostly unaffected. The 'call me queen' thing gets on my nerves a little, but she moans at *alllll* the right times, and arches her back in *juuuust* the right way, and doesn't ask for a single thing. Nothing. She wants nothing from me.

It's not just nice, it's satisfying.

I lean into her neck and she stirs a little, still half asleep. When I kiss the tender skin just below her ear, she sucks in a breath and lifts her chin up. When my hand slides over her hip and slips between her legs, she whimpers a little.

Callistina's eyes are closed. I know this because she doesn't ever open her eyes when we fuck. She doesn't want to look at me. I am Eros, after all. And the sight of me is intoxicating.

It's just a side effect of who and what I am.

She can control her infatuation when she's fully awake and dressed up as the folly queen, but in the middle of the night and stripped of her costume, she's vulnerable.

I give no fucks if she wants to look at me. I don't even care if she's pretending I'm someone else.

It's just fucking and we both know this.

I slowly push a finger up inside her and she gasps. But she doesn't ever tell me to stop. She lets me get her off—which I always do first—and then she climbs in my lap, eyes still firmly closed as she pushes her tits into my face and fucks me until I'm spent.

It happens like this every night. Every time.

And tonight is no different. I finger her for a few minutes, she gushes all over me as she comes, and then I sit up, she climbs in my lap, and we fuck 'till we're spent.

This is how I end every day.

And I'm starting to get tired of it.

All of it.

Which brings me back to my point about the reality check. A man—even one who is a god—needs to come to terms with things eventually. And this eventuality is starting to hit me.

This town has no location on a map.

I cannot leave, I cannot move forward, I cannot do anything but exist in my current state.

And this is not enough for me.

CHAPTER TWO - CALLISTINA

J **wake with the sun**, as queens do, and leave the bed I share with the god of love. He sleeps until noon, which is really the only thing I like about him.

Well, the sex isn't bad, either. And the night is a precarious time for me. It's when the veil of illusion is thin and see-through. The sun makes everything better.

In order to get out of the bed I have to slither out from underneath Eros's possessive arm and slide my body over until I can swing a leg out.

Every time I do this, I hold my breath, wondering if this will be the one time I wake him.

But it's a needless worry. He never does wake.

When I'm free from his bed I go into the bathroom and start a tub. It's not a very grand tub—in fact nothing in this town is very grand—but I've gotten used to the dingy, shallow basin and have decided to make the most of it.

There could be no washtub at all. I could be forced

to take, God forbid, *showers*. Like a common peasant. Besides, the dragon-girl at the feed store cooks up soaps and lotions. And she gifts me a bubble bath scented with rose hips and lavender every time I wander in there.

It might be, quite simply, the most divinely scented concoction I've smelled in my entire life. And I come from a palace.

This one small addition to my bath routine has elevated the experience to a level that is comparable to a Fireday Saturnalias. In fact, I think the rose hips and lavender bath is better than the sex with the god of love himself.

It's so strange and so disproportionate—I mean, sex? It's definitely one of the more enjoyable moments in life —but it's so disproportionate that I start to wonder if the dragon-girl is putting magic into those bubbles.

She could be. She *is* a dragon. But it's a recessive trait that has mostly gone away since that dragon-man left her alone and retreated to... whatever hovel he's living in these days.

Still, the girl—Madeline, her name is—must have some alchemist lineage.

I myself have alchemist lineage. As First Daughter of Saturn and the great alchemist, Ostanes, it was my fate to be groomed to be one of the best alchemists in all the realms.

But I cannot make rose hips and lavender smell like *this*.

I love it so much I fill up my palm and hold the viscous liquid under the rushing water *twice*! Two fist-

12

fuls! It makes a spectacular cloud of bubbles that hides all the dreary, dingy parts of the too-small basin.

And thus, this is how I start the daily delusion.

Imagining myself in the royal bathroom just off my royal chambers with all my attendants in attendance. Waiting on me hand and foot. Scrubbing me, and washing my hair, and carefully drying me off with fluffy things. Then dressing me in fabulous gowns made by the royal tailors.

I close my eyes as I bathe. Picturing all this. Picturing my old life.

It's a fantasy. I know this.

But it's still better to live in the fantasy than admit that it's all gone.

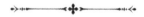

WHEN I'M DONE BATHING, I get out and dress myself. I pick up articles of clothing from the various shops around town. Today I am wearing an electric-blue dress with poufy sleeves. The girl at the shop said it was a prom dress, but I don't know what that is. I was just in the mood for blue when I picked it up. Blue the color of the electricity that used to spit and crackle inside the glass globes that dotted the palace hallways in the night.

I have a pair of green shoes but you can't see them, as the dress was tailored for an Amazon and I am quite dainty as a human. It drags on the floor as I walk. And since I have worn the prom dress dozens of times, the hem is torn and ripped and discolored from the muddy roads.

I affix my golden antlers to the top of my head next. Having twenty-two points makes them quite heavy and so I have to tie the leather string under my chin, which holds them in place very tight. Tight enough that I've developed a callus there.

Next come the blocks of wood. In my real life I had paws for feet, but my imagination was not resourceful enough to come up with a way to simulate paws, and so I must settle for hooves. Or blocks of wood, as it is.

Finally, I put on the fur coat. It was the only fur in town—I looked everywhere. Stealing into houses at night, checking closets. I scoured every shop and, indeed, this was the only one. It's leopard. Real leopard. But it's also a hundred and twenty years old. I found it inside a trunk in the attic of an abandoned house. I know it's real because it came with papers and photographs of some man on safari a long, long time ago. It's moth-eaten and missing large patches of hair along the insides of the arms and... well, pretty much everywhere. It's basically a skin at this point.

But one works with what one has. And this is all I have.

I check myself in the mirror one last time, and then, satisfied with my delusion, I grab my broomstick scepter and leave Eros and his apartment behind.

DOWNSTAIRS THE BAR IS EMPTY, but out on the streets there are many humans going about their day. They like to rise early, for some reason, and they open up the shops. There is a coffee shop, and a candle shop, and a car mechanic's garage and other stupid places like that, which all require a human to attend them.

Some of the humans take their cars and leave the town. They go to work in places called Bedford, and Windber, and Somerset.

I'm fascinated by this tradition. Leaving town to work. How interesting.

Of course, neither the monsters—of which I am one —nor the god can leave Savage Falls. There is a fog around the town. A magic fog that traps us in a cloud of nothingness should we stray too far outside the city limits.

Humans though, at least the ones who live here, can just go on down the road like it's nothing. Of course, there's always a bit of a challenge finding their way home once they leave. Which is why the human population has dwindled down to a mere couple dozen since the monsters came to town several months ago.

What happens to them out there, I have no idea.

I don't actually care, either.

We had humans in Vinca. They were a middle-class species, something far below the royal beasts such as myself, but certainly higher up than the peasant chimera like satyrs, or even the wood nymphs, who—while certainly desirable for the wood wine they produce, which can be used to open magical doors—are a lowly, inferior class of magical person.

I wish that the wood nymphs were not here. They are a part of my history that I would rather forget. If they were making wood wine, I would reconsider my opinions of them. But they are not.

So, as part of my delusion, I cancel them out. I do this by wiping my mind of all thoughts and saying the words, 'You shall call me queen!' on repeat, whenever one looks in my direction. I give my broomstick a bang on the ground to punctuate my madness. Typically, they shoot me a concerned look, but quickly redirect their attention elsewhere.

I've done this to everyone in town at this point so I'm mostly ignored as I walk up and down the same four blocks that comprise the tiny downtown area of Savage Falls.

Of course, I do interact with the dragon-girl so as to continue my bubble bath transactions, but other than that, I'm happy to be the town eccentric who is ignored.

However, this general acceptance of myself—which feels so fresh and invigorating each morning when I put on the costume—typically becomes exhausting and monotonous by late afternoon.

I have doubts. And regrets. And I feel like something is crushing me from the inside out.

This crushing thing has no name, nor do I fully acknowledge it. One equals the other, after all.

I push it down and hide it in the dark spaces where it belongs.

Not because it's evil, though I have done many evils in the name of this crushing thing. But because it is painful. The kind of painful that might break a lesser, weaker person right in half.

I typically spend the mornings scavenging in the empty houses. Every week there is a new one to look through. Someone goes off to work and doesn't return.

This week it is not a house but a shop called the Kitchen Sink. I have not been in here before, but yesterday I heard some whispering about a man called 'Big Jim,' who is... possibly dead? The whispering people didn't seem sure. They wanted to go into his shop and take things, but their uncertainty prevented them from doing so.

I have no idea why they fear this man, nor do I care about the life status of Big Jim. I go right into the Kitchen Sink and begin to peruse the shelves. There are weapons in here. And backpacks made of thick canvas the color of dreary olives. Little containers, in the same dull color, that hold water. Various electrical mechanicals. Food wrapped up in silver packages. And on an endcap a book of maps.

All these things feel quite useful in a wild way. A way that intrigues me and makes me yearn for the open road. For an adventure. A trip into the great unknown.

But there is no adventure for me.

I will be stuck in this town for all eternity.

So I leave the shop and wander back down to the bar.

It takes a moment for my eyes to adjust to the shadows once I step inside, but I sit at the same place every time I come in so I head in that direction with the sunlight lingering in my vision. When I get to my stool, I take off the leopard coat and drape it across the back, then settle and sigh, my feet weary from all my aimless walking today.

The bartender, who is a gigantic bear-faced chimera who looks much more animal than the human he's been mixed with, slides a glass of whiskey down my way without comment. It's my usual. Sometimes it's a very nice whiskey. Sometimes it tastes like shit. It all depends on how well the shelves are stocked. And oftentimes they are not stocked well at all, since it's the job of the eros humans to procure and deliver supplies and, as we all know, getting home from the outside world can sometimes be a problem.

I don't participate in much as far as the community goes. I walk. I scavenge. I drink. I go back to the apartment and sleep. Eros will join me in the middle of the night. He usually wants sex, but the nice thing about having sex with Eros is that he has absolutely no expectations. It's a physical act and nothing more.

And it suits me.

This whole life is starting to suit me.

In fact, I'm beginning to forget what it was like to be a queen with her day scheduled down to the very last moment.

Perhaps that whole life was a dream?

The longer I sit in the bar, the more this dream fades. One day, I think, it will vanish altogether.

I sit on my stool sipping whiskey until the sun goes down.

This is my signal to end the day.

I follow the sun and go upstairs to bed. I'm not really tired—it's more like a weariness—but sleep comes easy to me these days, so why fight it?

A heavy sigh comes out as I set my broom-handle scepter against the wall and toss the leopard coat in the general direction of a chair, but it misses and falls to the floor in a heap. Then I slip my arms out of the blue dress and let it slide to the floor where it lies, like a puddle, at my feet, until I step out of it. The antlers come next. Another exhale comes out when I untie that string, but this one is relief. Carrying a rack of twenty-two points around on the top of my head is tiring, after all.

It never used to be. When they weren't affixed there with string, but were a part of me, like my heart or my bones. But it is definitely tiring now.

When I am stripped down to my skin, I slip into the bed I share, kind of, with the god of love. We both sleep in it. And have sex in it. But we don't really share it. There are a few hours during the night when we're both here in the same space. Not talking, or commiserating, or supporting one another—it's not that kind of 'share.' It's just… existing next to each other.

I tell myself I like this way.

I like being alone. Singular. Solitary.

Who in this world, after all, could possibly relate to me?

So I like it this way.

I WAKE UP SUDDENLY, sweaty and breathing hard, sitting up and holding my chest with both hands as the memory of the dream comes back.

It takes me a moment, actually, to realize that it *was* a dream and I am now awake.

And then I breathe through the residual fear until that too withers.

It's not what's happening in the dream that frightens me, which is the destruction of Vinca. The utter demolition of it. Buildings cracking in half. Boulevards flooded by the engorged river. Humans and chimera screaming as fireballs come hurling down from the sky, blowing them into bits.

I knew all that happened. Well, I knew Vinca was destroyed. The particulars were left up to my imagination.

No. The frightening part is the *face* of that destruction.

A bull god. Golden and black. Terrifying and destructive.

Not just any bull god, either, but *the* bull god.

The Apis bull.

In my time as queen there was no bull god. He was destroyed—dismembered, actually—thousands of years ago, his individual body parts sealed inside jars that were then taken to the far corners of the realm and hidden away so he might never incarnate again.

So what could this dream mean?

I get up from bed, naked, and go downstairs to the bar. It's empty, but the jukebox is playing that stupid song about a ball and chain that Eros loves so much.

I grab a bottle of whiskey from the shelf and take it back upstairs. Then I climb out the window and carefully navigate the rickety and rusty stairs to the roof.

This is where I find Eros. He turns to study me, looking moody, and volatile, and handsome, of course, with his giant black bat wings contrasting sharply with his blond hair and green eyes. He's standing on the edge of the building, looking down, perhaps contemplating suicide. More likely not, though. More likely he is just wondering how the hell he got here like all the rest of us.

He watches me approach with narrowed eyes. "What are you doing up here?"

His strange Pennsylvania accent intrigues me, but I ignore him, walk to the edge of the roof, and then sit down with my feet dangling over the edge. Then I tip the bottle to my mouth and take a long drink.

I sputter a little bit when I pause to wipe my mouth, then take another.

"Hel-looo? Are you deaf?"

"Which do you think is more likely, god of nothing? I am suddenly and inexplicably unable to hear you? Or I am ignoring you?"

"Well, well, well. She talks."

"Of course I talk. I talk every day. I have never pretended to not talk."

"So you say. But the only thing I've ever heard come out of that mouth of yours, aside from moaning, of course"—he stops here, and I find him grinning down at me when I look up—"is that whole spiel about calling you queen."

I look away and take another drink of my whiskey, saying nothing in response.

"Do you realize you're naked?"

I huff. "No. Eros. I'm a literal idiot who can't tell if she is wearing clothes or not. Thank you for letting me know."

"You're so fucking weird."

I say nothing. Just continue to gaze out across the low rooftops of the little town, focusing on the tops of trees and the foggy sky in the distance.

"If you just want to ignore me then why did you come up here?"

I sigh, already tired of him. "Because I had a bad dream and I need some air. But I didn't realize you'd be up here, so it was probably the wrong choice."

"Bullshit. You knew I would be here." I don't look up at him but I can tell he's smirking. The unfortunate thing about Eros is, smirk or smile, he is always alluring.

He's also correct. Unfortunately. And I don't have the energy to lie to him right now, so I just admit it. "I wanted some company."

"I'm not really the best choice when it comes to company."

"No, you are not. But I had a nightmare."

Eros sits down, dangling his booted feet over the side of the building as well. He's not very close, but he takes up a lot of space with those wings. And as the right one brushes up against my bare shoulder, I shudder. Chills run up my spine and little bumps burst out all over my naked body.

"Do ya wanna tell me about the nightmare?"

"Not particularly."

"Do ya... want me to shut up and just make ya feel safe?"

"That sounds acceptable."

"Can I have some?" When I look at him, he's pointing to my bottle of whiskey, so I hand it over. He studies the label. "The Busker. Never heard of it."

"Are you a whiskey aficionado?"

"Not particularly, but we get all kinds through here. Almost never the same thing twice. And this one is new."

I study him as he takes a sip, then lets out a breath. "Well?"

He shrugs. "Seems fine to me." He hands back the bottle.

For an outcast god who has been shit on his entire life and therefore should have several addictions as well as a personality disorder, he doesn't often partake in the drinking. Not the way the satyrs do. He doesn't spend a lot of time in the bar with the people and chimera, preferring to keep to himself most of the time, giving off an air of... 'heavy is the head.'

Which I can relate to as well.

We stay quiet after that. Just gazing out at nothing.

I don't know what he's thinking about, and I have no interest in asking, but the images from my nightmare are still running through my mind on repeat.

That bull. Apis.

Of course, I knew he was part of this. Whatever 'this' is. A curse, maybe? A punishment? Perhaps just a fog? It's hard to tell. But I knew he was involved. Pell, the Monster of Saint Mark's, told a tale about him to Eros weeks back after we, meaning myself and the other prisoners from the Bottoms, were freed from that dungeon.

So it should not come as a surprise that Apis has invaded my dreams.

I just don't like it. "Vinca," I say into the dark silence.

Eros turns his head to look at me. "What?"

"My nightmare was about Vinca. But… it wasn't so much that it was destroyed." I look at Eros now too, meeting his gaze. "We knew that, right? The skull and crown? Tarq?"

Eros nods. "Yeah. It's too bad about that. I could've used Tarq."

I almost snort here. "To do what? Make a godling? With Pie?"

"Well, that was the initial plan, as you know. But not anymore. I've let Pie go. I'm not gonna think about that girl ever again."

"Another Pressia, is she?"

"As if you know anything about me and Pressia."

"I know you're infatuated with her."

"Infatuated?" He says this with incredulity, then lets out a chuckle. "I would not call it infatuation."

"What would you call it, then?"

"How about we stick to the topic at hand, which is you and your nightmare?"

It bothers me that he still thinks about Tarq and what Tarq could've done for him. Which was, specifically, give him the genetic material to make a godling. Of course, he'd have to find another Pie to complete that process. A lion*ess*. A Second Daughter gryphon chimera from the House of Fire, to be specific.

Good luck with that. There is only one Pie. She and I are very close relations. Half-sisters from the same father. But as First Daughter, I was made from the genetics of the great alchemist, Ostanes. I was to be her apprentice. And as Second Daughter, Pie was made from the genetics of all the gods and goddesses combined. She was to bear a godling that would rise up and reunite all the discarded pantheons with the human world once again. A god of gods.

I don't often wonder what my life would've been like if the man sitting next to me, the man I share a bed with, hadn't ruined it by kidnapping my little sister, Pie. Would I have gone on to do great things? Would I have been nicer? Gentler?

It's not likely. I was, for all intents and purposes, ruined long before Eros showed up. I just didn't realize it for many years afterward.

The moment Pie told me about the magic that happened in the throne room where she was gifted a bag of rings that could open doors to other realms by the god, Ptah, everything that happened next was set in stone.

I didn't understand a single word of the madness spilling out of her mouth that day. But she said a lot in just a few minutes. She told me the spell Ostanes used to bind her magic into a bird.

I would obsess over Pie's words for nearly two decades, trying to understand what happened to us that day.

Well, that's how it started. Innocent enough.

But it turned into something else entirely. Something very, very sick that I—

"Ya know," Eros interrupts my thoughts, "this is the first time you've ever spoken to me. As far as making sense goes."

"Hmm. Well, it wasn't planned. I wouldn't take it personal."

"Why do you pretend?"

I turn my head to look at him. "Pretend? Pretend what?"

"To be crazy. Why do you wear those stupid antlers and that mangy coat? You do realize the wooden blocks make no sense, right? You didn't have hooves and they look nothing like paws."

"Well, thank you very much for your astute observations." I sigh and roll my eyes.

"I'm not trying to be a dick, or anything. It's just… I've been fucking you every night for almost two months and the only thing you've said to me in that time is, 'You shall call me queen.'"

"I'm not sure what you're looking for here, Eros."

He gets to his feet and stands next to me, looming over me so I am compelled to look up at him. "Thank you for the conversation, Callistina. That's all I was trying to say."

And then he turns and climbs down the rickety and rusty stairs.

Leaving me behind.

CHAPTER THREE - EROS

allistina never came to bed last night. This bothers me because I can't tell if she did that on purpose because we had that uncomfortable conversation, or if she regularly finds another place to rest her head and I just haven't noticed.

Shouldn't I notice if the woman I'm fucking stays out all night and doesn't come to bed?

I think this is a given.

So I am bothered.

Being bothered also bothers me and so there is nothing left to do but make a decision and put her out of my mind. The decision is that I will not allow her to sleep in my bed again.

Well, maybe eventually I could see her coming back. But she needs to give up the fucking costume and start acting like a normal human being. I do get the irony because she is not human. But the truth is that while she wasn't *made* human at birth, she is a human *now*, and that's all that matters.

When assholes curse you and rearrange your life you have two choices: Suck it up and do your best, or dwell and be one of those victim people.

If she chooses victim, I'm just not interested. I can't deal with people who give up so easily. I mean, how could I ever count on, or trust, or respect, a defeatist?

It's counterintuitive and not aligned with my own sense of self-preservation.

And I also get the irony that I was perfectly fine with her choice until last night, but that's because I really thought she was insane. Now that I know she is just prolonging her acceptance of the inevitable, I'm not inclined to be so accommodating.

At any rate, I will not be fucking Callistina anymore until she gets her shit together. And I have a sudden urge to go tell her this. Like an ultimatum.

But that feels like I *want* to tell her this so that she might object and we might fight.

You don't have to be the god of love to understand that fighting with someone about how you will not be having sex with them is just a whole bunch of bottled-up sexual tension. And while I might be wandering a bit aimlessly these days, what I am not doing is planning a future with the former Queen of Vinca.

I say this—internally, of course—all the way down the stairs of my apartment. I am not planning a future with the former Queen of Vinca.

I am not planning a future.

I am *not* planning a future.

I am *not* planning a future with the former Queen of Vinca.

Four times feels sufficient. So I let out a breath and push open the door that will take me into the bar. Immediately, I'm scanning the room for her presence.

Eros. Get a hold of yourself. You are not obsessed with Crazy Callistina.

I don't get obsessed with anyone. It's part of my curse. But what I am inclined to do at times—perhaps times such as this—is dwell on certain individuals. Purely for selfish reasons, of course. Because I am nothing if not selfish.

But at any rate, Callistina is not in the bar. There is no one in the bar.

So I go outside and take in the morning. Well, not really morning, actually. I don't do mornings and the sun above tells me it's noon.

That's when I notice Darrel, AKA Batty, walking up the sidewalk in my direction. I pause here and watch him because he's watching me. That can only mean one thing. He needs something. Probably for that little dragon girlfriend of his. Who is one of my descendants, obviously, since everyone in the town of Granite Springs came from me. But fucking gods above, how the hell one of mine came out part dragon is beyond even my celestial comprehension.

Darrel nods his head at me as he approaches. "Hey, Eros."

"Hello, Darrel. How can I help you?"

He makes a face that comes with an uncomfortable smile. "Well, since you asked, I could use a little help in the love department."

"How so?"

"Madeline. She..." He looks over his shoulder in the direction of the feed store where little Madeline works, then blows out a long breath. "She's... being weird."

"Well, Darrel, I'm not really sure what you mean by 'weird.' But you know that, so how about you just get to the fuckin' point and tell me what you need."

"I need you to..." He looks over his shoulder again, then back at me. "I need you to shoot her again. The arrow. It's wearing off. Her scales are coming back. Not like they were before you shot her, but a little bit here, a little bit there. Ya know?"

"That's ridiculous. My arrows do not wear off. They are eternal unless I interfere and shoot her with the antagonist version. Which I have not done, I assure you."

"Well, then why isn't she... you know... into me enough to keep her curse at bay?"

"Perhaps because you're just too ugly."

Darrel blinks. "What?"

I sigh. "I'm just fuckin' with you, brother. But listen, that arrow I shot was under duress. Do you recall that day when Saint Mark's Sanctuary came tumbling down and you and your ilk came into my town looking for a place to settle?"

He shrugs. "Well, of course I do."

"And do you recall that I was in the middle of compelling Pie and Pell to bring me Tarq so I could make a little godling that could then be sacrificed for powerful magic to break my curse?"

"Uh... yeah. I guess."

He probably didn't really understand that part. It's

not like he's my second in command or anything. He's just one of the more intelligent and rational monsters, so I have higher expectations of him.

"Well, upon the sight of you carrying the little dragon-girl covered in scales, I was… well, distracted."

"OK." He's not sure where I'm going with this.

"I had other things on my mind. That's all I'm saying. I wasn't capable of pulling together a bunch of magic to turn you into the man Madeline really and truly loves." He's still not getting it. "*Darrel,*" I say, my voice stern and this word snappish. "She wasn't in love with you, brother. She was in love with Tomas. He was the one who could cure her, not you."

He sighs. "Right. *Tomas.*" That name comes with a little sneer. "But your arrow should've compelled her to love *me*, right?"

"Does she not love you? Because that wasn't your complaint. Your complaint was that she doesn't love you *enough* to keep her curse at bay. And my answer to you is… well, the plain and simple truth is, you're just second best."

Now he's makin' an angry face at me. "So what are you saying?"

"I'm saying you might have to put up with a scale or two, OK? That's what I'm saying. You're expecting perfection and I just can't deliver. Not because I am not powerful, but because she was in love with another man when I shot her." I tap my head. "And that memory is still there."

"Can it be erased?"

"Of course it can. People fall in and out of infatuation all the time. If her curse is coming back then she's not in love with you. She's infatuated. And I could, of course, do that for you. Erase her memory of Tomas. *Again.* But it's always gonna wear off, Darrel. Until she really loves you of her own accord, her curse will never be truly gone."

Darrel's face morphs into a look of defiance. "You just told me your arrows don't wear off."

"They *don't.* She *does* love you. It's just not *romantic* love, Darrel. It's more of a... *friendship.*"

"Hmm." Darrel considers this. "Friendship, huh?"

"That's right. Love comes in many forms, my friend. And her love for you is just not enough."

He stares at me as the reality sinks in. As it always does when someone asks me for a love arrow and hasn't come to terms with the consequences of the compulsion spells.

You always get what you ask for, but it is never what you expect.

People, all species, are constantly surprised by this.

I just don't understand how everyone is so dumb.

I clap him on the shoulder. "Good talk, brother. Now." I straighten up and clear my head of his petty problems. "I will gladly shoot her again for you."

He brightens. "You will?"

I shrug. "Fuck it. What do I care if you prolong the inevitable? Sure I will. But I want something in return."

Darrel looks a little taken aback at the thought of him being useful to me. "Uh. OK. What do you need?"

"I need to know how the hell Callistina got turned into a human."

I really didn't expect to say this. I mean, I did say that mantra. Four times. I am *not* planning a future with the former Queen of Vinca. But I'm justifying what comes rolling off my tongue as the past, not the future.

Though I am not planning a past with the former Queen of Vinca, either.

"I need to know what happened with her and Pie. How did she come upon her curse?"

"Well…" Darrel thinks back. "We went to Vinca to steal the wood nymphs"—he pans his hand to a group of them hanging out in front of the diner as his Example A —"and make Tarq the king."

"As one does, I suppose."

"Right. So… Callistina was waiting for us. Like it was a trap."

"Isn't it always a trap, Darrel?"

"Uh. Sure." Darrel nods. "It is. It always is. But anyway, Callistina killed Pie's bird. And this riled Pie up and she cursed Callistina."

"*Pie* did? Well. That surprises me. I didn't know she had it in her. She's so fuckin' sweet."

"Yeah, well. Not always. She had her moments there, at the end. Anyway. Pie spelled her."

"What was the spell?"

Darrel thinks back for a few moments, making a face of concentration. Then he brightens and snaps his fingers. "'A horn, a hoof, an eye, a bone.'"

"Oh, *that* one again." I roll my eyes.

"'A bitchy queen on her makeshift throne.'"

This part makes me laugh.

"'Her sins are mine to keep and hold. In debt she goes in my control!'"

"Whoa!" I exclaim. "Four little lines did all that?"

"Four stupid lines from *Pie* did all that."

"Right." I nod. "She is a spectacular speller. So Pie put Callistina in debt, huh?"

"And locked her up in the Bottoms prison. And when she got there, she was a human. All magic stripped. This is a type of torture for a creature like Callistina."

"Wow." I actually have to take a moment to consider all these new facts. "My little Pie certainly did find her power."

"Oh, she did all right. But in all fairness, Callistina *did* kill her bird."

"Which only made Pie *more* powerful."

"Correct," Darrel says. Then he blows out a breath. "Anyway. About that arrow."

I SHOOT **the poor dragon-girl** again and Darrel seems satisfied with this. And by this time, it's full-on afternoon and I have yet to see Callistina.

I'm not obsessed with her. I'm just curious now. About where she's staying, of course. But also… that curse of hers. It's changed things, I think. I just need to work out *how*.

Because one does not just go from being First Daughter Lion*ess* of Saturn in the House of Fire to being a human. It's not possible. This is genetics we're talking about. She was bred to be a certain thing and it was not a human. So her true self still lingers. But how to unlock it?

Better question—*should* I unlock it?

I know it would make her happy, but what would be in it for me?

In order to figure that out I need to know what I want. And I'm not sure. All this time—all these thousands of years—I wanted to be the god of gods. The head of all the pantheons. The one who pulls the puppet strings.

I possess the power to be that because I possess the power of love.

When mutual, it's heaven on earth. When one-sided, it can tear you apart. There is no greater weapon than the heartsick soul. That is the power I wield, for I *am* the god of love. No one has power like me. No one can poison a heart and pollute a mind the way I can. That's why the gods kicked me out. That's why they made me fall.

I already *am* the god of gods.

What I *am not* is free to take that position.

And the funny thing is, I was so close. If only Pie hadn't taken Callistina to the Bottoms, then Tarq would not have been king and Vinca would not be ruined. And if Vinca wasn't ruined then Tarq might be alive.

But it didn't happen that way so the probability that Tarq is my path forward into a future where I wear the ultimate crown seems fairy remote.

I had Pie. I had her practically in my hand. Now I do understand that Pell would've put up a fight. He was making deals though, wasn't he? He was going to give me a door to the Apis bull. Which is… interesting. Pell claimed that door was a direct line back to the old gods, but it was a guess.

Maybe he was right. And if so, well, that door would've been useful. I would've had to fight hard if I took the door. It would've been a long, messy war with those old gods.

Still, it was a good offer. And the gods of old have been out of favor for so long now, they're not what they used to be. Perhaps Saturn is, since he's kept a cult going all this time, and worshippers are how these gods get power. The door to the Apis bull might've been the better way to go.

Something compelled me to not take that deal Pell was offering. I pause to think here, because I can't remember why I lost my fucking senses and didn't grab that door when I had the chance. Or Pressia's books, for that matter. Pell said something about her books being in his apothecary at Saint Mark's.

No. He called it *her* apothecary. Pressia's apothecary. She's been hiding at Saint Mark's all these eons. Existing in some sort of time shift, maybe, or on an alternate plane of existence. Writing her little books and doing her little spells like nothing and no one can touch her.

Pressia. The one who made me love her. Her magic is… significant. A better word might be formidable. She used that magic to spell my heart. Much like I just used an arrow to spell Madeline's.

Pressia is the one who stole my heart and then broke it. She is how the gods ruined me.

But I've been thinking about this ever since it happened, which is a long, long time. The feelings I have for Pressia are definitely more along the lines of hate. And hate comes with very specific feelings.

And wants. Maybe even needs.

In my case, these wants and needs fall along a path of revenge. And I think part of my current state of uneasiness is the fact that I've got power all around me in so many different forms. Just waiting to be used.

I've got the Queen of Vinca, for fuck's sake. Plus all that comes with her bloodline.

I've got a small army of monsters and wood nymphs.

I've got some semi-human descendants—one of which is a fuckin' dragon.

I've got Batty. Darrel, whatever. And if I remember correctly, he was some kind of chimera dissident leader back in the ancient times.

In addition to all that I have Tomas, the god of happy endings. He's probably warded from me these days, but not heavily. I could find him if I wanted to. And he could find Pressia. I know he could. He was kinda hinting at that the last time we spoke.

So perhaps my sense of unsettlement is more about how I'm unable, or unwilling, to use all this power and all these resources to bust myself out of this fuckin' curse?

Alternatively, perhaps I just need to get laid a little more. With a woman who actually appreciates me.

But this town has few choices. Which is why I sleep with Callistina every night.

Or, as it turns out. *Not* every night.

Where did that crazy queen go?

I should find her. Because it is not Tarq who is my path back to the gods. Not Pressia, either. Though I hate her, and would end her given the chance, she is but a side quest at the moment.

It's Callistina I need to figure out.

I get caught up in my thoughts for a while, the past running through my head. Whirling around. Spinning and turning. Inside out and upside down. I'm trying to fit all these pieces into some kind of order.

A plan begins to form too. Nothing spectacular, but all the bits and pieces of past events and choices suddenly start adding up to something.

A former queen.

The House of Fire.

Royal beasts.

Might I be able to whip up a little quid pro quo?

I FINALLY FIND **Callistina** tucked away in the abandoned bookstore. She is sleeping—naked—on a blue velvet divan in a corner, lying on her side with her hands tucked under her cheeks. Her face is calm and sweet and there are no antlers on her head or wooden blocks on her feet to mess up the illusion.

The person who used to run this store left the fog a couple weeks ago and never returned. Probably got lost. It's a risk they take.

But anyway, after checking every single fucking store, here Callistina is.

I clear my throat. Then wait for her to stir.

She doesn't. So I clear it again and say, "*Callistina,*" in a commanding voice.

This time she groggily opens her eyes. It takes another moment for her to focus on me and then she spits, "You shall call me *queen!*"

"Come on. I know you're faking it. Just knock it off already."

She glares at me, then gets up, standing mere inches away from me... naked. Which, not gonna lie here, is putting me off my game. She sets her jaw and through gritted teeth she hisses, "You. Shall call. Me queen."

"Fine. You're the fuckin' queen. Why are you sleeping in the bookstore? Is this where you were last night?"

"You—"

"My queen! My fuckin' queen!" I pan my arms wide and turn in a circle. "Did you sleep in here last night?"

She picks up that ugly blue dress off the floor and slides it over her head. It's like ten sizes too big. And

41

then, without saying another word or giving me another glance, she walks away.

"Callistina!"

She growls, but doesn't even so much look over her shoulder. Just hits the front door and exits.

What the hell?

I go after her and by the time I get outside, she's already down the road.

For a moment I consider giving up. But then I have a little pep talk with myself. "If becoming the god of gods was so damn easy, Eros, then everyone would be the god of gods, wouldn't they?"

This is true. Big rewards require big effort.

I have a feeling about Callistina's nightmare. Specifically, that it might not be a nightmare, but a glimmer. A hole in the fabric of time, if time even exists. Which is questionable.

But anyway, I would like to find out more about her glimmer, if that's what it is, because I could find a good use for a glimmer. Foresight and all that. It's useful when making big plans.

So. Right. I let out a sigh and continue after her as she disappears inside the bar.

When I get inside the bar, she's already heading up the stairs to our apartment. There are a few people in the bar now, helping themselves to whatever whiskey we've got on the shelves, but I ignore them as I pursue Callistina upstairs.

Inside the apartment she has hastily pulled her crazy self together. Already wearing the mangy coat and her wooden blocks, she is standing in front of a dirty mirror positioning her antlers when I arrive and sigh. Because I'm tired of her little game.

Maybe she's really not worth the trouble?

I *might* think that. But she talked to me last night. Nearly a real conversation. We were talking about her nightmare and then we got off track because of Pressia.

Typical.

"You were gonna say something last night." I look her in the eyes using the mirror. "About your nightmare. You said..." I have to think for a moment to play it back. "You said it wasn't so much that Vinca was destroyed, because we knew that already when Pell came back with Tarq's skull and crown. But then you never finished your thought about why it bothered you enough to come up to the roof."

She only meets my gaze in the mirror for a moment, then goes back to ignoring me. Tying the string that holds her antlers on under her chin.

I'm really getting frustrated now. But I can do this. I can get her to talk. To be sane. To give me answers. Answers she has and I need.

But a new tactic is required. So I say, "OK. Fine. You be you, Callie. Can I call you Callie?"

"You shall call me queen." She's not angry though. The words are calm and a little bit soft.

"Don't you want a second chance, Callie? Wouldn't you like a do-over? A fresh start? Pie got one. Two, actually, if you count her life in the Realm of Pennsylvania. And now look, she's probably married by now."

This gets Callistina's attention. Her eyes flick up to meet mine in the mirror just as she pulls the bow tight under her chin, then quickly return to their previous focus.

Still, I got a reaction with the Pie thing. So I keep going in this direction. Because I know she's faking. And she knows I know she's faking. "That's right. I bet they got married. Maybe even having kids by now—"

Those words are barely out of my mouth when she turns, eyes blazing, and slaps me across the face. "*YOU SHALL CALL ME QUEEN*!" She screams this at the top of her lungs.

And when she does this, I feel like the world blinks. Like the sun just shuddered, or something. Going pale, then dark, then bright again. And I'm so stunned, I take several steps backwards and look around, trying to find the source of the interference. Which offers Callistina a way around me and she does not miss her chance.

The next thing I know she's cloppin' her wooden-block feet across the floor and down the stairs to the bar.

Well. That was an unexpected turn of events.

What it means, I'm not sure.

But I'll take it.

All change is good, isn't it?

CHAPTER FOUR - CALLISTINA

*E*verything in the room is buzzing and my head is pounding to the beat of my heart. I know my face is flushed red because just looking down at my arms, I see that *they* are flushed red.

And the *anger*! I want to kill him. I want to go back upstairs, open my mouth as wide as I can, and tear. His. Throat. Out.

And this urge shocks me. Utterly shocks. Yes, I was a bitch of a queen. I understand that. But I have never wanted someone *dead*. I have never wanted to kill someone with my *teeth*.

Until now.

There are more people in the bar now. Several of Eros's townspeople and nearly two dozen monsters and nymphs. There is an air of easiness in the bar. Friendship, even. But as soon as I am noticed they all stare at me and go quiet.

I pass by them without a word, but just as I get to the front door and my hand is reaching for the doorknob, someone behind me—a wood nymph, I think—says, "That's right, bitch. Just keep going. You're not welcome here."

Everything that happens next is just instinct. I turn. I glare. And then I growl, "You shall call me QUEEN!", snarling my teeth like a lioness in the wild.

There are some snickers from the back, but then... then the lights crackle. And all the hairs on my body— few that they are—go stiff and prickle up. At the same time the filaments inside the lightbulbs brighten and dim, giving off a bit of a blue glow. A glow that's very much akin to the color of my prom dress. It doesn't last long. It only stops what's happening between me and the wood nymph for the briefest of moments. But it's enough.

I don't know what it means. Do I have voice power, the way Pell did? The way Eros does?

Doubtful. I think I would've found that out before now, if it were the case.

But it is interesting that my anger and frustration has such an effect on light. Because the light dimmed upstairs as well when I yelled at Eros. Only that time it was the sunshine, not the electricity. Which has to have been a coincidence. A cloud, perhaps? Meandering its way across the sky? Just so happening to pass in front of the sun at just the right moment?

That's probably it.

But this? No. This is something else. And everyone in this bar realizes it at the same time. The wood nymph who was sneering at me has gone utterly pale. She swallows hard. Like she's gathering her nerve.

She doesn't call me queen, but she doesn't manage the courage to say anything else, either. And no one is snorting or chortling now.

I have worn out my welcome, but that's just fine with me. It's time to go, anyway.

When I get outside it's too bright and my head is pounding. So I walk down the street where I know the town limits are. And then, when I get there, I slip into the fog.

It's thin at first. But it thickens only a few yards in and becomes swirly around my feet. I stop here, afraid that if I go much further, I might get lost and never find my way back.

Then I slump to the ground, lie back, and stare up at nothing as I play those few words back on repeat.

Maybe even having kids by now.

Maybe even having kids by now.

Maybe even having kids by now.

It echoes in my head over, and over, and over.

I had children. Many of them. It's possible to do that in Vinca because of the alchemists. Lyrica didn't put them inside me, she harvested them and grew them in the lab. Many, many times. And Tarq too. He was the other half of my equation, after all.

The babies were grown in glass tubes. First very small tubes, thin as claws. If they made it past the first stage and everything checked out, they would be flushed into bigger tubes about the size of drinking glasses. If they made it past stage two, they were in the final tubes, which were the size of a baby chimera.

There were hundreds of such tubes.

And they all died just a few weeks into stage three.

Of course, I never felt like a mother. How could I? There was never any baby inside me. So the pain, while there—manifesting as disappointment, naturally—wasn't as bad as it could've been.

That's what Lyrica, the Royal Alchemist, used to tell me. "We always knew it was risky, my queen." That's what she used to say. "I'm so glad you never got your hopes up."

It was common knowledge that chimera, while not sterile, cannot just mix with anyone and expect good results.

Most of them have better luck than I did, though. Tarq was a breeder, but I was never meant to reproduce. That was Pie's job.

So I just wasn't good enough.

Maybe even having kids by now.

But if Pie and Pell are having babies, I'm certain they will be born and they will be born healthy. Because Pie was made to breed and has genetics from all the gods. Pell has the blood of two gods in him, as well. He's been mixed with animals—obviously, since he's a satyr—but he was meant to breed just like Pie.

Not me, though. I was meant to study alchemy, not be a royal beast and rule the land of Vinca as queen.

Eros derailed my whole life with his stunt. And now look at him. No remorse. No regrets. He certainly doesn't think about me and how he ruined everything. My whole future, stolen in a matter of moments. Selfish moments.

And now I'm stuck here, in some in-between curse world, as a human of all things.

A vapid, magicless creature with no skills, no plans, and no future.

I might as well be back in the Bottoms.

Because despite Lyrica's warning about hope, I had it. I hoped. And when she figured this out—well, I was deep into my mean queen years by this time. Bitter, and angry, and petty. So when she figured out it was due to all the failures, she made me a promise.

"We will find Pianna, my queen," she said. This was what we called Pie before, because we didn't know she was Pie, and Pianna was her given name in the House of Fire. "And we will pair her up with Tarq, just as it was meant to be, and that little godling will be born. And it will be *yours*."

Mine.

I had hoped.

But it was stupid.

Because nothing good ever comes from hope.

I blow out a long breath and let the fog cover me, letting the nothingness make me disappear.

Maybe I should just stay here?

Maybe I should get up and walk further into it?

Maybe I should get myself lost and never come back?

Why not? Why not at least try? It's not like this life I'm living has any kind of future.

So I close my eyes, and relax my whole body, and let the cool fog take me away...

*The next thing **I know*** I'm standing on the Riverwalk in Vinca and people are bustling all around me. An immediate sense of relief floods through my body as I take in the city that has been my only home for the last two decades.

It's the same as it was when I last saw it. A vibrant place, sunny and bright, with chimera and humans going places and doing things. Getting coffee, and talking, and laughing, and being normal.

When I look down at myself, I am... I put a hand up to my mouth because I suddenly want to cry.

I'm *me*. Real me. A lion*ess* with paws instead of feet, and claws instead of fingernails, and covered in velvety golden fur. And when I reach up to the top of my head, there they are! My magnificent antlers!

I am dressed in royal garb. A short skirt with layers, and layers of mustard-yellow chiffon and tulle, with the markings of the Royal Beasts embroidered along the hem in gold thread that shimmers in the sun. And I'm wearing the royal jacket of that year's fashion with a light-blue camisole underneath. My satin sash is smooth and the color of beeswax, covered in medals that celebrate all the things I learned that first year— sewing, and singing, and playing the pintar.

I recognize the outfit. It was my favorite many years

ago when I was just a princess and not a queen. Before I was sad, and broken, and mean.

This is my first year in Vinca. The fog has taken me back in time and this is such a respite from my real present-day life that I sigh and take solace in the sparkling, silver river that is crowded with activity. Houseboats lining the stone banks, and barges slowly meandering their way around the serpentine curves, and fun boats filled with happy people dancing and laughing to music.

They were grooming me to be the queen from the moment I arrived. And that's what queens did back then. They dressed in high fashion and had hobbies that pleased the men.

At least, that's what they did before *I* ruled. Queens were ancillary to kings. They had their ladies, and their guards, and their hobbies. They held dinners, and tea parties, and dances. They were polite, and pretty, and soft.

Tarq would've been learning his duties during this year too. All the things he would be expected to do. All the important Royal Beasts he would be expected to negotiate with on behalf of the people of Vinca.

I stand in place, smiling like a dumbstruck simpleton. Because it's here. And I'm here. And it hasn't been destroyed and neither have I.

But as I stand there taking it in, clouds quickly form in the sky. They swirl and make it dark. People change right in front of me. New fashions appear on the humans and chimera and then disappear just as quickly. Businesses close, change, and then go empty. The sky grows darker and darker, changing dramatically as time moves forward.

There was no dragon.

And then, one day, there was.

I wait for it. Her, I mean. I wait for her.

And this is when I realize the truth. This is the moment when a piece of my puzzle falls into place.

I didn't know who that dragon was back then, but I do now. Because I met her, in human form, in the foggy town of Savage Falls. She runs the feed store.

Madeline is my dragon and this is the very first Fireday of my rule in the city of Vinca.

She appears in the sky, circling.

I watch as human and chimera alike scurry around. They are all wearing clothes. Which is fine if you are human.

But animals do not wear clothes. Animals wear fur.

I look down at myself and find that I too am naked. Because this is how it's supposed to be. We should not have to put on clothes. That was my decree. That the beasts be free.

That's how Fireday started. That's how I started.

But I ended up a sad and defiant gryphon-chimera princess.

And Tarq ended up an overly ambitious minotaur-chimera prince.

All we needed after that was the alchemist, Lyrica.

And the dragon—Madeline.

She flies low. Sweeping down towards the river. Mouth opening. And then… everywhere, fire.

People are screaming. Horrific screams. The fire

billows out, growing into a cloud and covering the city with searing heat. Charring bodies and buildings alike.

I look up at the palace and find Tarq on a terrace. He's yelling. The Skull King, that's what I called him that day. He's telling me to stop. To make Madeline stop.

But I did not make Madeline stop.

*I SIT UP, **coughing and sputtering**,* the taste of smoke in my mouth, smelling of sulfur and covered in ash.

"*Callistina!*"

Someone is calling my name. No. Not someone. Eros is calling my name. "Callistina! Where are you! Can you hear me?"

I'm in the fog. Surrounded by a cool, swirling mist.

"*Callistina!*" He calls and calls for me. But I can still smell burning flesh and even if I wanted to answer him, I can't. I can't shake the dream, or vision, or memory— whatever the hell it was.

It's still fresh in my head, filling it up with images of my city. My beautiful city. Turned black and charred that summer.

It recovered.

But no one ever forgot what I did.

Or *how* I did it.

I became queen that day. Declared myself such and put crowns on my head. Many, many little crowns perched upon the tines of my antlers. I was too young to understand that I was being used by the royal alchemist, Lyrica, and the Alchemist Guild. Still, it doesn't excuse what I did. What I agreed to. And how I kept the Fireday threats going year after year. Continuing a tradition that started out as a way to free the chimera of human expectations, but turned into a way to subjugate them instead.

"Callistina!" He's still calling for me.

Vinca was supposed to be my new life. My good life.

But it was just another Caretaking Ceremony.

Just another way to be exploited.

All Vinca really was, when I think about it with rational detachment, was a nightmare. Two long, dark decades of misery and suffering. Mine. Theirs. Everyone suffered.

"Callistina."

I look to my left and there he is.

Eros. The man who did that to me.

The god who ruined me.

CHAPTER FIVE - EROS

"*D**idn't you hear me calling you?*" I growl this at Callistina. I'm angry because I've been looking for her all afternoon. Someone said they saw her walk into the fog. And what do I care if she wanders into the nothingness? I don't. I really don't. But she's not getting out of this curse that easy. If I have to live with it, so does she. So does everyone.

Callistina, as per her usual self, is indifferent to my anger. Which makes me hotter.

But then I notice that she's covered in ash, her mangy coat is black, and she smells like sulfur. "What the hell happened to you?"

She's lying down in the fog, most of her body covered by swirling grayness. And she doesn't get up, or try to explain, or do anything, actually, except close her eyes and sigh. Like I'm not even here.

"Callistina. What's going on?"

Nothing from her. It's like I'm not even here.

And now what do I do? I've found her, but she obviously didn't want to be found. I look over my shoulder, back the way I came. There's a swirling gap in the fog, like a pathway, that shows me the way back. But I can tell it will close up soon. The fog doesn't stay still for long.

I lean down, slide my arms underneath Callistina's body, and pick her up.

She's frowning as I stare down at her face. But that's the only reaction she gives me.

"It's OK," I mumble. "I've got ya."

And then I take her into the fog, back the way I came.

When I exit the forest that surrounds Savage Falls it's late in the day. Much later than it should be. Like I've lost time. The sun is nearly gone—the sunset completely over—and people and monsters alike are walking the sidewalks or hanging out in front of the diner and the bar.

They watch me as I approach, holding the insane queen in my arms, but no one says anything. They don't really talk to me. They avoid me, actually. Maybe out of fear, but the more believable explanation for this shunning is that they just don't like me.

Or Callistina, for that matter.

So they don't say anything when I push past them and go inside.

I take her upstairs to the apartment and when I set her down on the couch, she doesn't even open her eyes. Just folds herself up and pushes her face into the cushions.

"What's wrong with you?" I don't know why I bother asking. She's not gonna answer me. And she doesn't. It's a dumb question, anyway. Callistina used to be a queen and now she's… this. Human, but not really human. Something in between.

She's not adjusting to the change very well. And left to her own devices, she's going to fade. Like an old god without a cult.

I pause here to consider my options with her. It's a complicated puzzle. But my options aren't complicated at all.

Either I take care of her or I let her go.

I go into the bathroom, start filling it up with hot water, and dump a bunch of bubbles under the tap as I do this. Do I know who Callistina is or what motivates her? No. Not in the least. But she takes a bath every day in this tub. She fills it with bubbles, and slides under the water, and she stays in there for hours sometimes.

It's the only way I can think of to snap her out of this surrender right now. If I walk away from her, she might leave again and go back into the fog. She won't die. I don't think. But she might disappear and I'm just not sure I'm ready for her to disappear.

Callistina is no longer a queen but she is, and forever will be, a royal beast. Hell, who knows what kind of potential she's got locked up inside her. What kind of god would I be if I didn't uncover that potential?

I can't let her go without fully exploring how I might use her.

Also, I've gotten used to getting laid every night.

When I come out of the bathroom it's clear that

Callistina hasn't moved. So I pick her up again—limp in my arms—and take her into the bathroom, setting her down on the counter.

She sighs, but her head is hanging low and I'm fairly certain that her eyes aren't even open.

"You like the bath, right?" I ask her, untying the wooden blocks from her feet. They drop to the floor, one, then the other, with a loud *clunk*. Then I take off the charred leopard-print coat and toss it out into the hallway. The antlers come next. I untie the string under her chin and lift them off her head. There's nowhere to put them in the bathroom, so I take them out into the main room, kicking that stupid coat along as I go, and set them on the table.

When I get back to the bathroom she's standing up, facing the tub, taking her dress off. She wears something different underneath the coat almost every day. Today she's still wearing yesterday's outfit, the bright-blue atrocity that is ten sizes too big.

She stands there, naked, with her back to me. Her clavicles and scapulae are clearly visible under her skin and even though I can't see the front side of her, I know her ribs would be prominent if I could.

Has anyone been feeding her?

But it's a dumb question. Who the hell would be feeding her? I'm the only one who pays any attention to her at all and I certainly haven't bothered to feed her.

"OK," I say, my head clearing, a course of action in place. "I'll leave you to it."

Callistina doesn't respond, of course. Just steps forward and gets in the tub.

But I catch her catching my eye just as I pull the door closed.

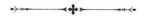

*It's **busy inside the diner***. People, and monsters, and nymphs alike are all sitting around having dinner. I go up to the counter where a human waitress wearing a nametag with the word 'Sassy' printed on it smiles at me, pad and pencil ready to take my order. "What can I get you, sweetie?"

I sigh, not in the mood for the local color right now. "Two cheeseburger specials, well done, extra cheese."

"You got it, hun. Would you like drinks?"

I nod, thinking. "Strawberry shakes."

"Comin' right up." Then she turns and places my order on the rotating check-minder.

I turn and lean against the counter, taking the place in. These are my people and it's still kinda weird. Before this whole Saint Mark's thing, and the end of Tomas's happily-ever-after game, it was just me here. Sitting in my bar, barely existing, as the neon sign outside crackled and sputtered to the beat of 'Ball and Chain.'

Granite Springs and Savage Falls were two entirely different places, existing on two entirely different planes. But it wasn't always that way. Long ago the fog was thin. That's how these people started. I fucked some random human all that time ago, and the rest, as they say, is history.

All these humans are my descendants. Little bits and pieces of god in them.

My eyes find Darrel, who is sitting with the girl from the feed store, and I pause for a moment. Little bits and pieces of god and other things, obviously. The dragon girl is a precarious situation. One that might not have a happy ending.

But that's a thought for another time. She looks normal enough right now. Of course, I did shoot her with an arrow just this morning.

There are many monsters in here too, most of them in groups of five or six, but a few have paired up with wood nymphs. I'm not exactly sure how many wood nymphs are left in town—a dozen maybe? Most of them elected to go back to the world where magic lives via Pie's doors.

It's unsustainable. That's all I know. They are satisfied at the moment because it's all new and different. But it won't stay that way forever. If anyone understands the dangers of boredom, it's me.

"Here you go, baby. Would you like ketchup?"

I turn and find Sassy packing up a white plastic bag with two takeaway containers. "Sure."

She throws in a couple packets, then adds some mustard too, even though I didn't ask for it. "And here's your shakes." She places them in a cardboard drink holder. "No charge, cutie-pie. Have a nice night."

I nod my appreciation, then take the food and drinks and walk back to the bar.

Inside it's loud and crowded. It's quiet in here during the day, but at night it's almost always rowdy. They like the drinking, and pool tables, and jukebox, and darts.

For now.

But it's gonna get old real soon.

I ignore everyone, and they ignore me back, as I go back upstairs and enter the apartment. The door to the bathroom is open and there's a cloud of steam hanging in the air in front of it.

I find Callistina back on the couch, wrapped in a towel and folded all up the same way she was before.

"I have food," I say, setting it all down on the coffee table.

She doesn't move.

"Sit up, Callistina. You need to eat something."

I'm expecting a fight over this. Or indifference. But to my surprise she actually does what I tell her. Her eyes meet mine. They are... well, they're kinda hard to describe. They could be brown. They're just not. But they're not quite yellow, either. She looks right at me as she adjusts her towel, and then says, in a low whisper, "You shall call me queen."

"Right." I chuckle a little, but it's mostly out of frustration. "My queen. I didn't know how you like your burger, so I just got it well-done with extra cheese, since that seems to be the standard operatin' procedure these days."

Her eyes dart to the food on the table and she lets out a long breath.

I open up the containers and then hand her a burger that's halfway wrapped in paper. Which is a nice touch from this diner, I think, since you can hold the burger without getting your hands dirty.

She looks at it for a moment, then takes a bite. It's a small, tentative bite. But as she's swallowing, I catch a smile.

"OK." I take my burger and lean back on the couch, kicking my feet out to stretch my legs. "It's funny," I say, "that we've been living together for a couple months now and I've never seen you eat. Have you been eating, Callistina?"

She doesn't look at me. Her answer, as she chews on a French fry, is simply, "You shall call me queen."

"Yeah. I keep forgetting." Whatever last night was, it's over now. She's not going to talk to me. Not tonight, anyway.

I finish my food first, but she's only about a minute behind me, so I clean up as she polishes off the rest of her burger. When I turn back to her from the small kitchen, she has dropped her towel to the floor and is already climbing into bed, naked.

Now this isn't anything unusual. It's been going on for nearly two months. She and I are... uh... well, I'm not sure what we are, I just know we've been sleeping together this whole time. Beyond that, I haven't given it much thought. And I'm pretty sure she has given it zero thought.

But now, for some reason, after I rescued her from the fog and we had a bite to eat together, it feels much more intimate than it did and I'm not sure what to do.

I would like to fuck her. Which is what I normally do. But today doesn't feel like a normal day.

She's already under the sheet by the time I'm having this internal debate, so obviously, Callistina has no opinion on this.

I shrug and throw up my hands. Then I turn the lights out, strip off the boots and pants, and get in bed next to her. I'm lying on my back, wings pressing into my shoulder blades, and staring up at the shadows on the ceiling, wondering what to do next.

That's when I hear her sniffling.

She's crying.

As a rule, I don't respond to crying women. It's a hassle that I just don't have the patience for. And if she had started crying two nights ago, I wouldn't even hesitate. I'd get up and walk out. I'd find another place to sleep. I am not the kind of god who *soothes*. That's not my thing.

I don't have any intention of soothing Callistina tonight, but I don't have an urge to get up and leave her, either. So once again, I get caught up in overthinking things.

But just as I'm about to close my eyes and sleep, pretending none of this is happening—just get this day over with so I can start a new one—she turns over and reaches for me. One hand snuggling up under my shoulder, the other stretching out across my chest, her head positioned somewhere in between.

I go stiff, but she begins to cry harder.

And then I'm right back to where I was.

Why is she here?

What is she doing?

What am *I* doing?

That last question is the most important.

What am I *doing?*

CHAPTER SIX - CALLISTINA

*C*rying *is a weakness* I don't display. In the twenty years since my little sister was pulled out of her world and thrust in the human one by the man lying next to me in bed, I have cried a total of four times.

The first was that very night after Pie was stolen. I was overwhelmingly sad. And worried. And... well, really just sad. I had no idea what was coming for me. It didn't even enter my mind that I would be required to take Pie's place as the Vincan princess. It's just not done. That's not how it works. We were sisters in a peculiar way, after all. Of course we shared some genetics, but that's not what made us sisters. I share genetics with thousands of gryphon chimera who came before me. What made us sisters is the simple fact that we shared a specific living space in the House of Fire palace where Saturn's word was law.

I was not meant to birth godlings. I was meant to make potions, and write spellings, and pore over pedigrees, and breed future generations of gryphon chimera for the House of Fire.

That was my place.

So on the night of Pie's disappearance I wasn't thinking about what the King of Vinca might demand and lamenting my future in the capital city. I was crying because my little sister was taken through a magic door against her will by—well, from my point of view, it was just a disembodied *hand*—and then followed by a no-good, narcissistic, fade-away god who was going to ruin her.

I was crying for Pie. Her life was over. Her future stolen.

The second time I cried was when Tarq relieved me of my virginity just a few weeks later. It wasn't him, not really. It was everything. There was an inspection to make sure I was, in fact, a virgin. And there was an audience.

I cried because I was embarrassed.

The third time I cried was at the king's funeral the following year. He was a good man. He really was. And even though I was still quite young and didn't have a keen grasp on the nature of the world outside the palace, I knew in my heart that most men were not good. 'Most *people*' would be the more accurate way to say that. It's really got nothing to do with men. It's just *people*. They're imperfect.

I, myself, am a prime example.

The fourth time I cried—the last time, up until tonight—was when Pie banished me to the Bottoms prison just a few short months ago. It was overwhelming because my beautiful, mature, magnificent gryphon chimera body had been turned into... well, *this*. The skin suit I am currently wearing. Human, powerless and ordinary, and not in the least spectacular.

It was quite a shock and I cried because I was humiliated. Even more so than when Tarq took my virginity. Everyone in the consummation bedroom was a royal beast. It was all very cold and professional—still embarrassing, but not nearly the level of humiliation I felt when I found myself in the Bottoms with common monsters. Common monsters who knew me. Knew *who* I was, and *what* I was, and could appreciate both the irony and the significance of me finding myself stripped of power, and magic, and beauty like a common criminal.

So I cried because I was put in my place. Shoe-on-the-other-foot kind of thing. *Ha, ha, ha. Look at her. She got what she deserved.*

It's humbling. Now, at least. But back then, on that first night, I would've chosen death over the laughing and jeering of the entombed criminals all around me. The pointing and sneering, the jokes at my expense. And the miserable conditions. I kept telling myself, *She won't leave me in here. She wouldn't do that. She's my sister.*

But I am her sister too, and I killed her little magic bird. Which was just a spelling that was locking up her power. Except that's not who Pia was to Pie. Pia was her best friend. And I killed her.

So Pie did leave me there. She didn't come back. Not once. Not even to argue, or express her hatred for me, or even to curse me again.

I was no one to her.

It was a bad time.

The only reason we all got out of the Bottoms was because the whole curse of Saint Mark's was falling apart. The prison literally crumbled around us and when the dust settled, we found ourselves in the ruins along with all the other monsters who were living there at Saint Mark's, though not as prisoners.

Tonight, though, is different from all those other times I found tears rolling down my cheeks. I'm not even sure what this emotion is aside from gratefulness.

I hate to admit it, but that's the overwhelming feeling I have inside my heart right now. I am grateful that Eros has taken pity on me. That he came looking for me in the fog, and took me home, and ran me a bath, and brought me food, and even got into bed next to me. Because I was positive that he would sleep somewhere else tonight.

Not to punish me. I'm really not worth his thoughts of punishment. I'm really not worth any of this.

But Eros didn't leave me. He got into bed.

And when I turn and snuggle into him—desperate for... well, everything—affection, validation, friendship, warmth, tenderness—he doesn't push me away when I reach for him.

This is the saddest thing and makes me cry harder. Because I'm not getting any of those things I crave. He's not offering affection, or validation, or friendship, or warmth, or tenderness.

He's merely putting up with me.

And my life is so miserable, and my ego so

destroyed, and my sense of self-worth so diminished that his indifference is *enough*.

I let out a sigh of relief.

I am pacified.

Which makes this the most pathetic moment of my entire life.

Eros clears his throat. "Ya know... I didn't really understand what I did to Pie that day."

I blink. Making the water pooling in my eyes slide down my cheeks. Then I run these words back in my head.

What is he doing? It this a confession? I tilt my chin up and look up at him. He's not looking down now, though. His eyes are on the ceiling. But I'm sure he can feel my gaze.

"I was wrong. To do that, ya know. I mean, it didn't even pan out. If I had gotten her little bag of magic doorway rings, at least I could justify it. I could make excuses. But the rings were gone. They were just gone. And I knew, the moment I realized they were missing, I knew I would never get my hands on those rings. It's even possible that Ostanes, that bitch, put that little birdie curse on Pie to steal her magic just so I would never get it. Like she knew. Like she had an oracle, or something."

"Hmm." This sound actually gets past my lips. Eros goes still when I make this noise. Like I am some small fawn in the forest and might spook if he moves too fast. Like I might have more to say about this than some small 'hmm.'

But I don't. So after a few moments, he continues.

"'Hmm' is right. I only know of one oracle and her name is Pressia."

Pressia was made and raised in Vinca until the age of seven. She was destined to marry Pell, the godling who was raised in the palace of Ptah and made by the hand of Ostanes, just like I was.

But not like me at all.

The marriage was called off because Pie disappeared.

And then, the way the scribes tell it, *everyone* started disappearing.

Pressia disappeared from her quarters in Ptah's royal palace where she was waiting to be married to Pell. But with Pie gone, Pell was to be a sacrifice to get his magic and use it on some future endeavor.

His disappearance is still a mystery to me. No one bothered to fill me in because on my side of things it was all about Pie.

I had never thought much about Pressia, but clearly she is an integral part of Eros's past.

People were still talking about her disappearance when I arrived at the Vinca Palace with Tarq and the king.

Though I did not know she was an oracle. Her alchemist—the royal alchemist, Lyrica—was also my alchemist once I became princess. Lyrica was very angry and bitter after losing her prize creation right out from under her nose. She fumed about it for years. I don't think she ever got over that, actually.

"Pressia is an interesting woman," Eros continues. "She looks human. Almost nymph-like in her beauty.

But she is neither nymph nor human. She is a cross between a goddess and chaosius."

I've never heard that last term.

He must know this somehow, because he elaborates. "It's a... an ancient sort of chimera. One of the first, actually. From the primordial days of Chaos, who is, in a technical way, my father."

Well. I didn't know that. I admit, I have not spent much time thinking about the origin of Eros. I was brought up being told that he was god of nothing. At one time, he controlled love, but he was banished into the Fadeaways long before I was born.

Eros keeps talking. "There are many ways to make breeding chimera. But using a chaosius is the easiest. These offspring will always be fertile. The catch is, there is no way to predict what they will look like, or how smart they will be, or what kind of power they will have. It was done a lot in the beginning of time. That's why there are so many different species of animals in the realms. Everything comes from a chaosius. Little Pressia was the first offspring from this genetic line to be born in thousands of years. Since the first gods were made, in fact. She is very special. And powerful. And pretty. If she and Pell had a child it would've been something spectacular.

"As it happened, though," he continues, "they didn't. And Pressia went missing the same day Pell went missing, which was the same day that Pie went missing. And Pressia's special powers turned out to be divination and prophecy. But somehow, she got herself a door *and* a key. She's been travelling through time. I met up with her once."

Well. This story is taking a turn I didn't expect. He's about to tell me something personal.

"She disappeared when she was a child, of course. Long, long after I had already been banished. But I bumped into her far, far, far into the future. I found a door in the early days of my banishment. Rather, a door was presented to me and I walked through it. It was a trap, of course."

He pauses here and I can feel him looking down at me. "They're all traps. Remember that, Callistina." I don't say anything so he just keeps going. "On the other side of my trap door was this woman, dressed in a flowing, light-green dress, with long, golden hair pulled back away from her face with gold chains, and a face so sweet you'd never even suspect the evil lurking underneath. But she *was* evil. She used me. She lied to me. She made me vulnerable. And in that vulnerable moment, she put me here."

He stops. I figure it's a dramatic pause, maybe. But it lingers too long for that. I conclude that he's waiting for me to urge him on, which I will not do directly, but I do say, "You shall call me queen," to let him know I'm still listening.

"Right." His chuckle is laced with cynicism.

And then I realize he wasn't waiting on me to let him know I was listening. He was caught up in something. He was caught up in his past.

"She was controlling time, Callie." I hate that name. "And memories. And she trapped me here with a song.

That stupid fuckin' song that plays even when the stupid jukebox is unplugged. She sure is my ball and chain. Anyway, once I was here, she presented me to the Court of Succession and I was formally banished into the Betwixts of Time. That is where I live still. The Betwixts of Time. Everything that I have done—that you know I have done, that everyone thinks I have done —has been done in the Betwixts of Time. It's not an absolute place. The fog is thin, at times. And I walk through it. That is how I got to the human world. That is how I met Lisa, the woman whose hand appeared that fateful day of Pie's Caretaking Ceremony and pulled her through the door. That is how I exist, and have existed, since nearly the time I was made."

It's an interesting story. Somewhat familiar too. And it calms me greatly and settles me too. So I am no longer crying.

Maybe that was his point. That's what I'm thinking when he says, "I didn't know any better. When I ruined Pie's life, I didn't know any better. And I'm sorry about that. And how what I did may have affected you."

My forehead furrows as I parse his words. Did he just… apologize to me?

I open my eyes and stare into the darkness. My head is resting in the crook of his arm, my own arm thrown over his chest in a possessive way I don't really mean. I'm simply clutching at him right now. Looking for some kind of stability that might keep me from actually going insane.

Or I was, before he started telling me his story.

Now I'm not sure what I'm doing.

The next thing I know, he's pulling me on top of him. It's a position I'm familiar with. This is how I have sex with him almost every single night. But tonight, I'm afraid.

Not because we're going to have sex. I don't care about the sex. But because when I am in position—his naked hips between my open legs, my hands pressing down on his chest—he's not putting himself inside me. Not the usual way, at least.

He's looking me in the eyes. Staring at me. Putting himself inside me that way instead.

I'm frozen. Unable to move. Unable to make a decision. There's a part of me that just wants to get up and walk out. Just leave. Because he *sees* me. And I don't want him to see me.

But there's another part of me—a much larger part of me—that wants to stay right here with him forever. Let him gaze right into my soul with those green eyes of his. Regardless of the consequences.

Because to look Eros in the eyes is to adore him. It's inevitable.

Except he's not trying to cajole me into loving him. Not yet. He's still talking. "Don't give up on my account. Don't lie down in the fog and fade away because of what I did to you. Or because you're stuck in this place. Or because you have to live inside this gorgeous body of yours that you hate with a passion. Don't give up, Callistina. I'm just not worth it."

Then he reaches up, and places his hands on my cheeks, and urges me to lower my lips down to his.

Which I do. And then he kisses me until I fall in love.

I know what this is. I know it's his magic. I know I don't love him and he doesn't love me.

But I want to believe it. Because I have nothing and no one left.

And so I do.

I believe it.

*I WAKE **up screaming*** like a raging lunatic. Reaching for something.

The nightmare is still fresh, convincing me I'm still there. But this time, the face of this destruction is what dominates my illusion. He's so real I want to reach out and touch him. Apis. The bull. The god. The one who never dies. The One Who Lives. Those words are on my lips and then they are spilling out of my mouth, and I am reaching for him…

Only it's not him at the end of my fingertips.

It's Eros. God of nothing. "What's wrong?" His eyes are wide and he's shaking me. "Why are you screaming?"

I wish that the illusion would shatter with his words, but they only make it stronger. In fact, I'm not in the apartment over the bar in Savage Falls with Eros, I'm still there. In Vinca City. Standing on the riverbanks as fireballs rain down. People burning all around me. Charred bodies and otherworldly shrieking.

When I look up, there she is. Madeline. It's Madeline up there, her blood-red scales tinged with an orange glow that is a direct reflection of the flames gushing out of her mouth like an ancient geyser as she burns my city to cinders.

And then I see him too. Not Apis, but Tarq. He's a skeleton. Nothing but horns, and hooves, and bones with a magnificent golden crown on his head.

The Skull King.

"What?" Eros is shaking me harder now. "What? Callistina! What are you doing?"

I think it's fairly obvious that I'm having a nightmare, but considering the fact that I'm awake, with my eyes open, looking at him as he looks at me, I suppose I can't blame him for being confused.

I blink. And then they're all gone. The One Who Lives. The Skull King. Madeline.

Vinca died the same way it started under my rule.

But why do I have to see it?

Better question is... who is sending me this message?

I push Eros away from me, get out of bed, and go searching for yesterday's dress, which also happens to be the day-before-that's dress as well.

I find it in the bathroom, but when I pick it up, it smells like the fog.

"Callistina?" Eros has followed me.

I ignore him. But I would like to borrow some of his clothes, so I drop the dress back onto the floor and go searching for a t-shirt. Which he doesn't seem to have.

And now that I think about it, he hasn't been wearing shirts since I arrived.

Reluctantly, I put the stupid dress back on, then sit on a chair in the living room as I strap the wooden blocks onto my feet.

"Come on," Eros says. He's very annoyed with me right now. "You're still gonna wear that shit? Callistina! You're not insane. This is an act! Just stop."

I stand up so I can look in the mirror as I attach my antlers. Eros is trying to make me meet his gaze with my reflection, but I don't give in.

He was considerate last night. I'm... thankful, I suppose. But I don't want to talk to him. I don't think I will come back to this apartment, actually. I don't think I want to see him again.

He's talking to me this entire time. Blah, blah, blah—"you're being dumb." Blah, blah, blah—"I can see through you." Blah, blah, blah—"Just *stop*."

But I don't respond to any of that.

I simply adjust my antlers one final time, then turn to the door.

"For fuck's sake, Callistina. You're really walking out?"

Well, if he was doubting me, those doubts probably disappear when I walk through the door and leave him standing there in the middle of his apartment, naked.

*It's **late morning*** when I arrive at the feed store, so there are several other people inside. Local people. Human people. I pretend to peruse all the various things sitting on shelves as Madeline chats her people up and takes care of their needs.

Eros did not follow me out of the apartment. I think this really is the end of us.

I'm OK with that.

Madeline thanks her last customer, a farmer type, who leaves, jingling the little bell over the door as he goes. Then she walks over to me. "Good morning, my queen."

She has always called me queen, so I never have anything to say to her.

"Are you out of bubble bath already?" Then she smiles at me, chuckling. "I'll go get you another bottle. Be right back."

I love Madeline. Love is a strong word, I know that. But there is no one else in this town who will have a conversation with me, or smile at me, or give me free bubble bath just to be nice. So I have decided to love her.

Which is why the nightmare is so terrible.

She's not a dragon now, of course. But I know that deep down she *is* a dragon. It's under control somehow. Magic, probably.

What really doesn't make any sense though, is how Tarq, or Apis, or both take control of her and destroy everything. Because when I left—rather, when I was pulled out by Pie and put into the Bottoms prison—I was the only person who could get anywhere near her without being burned alive.

The timeline is another concern of mine. Because I can't quite make sense of it. I fully understand that time is fluid. It comes and goes. Stops and starts.

But, from what I can gather, Madeline has always been here. Relative 'here.' Granite Springs, Savage Falls, Granite Falls, Savage Springs. Whatever this place is called, she is from here.

So is what's happening in my time the past? Or the future? Or the present?

It's quite confusing and my head is pounding for some reason, so I'm not up to the task of parsing it out. I suppose it doesn't matter though. I don't really have a desire to understand anything these days.

It's been building inside me, this feeling of… well. It could be indifference or it could be surrender, I'm not sure. That doesn't matter either. The point is, I feel *done* here.

"Here you go." Madeline has returned and offers me the bubble bath in her perpetually chirpy tone. She has never asked for anything in return and I appreciate that so much. I don't have any money—I don't even know how it works here—so I can't pay her using that. But I can pay her another way.

I take the bottle and look her in the eyes. "Thank you, Madeline."

Her smile drops. In surprise, I think. Since I have never talked to her, not even to demand that she call me queen.

KC CROSS & JA HUSS

"I would like you to know," I continue, "that I will do everything I can to help you in the future. Or past. Or present. Whichever it may be."

"Oh." She touches her heart with her hand, her sweet face once again bright with optimism. "That's so nice of you. And... thank you."

She has no idea what my promise means. Perhaps she's picturing makeup tips, or fashion advice. That's probably what she thinks I'm referring to.

Certainly, she has no idea she will be breathing fire in great streams over Vinca City. Destroying it.

But this is what I'm referring to.

I will stop the destruction of Vinca. Somehow. Not for Tarq's sake, not for my sake, but for Madeline's sake.

I can't take back my evil past, but perhaps I can prevent Madeline from ever having one.

I think there is more to the fog. I think it might lead somewhere.

And so that is where I'm heading when I leave the store.

CHAPTER SEVEN - EROS

A **profusion of emotions** flood through me as I watch Callistina walk out of my apartment, those antlers perched precariously on top of her head, those wooden blocks on her feet clopping on the hard-wood steps as she descends.

"What. The fuck." I mutter this under my breath.

But it's not really a mystery, is it? She's crazy. Losing her royal status turned her crazy. And ya know what? It's none of my business. I don't even like her. Some-how, some way we got tangled up together after Tomas's whole Saint Mark's game ended and that's all this has been.

Not a relationship. Not even an affair. It's a fling.

Was a fling. Because it's over now.

I walk over to the bed and start ripping the sheets off. In fact, I'm gonna get rid of everything she has here. Including all that bubble bath. But as I throw the sheets on the floor, a feather floats upwards with a whoosh of air.

My eyes follow it as it floats and then falls, landing at my feet.

I reach down and pick it up. Twirling it in my fingers. Studying it.

Now, the logical conclusion when one finds a feather in their bedding is to assume it came from the pillow. But my pillows aren't stuffed with feathers, they're stuffed with down. And this feather—being a good eight inches in length—is not down and in no way came from a pillow.

It's also... gold. Which feels like both a reminder of the past and portents of the future.

All of which are disturbing.

I'm not sure where it came from, but finding it in my bed is so disgusting to me, I almost retch. I can't even think straight for a moment, that's how grossed out I am.

A feather. In my bed. Disgusting.

I look at the sheets and immediately want to burn them.

But I don't. Can't, really. Because it's hard enough to get a regular delivery of whiskey and food. Getting one of my human crossbred descendants to venture into a bed and bath store out in the wider world to pick me up some new sheets feels like an ask too far.

Instead, I drop them into the washer, add some bleach, press hot, and start the machine.

Feathers. No. I cannot abide them. I walk over to the window, open it up, and toss the feather into the wind, then quickly close the window and try to put that whole incident out of my mind.

Now where was I?

Oh, right. I go into the bathroom, grab the waste can, and toss all of Callistina's things into it. She's got a lot more here than I even knew. I throw all her stupid bottles of crap into the trash.

Fuck her. She's not even fun. She's... well, she is a little bit fun. In bed, at least. A smile slowly creeps up on my face as I remember all the times we've had fun in bed. She's a little wild. Of course, she doesn't say anything meaningful, and her eyes are always closed, but every once in a while, when she's climaxing, she will tell me to call her queen.

I don't really mind it during sex.

The last time we had sex she wasn't very excitable, but that's what makes it kinda interesting. The unpredictability is stimulating. She was slow and softer than usual that last time, those perfect breasts of hers taunting and tantalizing as she rode me. The expression on her face was calm and almost accepting. Like she had let her burdens go.

And I felt that way too, come to think of it. Untroubled and quiet. It almost felt a little bit like... progress. We had crossed into new territory, or set new boundaries, or maybe removed some boundaries.

I'm not quite sure of the specifics, but it felt like change. And change is good.

And then all that fog stuff. And the bath, and the food, and the cuddling.

My God, I cuddled with her. And told her a story. Though the story really was on point.

Regardless. For the first time, Queen Callistina was

vulnerable. That's the only way to describe it. She had come to her end and given up in the fog.

And what did I do? I pulled her out of it.

She didn't even thank me.

She woke up, threw aside all of the gestures I made yesterday, went back to being crazy, and then walked her ass out of here without a second glance.

It pisses me off. It feels a little manipulative.

Though I know what she would say to that, if she was inclined to say anything. She would say, "I didn't come to you, Eros. You came to me. I never asked anything of you. You take from me."

And maybe I do. But just because she doesn't ask for things doesn't mean she doesn't owe a debt when they are given. I didn't blink an eye when she showed up here. I didn't care if she slept in my bed, or bathed in my bathroom, or whatever else she's been doing on my dime.

It was all mutual.

But now I realize I was mistaken. It was not mutual. She was using me and it pisses me off.

This anger builds inside me until my whole body goes hot. And then I get this tunnel vision type of thing. Where the edges of my world go dark and only the middle has light.

And in this light, I see a place. Some place sunny and bright. A clearing in a forest, maybe, or the top of a hill. Someplace open like that. And then there she is. Callistina. The queen. In all her gryphon chimera glory —her golden velvet fur, and her yellow eyes, and her magnificent set of antlers that are not affixed to her head with string, but growing right out of her skull. Shining in the light. She is almost aglow, that's how much light is shining down on her.

She is so beautiful, so stunning and majestic.

But streaming down her cheeks are tears. Her long eyelashes are dotted with them too.

She is crying.

I reach for her, but as soon as my hand enters the vision, it all disappears.

Gone.

I find myself sitting on a throne, wondering what just happened.

And then I open my eyes and realize that I fell asleep and it was nothing but a dream.

UNFORTUNATELY FOR ME, it was not a dream. Well, maybe the part about Callistina, but my actual piece-of-shit life here in Savage Falls is all too real as I listen to the monsters and townspeople congregating in my bar downstairs.

Something has to give.

I can't do this anymore. Not only that, I don't *want* to do this anymore.

I'm at that point where one cannot continue. Where even eternal strife is preferred over mindless stagnation. When you know that moving forward is dangerous and fraught with peril, but you no longer care. You'd rather die than be stuck here.

That's how I feel. I'd rather die.

And since that is not an option, there is no relief. There will be no relief. This is what my eternity looks like. Me, in this foggy little piece-of-shit town, living above this bar, listening to these ignorant, foolish people and monsters complain about their stupid problems, all the while throwing darts, and playing pool, and drinking whiskey that is probably gonna run out sooner rather than later.

Then what?

Then what are these fuckin' monsters gonna do?

They're gonna lose their shit, that's what they're gonna do.

Lose. Their. Shit.

One of these days the last human resident of Savage Falls is gonna leave to go get cigs and alcohol and they're never gonna come back. They're gonna get lost in the fog. Or, hell, maybe they'll just decide, *Fuck this place.* Because that's what I'd have been thinking the very first day if I were one of the humans. *Fuck this place.* I'd have been outta here so fast.

The very same moment that this thought is occurring to me inside my head, I hear a commotion downstairs.

"Great," I mutter, then walk over to the door and pull it open. There's a fight downstairs. Because of course there is. I stomp down the stairs, come out of the hallway, and just stand there witnessing the complete disregard for my bar, the utter turmoil of all the various monsters in it, and the spilt beer and whiskey on the floors.

And that's it. This is the last straw. I duck out of the way as a chair comes flying in my direction, and then step forward, crossing the room until I'm in front of my throne. I haven't sat in it since that day that Pell and Pie showed up and took most of the monsters off my hands. The throne is a formality. A bit of pageantry meant to convey power.

It's nice, but I don't need it.

Still, in this moment I think these monsters need a reminder of just who and what I am. So I sit. And the moment I do, the room changes. It becomes bigger, wider, more important than just some little hick bar.

There is regalia on the walls. Banners and such, displaying the crest of my house. And in my hand is a bow. Not a shitty fucking longbow, either. I'm talking a shoot-a-bear-between-the-eyes-and-drop-him-dead kinda crossbow complete with titanium bolts tipped with tungsten that add weight and must be aimed just so.

But I am nothing if not a good aim.

I load a bolt and shoot the nearest monster. Now, when it comes to my power, it is limited to this realm right here where I exist. Not only that, my weapons are feelings. Love and hate. That's what I command. Some might think it's a small power. Most will admit that the broken heart can change the course of history, but they're only seeing the tip of the iceberg.

And ironically, love is infinitely more powerful than

hate. Love can ruin the world much quicker than hate. Because a man would do anything for love. *Any*thing.

Still, it is a hate bolt that I shoot now. Because hate manifests in interesting ways. It can be a blind rage. It can be calm and calculating. It can cause wars, and atrocities, and divisions just as well as love can. But in the name of hate, the rage turns inward on one's self.

And that's what happens to the big satyr I shoot. His hate is all-encompassing, his rage comin' out of his eyes like red heat. His face changes. Right before our eyes. And he turns into something hideous.

That's what hate makes you. Hideous.

The fighting has stopped by now and the monsters are staring, first at me as I shoot the bolt, but then at the target.

He was a monster already. He had fur, and horns, and very large teeth. But now he's something disgusting. The degree of ugliness that outwardly manifests after being struck with one of my hate bolts depends on how much animosity and rage one has cultivated over the years.

And this one, he must have a lot. Because his face begins to melt. He looks like hot wax. He is so full of hate, it starts dripping off of him. Sliding down his cheeks, plopping onto his shoulders, running down his hairy chest.

By this time, the monsters have noticed that something unusual is happening and begin shouting and roaring in surprise as one among them starts to liquify from the inside out due to his hate—and my tungsten-tipped bolt, which has pierced his little black heart.

I feel like the humans must know better than to start shit in my bar, because I don't see a single one in the room right now. But the monsters, they are taken aback, to say the least.

Now listen. I get it. Love and hate are good and all. They are powerful emotions. But how many ways can you possibly come up with to use these two itty-bitty things to create havoc?

Well, turns out, if you're an eternal god who has been banished into the fog with very few opportunities to do anything but plot your revenge, you become rather resourceful.

The hate-pull is one of the more gruesome ways I've come up with to make a point over the course of my very long life. And it certainly has the desired effect now. Because the fight is over and by the time their friend-foe—whoever the hell the monster was—by the time he's nothing but a disgusting little puddle on the floor, they're standing silent in a ring around him with mouths open like a bunch of ancient idiots.

"Now that I have your attention," I say calmly, but firmly—every monstrous face turns to look at me—"I would like to go over the rules." I place the crossbow in my lap and look every fuckin' monster in the eyes as I talk. "One. You are no longer allowed in my bar."

There is some grumbling, but it doesn't last long.

When they first got here, I thought it was kinda nice having people in the bar. I liked the hum of conversation and the laughter. But I'm tired of it now. "You're gonna have to find somewhere else to hang out. Two. If you ever"—I pause here for dramatic effect—"*ever*

89

destroy something in my town again, I will throw you into the fog and let you aimlessly wander for all eternity. Three. If there is one more fight"—I hold up a single finger to punctuate the point that this 'one' is a literal number—"one. More. I will liquify everyone involved. And maybe you think this might be an easy way out. Maybe you think you're tired of living and what the hell, let's make Eros kill us." I point to the puddle on the floor. "But he's not dead, friends."

There is a gasp as everyone turns to look at the puddle.

"That's right. He's still in there. He's trapped in his own hate. This is my version of Hell, you see. I have the power to send y'all to Hell. I don't like to do it," I tell them. "I don't. There is no joy in sending monsters to their own personal Hell. But you all are gettin' on my last fuckin' nerve. And when a god's peace is disturbed, he will do anything to restore it." I pause again to make a flourish with my hands. "So are we clear here?"

They just look at me.

"Are you gonna make me repeat my question?"

They start agreeing real fast, nodding and assuring me that there will be no more trouble.

"Wonderful." I smile at them, get up off my throne, hold my crossbow up—then make it disappear—and start walking towards the stairs that lead to my apartment.

They are holding their breath and just about to let it out when I reach the little hallway, but I turn in that moment. "And don't forget to clean up the mess before you leave. That includes the puddle that was once your friend."

Then I take my leave and retreat back up to my shitty apartment.

Where I exist in my natural state.

Which is singular.

Solitary. Apart. Isolated. Separate.

All words for the only one that counts.

Alone.

CHAPTER EIGHT - CALLISTINA

woman can only take so much. And I have found my limit.

This day. Right now, this moment, I realize that I have had *enough*.

While I hate the term 'victim' and would never, *ever* have referred to myself as one back when I was queen, the idea that I have been wronged is growing on me.

Furthermore, the idea that I have been wronged in such a way that the wrong can never be righted has also taken root.

There are not many options when one finds oneself the victim of circumstance, as I have found myself, on more than one occasion. You can rise up. Meet the challenge. Do your best.

And I feel like I had that spirit in me when I was taken to Vinca after Pie was stolen.

Or one can simply accept defeat. Normally I am not one to choose this path. But when a woman gets to the point where she has been stripped of everything she ever was and sees no possible way to make a change that will lead to an acceptable outcome, a reality check might be in order.

I walk down the road towards a little park on the edge of town and take a seat on a stone bench that was erected in the memory of that 'Big Jim' man. The bench declares that 'He was a giant among mortals. May he rest in peace.' Here, I do some real soul-searching.

Despite my rash behavior yesterday, one should not rush into one's end. One should think about it carefully. I think the fog is a plausible answer to my dilemma. It might not kill me—in fact, I'm quite certain that it won't kill me. That would make the choice so much easier, actually. No. It's not going to kill me. It's going to… release me. It's going to sever the tether I have to this world and allow me to wander. Aimlessly, I hope. Unconsciously would be a nice perk as well. If I could just start walking, and get lost, and wander, then wander some more…

Then maybe, perhaps, I might pop back out at some point in the future when this town is gone and this god has moved on.

That is my hope.

I choose defeat.

Because my wrongs cannot be fixed. I cannot go back in time and be the woman I was meant to be. Oh, and I know what the other strong women of the world would be thinking. 'Callistina, one only needs perseverance to succeed.'

But it's a load of bullshit, isn't it?

It's utter crap. I mean, there is no alchemist to

apprentice with here in Savage Falls. Not even a little herb store. What am I supposed to do? Walk around these hills chipping on rocks until I bump into a crystal?

There is no possible way for me to be the alchemist I was meant to be.

And I was meant to be a great one. I know it. I would've been so good. I was already making progress by the time I was fourteen. And just the week before Pie's Caretaking Ceremony I had discovered that my true magic was in using bottles.

I hadn't even told anyone yet, it was so recent. I only got to experiment with the bottles a few times before that treacherous Eros ruined everything. But I knew that my gift led in that direction and I was going to do great things with magic inside bottles. I was testing potions and had one in particular that really, really mattered.

My labmate—what was her name? Gods above, I have not thought about that girl in almost twenty years. Regardless of what her name was, she was properly impressed. Nearly green with envy. Hardly any of the apprentices discovered their true intrinsic potential until they were well past the age of sixteen and there I was—the one and only bottle-magic maker.

Sounds stupid when you say it like that, but it's actually quite powerful. I could put any potion at all inside a bottle and with the right additions, and a little bit of time, I could double or even triple the power.

And that was just my first set of experiments. I can only imagine how powerful my bottle magic would be now, after twenty years of perfection.

I resent this loss. I resent being taken from my true path and put on Pie's. I resent being mated to Tarq, and all those dead babies, and what I became because of it.

Fine. I will accept responsibility for my part in this outcome. I was a terrible queen.

This makes me scoff and chastise myself out loud. "Terrible, Callistina?" Then I huff. "Fine. I was an evil queen. There. I said it. I was an evil queen. But does fate not bear some responsibility for the monster I turned into? Can I not share some of this accountability? Was it really, entirely my fault when I was taken off my path?"

No one is here to answer me.

No one has ever been around to hear my confessions, or prayers, or begging for guidance. And that's part of the problem too.

I ruled an entire kingdom, had a royal guard, and that stupid alchemist, Lyrica, and the worthless Tarq—who left me to perform all the royal duties so he could be left alone in his pursuit of power. Power that was going to be much more than a king's, that's for sure.

I had subjects everywhere. People bowing to me.

But the entire time I was in Vinca, I was alone.

I almost never thought about my life in terms of solitude or companionship. What was the point? I was married to Tarq. I was the queen. It was a loveless marriage, of course. I never hated him, but in the later years he hated me very much because I discovered his greatest desire—his search for doors, first and foremost, but also his attraction to Nysta, who he was hiding from me.

His reasons to hate me were legitimate.

All of this is a very long-winded way of saying that I have nothing to live for. Nothing to look forward to. And maybe, if I had a God, I could find some strength within to persevere until I found my new purpose. But the gods are fake, and imperfect, and fallen.

If I were an alchemist, I could make my own god, perhaps. Isn't that the ultimate goal of all alchemists? Isn't that what they're doing with the genetics of royal beasts? Looking for the big magic? The magic that might break through and live on. And they will be the ultimate creators.

The god-makers.

It's what I should've been doing all these years but it's too late for that now.

And anyway, I've had enough.

I'm done. Regardless of who is to blame for what I have lost and will never recover, I am done.

So I get up and start walking down the road towards the fog.

I will walk in and I will keep walking.

This is my future now.

Fog.

THE SHALLOWS of the fog are in view when I hear someone calling in the woods.

I pause in front of the closed-up candle shop and look behind me, wondering if anyone else can hear it as well.

There are a few people on the streets. Mostly they are by the diner and the coffeeshop, which are both too far away to hear the shouting. So I turn back and look up the hill to my right where the woods are.

"*Hellooooo*!" someone is calling. "Is anyone *heeeeeeere*?"

Well. What is this all about? Did a human get lost in the woods? "Oh!" I exclaim this out loud. "Perhaps it is a townsperson who left to get supplies and then got lost on the way home!"

I gather up the skirts of my dress and head up the hill. My wood-block shoes are not very practical for hill climbing, but the shouting is getting louder and I don't want to stop and take them off.

"*Helloooooooo*!" the person calls again. And I am quite sure they are human and not monster by the accent on the word.

"Hello!" I call back. "Are you lost?"

"Oh, my God!" a man's voice calls. "Hello! I'm here!"

"Keep talking," I say. "I'm coming to find you." It's only now that I realize that I should be insisting they call me queen, but I'm excited about this strange turn of events. Life here is so stagnated that a random townsperson returning is almost like an adventure.

Well, not a grand adventure, but at the very least, it's a small escapade.

I'm still going into that fog. I think.

I'll decide later.

Right now, I am on a mission to increase the population of Savage Falls by one.

As soon as this thought enters my head, I see them.

Not one. But two! *Two* townspeople returning! Imagine the news they will bring! And possibly good liquor!

I take a deep breath and let it out, steadying myself. I have to stop being so chatty. I have a reputation to uphold as the town queen and my demand to be called queen will be seen, from their perspective, as a sign that they have indeed made it home.

So I do not say any more.

The two men and I see each other at nearly the same moment, and although I try to hide it, there is a smile on my face. I do not recognize them, so they probably disappeared into the fog just after everything changed.

Also, are they… men? Or are they boys? They are not tall, and muscular, and burly, as is my experience with men. They are kind of skinny and puny.

"Oh, my *God*!" one yells, his hand over his mouth as his feet come to a full stop on the side of the mountain. He has caught sight of me.

Then his friend says, "What the fuck is that? Am I drunk? Am I seeing this?"

And I realize he's talking about… me. Is he seeing me? What could that mean?

"Uh…" the first one says. He and I are staring at each other. "Uh… hi?"

I am puzzled. Trying to work out what is happening here.

I think they are too.

"Hel-*lo*," I say cautiously. "You shall call me queen."

They stare at me, blinking a few times. Then they look at each other and fall into a fit of laughter. They are saying things, but I can't quite keep up with the patterns of speech and certain words are not translating well in my brain.

But one thing is for certain. These puny men are not from Granite Springs. They did not wander off getting supplies one day and find their way home.

They are outsiders.

I peer over them and up the side of the hill and almost lose my breath when I see it.

Shimmering, right there in the forest.

A *door*.

"Dude," the second man-boy says, still laughing. "Tell me this is a joke." He points at me. "Tell me we did not just hike in the woods for two fucking days to find *that*!" He's pointing at me.

I'm not sure how to respond. I understand that they are making fun of me, probably because I'm wearing antlers on my head and blocks of wood on my feet, but I'm just not sure what to say back to them.

They are... outsiders. And they came through a magic door that is still *open*.

Suddenly my mind is whirling with questions. "Where did you come from? Are there any more of you?"

They are still laughing, but their fit is beginning to wear off a little. So the first one manages, "We came all the way from Pittsburgh, lady. Just because someone was in a bar last week and told us about a little town filled with walking, talking monsters that are half human, half animal."

"Did they?" I ask, still focusing on that door.

The second one says, "Yeah. But you're not a monster, you're just a crazy bitch. What is this? Some kind of weird cult?"

Cult. I consider this. It is, kind of, in a way, the Cult of Eros. So I say, "Yes. It's a cult," even though I understand we're probably not using this word in the same way. And Savage Falls is not, technically, a cult, since none of the residents worship Eros—a few of them are related by blood and the rest of us are just stuck with him.

Still, I feel this misnomer is accurate enough for the moment, and now it is my turn for a question. "Would you like to come into town for a drink?"

They both look at me in a new way now. I am wearing fake horns, a ratty fur coat, and blocks of wood on my feet, but underneath all that insanity is a very beautiful woman. At least by human standards.

This is how they see me now.

"Uh," that first one says. He looks at his friend and they have some sort of secret conversation with their eyes. *Should we, shouldn't we...* Then he looks at me and smiles. "Uh, sure. Yeah. Let's have a drink. Does the whole town dress like you?"

"Not exactly." And now it's my turn to smile. I extend both of my hands towards them. "Come with me, boys. Let me be your escort."

They shoot each other another look, doing something with their eyebrows. Like I just made them an offer of sex. Absurd. But whatever. I smile even bigger as they come down the hill towards me, turn around, and I take both of their hands.

"Are we going to a bar?" one asks.

"Is there food?" the other asks. "We're starving. We've been wandering in the woods for two days looking for you people."

I don't say anything, because we were not that far up the hill and the town is already visible through the trees.

"Oh, look," the first one says, pointing with the hand I'm not holding. "A candle shop."

"Oh, my God," the other one says. "I'm so pissed. Look, it's a road. We could've driven here, asshole."

"We needed the door, remember?"

"That door didn't do anything. It was just a stupid frame and we walked under it."

Interesting. They found the door open in the middle of the woods. "Pittsburgh, you say?"

"Yeah," the first one says. "We're both seniors at Pitt studying ancient history. What do you do, lady? And why are you dressed this way? Is it a festival day or something?"

I'm not sure what a 'pit' means in their language, but ancient history I understand. "Oh, ancient history. Then you're going to *love* this town." I snicker a little. "And I am the queen. You shall call me queen."

"Right," the first one laughs. "I mean, yes, my queen." He leans back to catch the eye of his friend, once again passing along some hidden meaning.

We are just about to step out of the woods when I catch sight of Batty—Darrel—coming out of the candle shop with a bag. It's been closed for weeks—that shop's owner went for supplies and never came back—but it's stocked with plenty of little luxuries. Batty must be procuring Madeline a gift. Which I like. Because I like her.

And he is the perfect monster for this moment.

Which is the moment when the man-boys catch sight of him as well and their feet do a full stop on the sidewalk as they stare at the monster across the street.

Batty is formidable-looking. He's almost a little Eros copy. Not as commanding, but he's had his moments in this shit show we're all playing bit parts in.

He is looking at us as well. His gaze finds mine, his eyebrows raised in confusion. Because he doesn't recognize these man-boys and he has questions.

"Hello, Batty," I say, which also takes him by surprise because I have never actually spoken to him. "We have guests. Can you help me? They would like a drink at the bar and I would like them to meet Eros."

The man-boys are shocked, having gone very still. The first one whispers, "Dude. Are you seeing this? Or is that last hit of acid comin' back to haunt me?"

The other one whispers, "No, dude, I see it."

Batty comes towards us, his face making an unfriendly expression. "Who the hell are you?" he demands.

The man-boys are suddenly shaking. I've still got them both by the hand. We all realize this in the same moment, and they start struggling to get free.

But Batty seizes their hands, twirls them around, pushes them to the ground, and kneels on their backs.

Then he leans his face down between them and growls, "If you move, I will dismember you."

They squeak and squawk, but having subdued them, Batty has refocused his attention to me. "What just happened?"

I point up the hill. "You shall call me queen."

"Callistina, I don't have time for your queen bullshit. Where did these people come from?"

My smile is sweet and my face is serene when I say, "You shall call me queen."

I expect the man-boys to give up this information, but they are in hysterics. Praying to their god, and begging for mercy, and all the other usual things that come spilling out of mouths when monsters grab humans and subdue them on the ground.

"Let's take them to Eros," Batty sighs. "He'll know what to do."

Which was the plan all along.

So I smile at Batty, like it was his idea, and say, "You shall call me queen."

CHAPTER NINE - EROS

"Hate is my soulmate, despair is my friend.
The fog is my solace, the darkness my end.
No love for me, this curse is eternal.
Hell is my home, my existence infernal.

"The road is long, and lonely, and sad.
The spaces between drive me wild and mad.
No reward is forthcoming, no prize in the win.
For there is no winning when you're neck-deep in sin.

"The gate is too narrow, too slim, too strait.
I'll never pass through, it is far too late.
I'll wander all lost and heavy with weight.
Hate is my soulmate, my soulmate is hate."

'm looking at myself in the mirror as I say these words. It's an old spelling, one cast on me by Pressia lifetimes ago. Well, what she did with this spell was quite clever, actually. Because she never said these words to me, she compelled me to say them to myself.

I was born with a curse of sorts—the god of love, who could not use his power on himself. Who could not compel another to love him. Or hate him, for that matter.

Now, on the surface, this is a very good thing. If my power could be used against me that would be a terrible weakness. One could, theoretically, steal my bow and arrow and just shoot the fuck out of me. Confuse me all up with feelings. Hate, love, what's the difference? They are both bad because they are both overpowering.

It would've made me terribly weak if I were susceptible to this emotional handicap.

But what Pressia's spell did, in all actuality, was *remove* love and hate from my whole existence. I could sleep with anyone I wanted. Woman, man—didn't matter, they all wanted me. And back in the beginning I didn't understand the depth of Pressia's insidiousness. Of what she really took from me that day.

She turned me in, is what she did. Sold me out. Ratted. Snitched. Betrayed me to the gods and goddesses. All of them. Not just one or two. No. All four of the succession pantheons were hunting me at the time and Pressia told them how to find me.

But just before I was caught, she compelled me to recite this spelling.

Hate is my soulmate. My soulmate is hate.

That... *that* was what burned me. Still burns me. She not only gave me up, she was playing me. The whole time, she was playing me.

Knowing what I do now, it makes a lot of sense. See, she can see through time while I cannot. So for me, what was happening was linear. I hadn't crossed her. I was just minding my own business.

But to her, I had already kidnapped Pie, ruined Pressia's wedding to Pell because of Pie's disappearance, and was already living in this godforsaken town. The ball and chain was in full effect.

When Pressia cursed me and turned me over to the gods I had already ruined everything.

And the funny thing is, I thought—all these years while I was biding my time in this foggy town—I thought that I was getting better. That I had matured. Grown into myself, as they say.

But the way I see it now, from the perspective of a man on the other side of time who can look back at his mistakes, I didn't get better. I got worse.

Which really surprises me because I really thought myself innocent.

But my timeline is not looking good. It's pointing to the fact that I've been an evil son of a bitch since I was born and I will remain that way forever.

I mean—I have to stop and laugh here—if a god cannot change his ways over the course of thousands of years, what hope, ya know? What hope is there?

There are loopholes, obviously, in this curse of hers. The human world. Which is not a place I belong. I tried with Lisa, I really did. If Pie had been useful, I might've even tried harder. But it didn't shake out. And I haven't been back to the human world since that door on the hill disappeared after Pie and Pell broke their curses and... well, went wherever they went.

Perhaps I should just give up. Stop trying. Fade away, the way I was supposed to, and... whatever, ya know? Whatever happens to gods when they fade.

And maybe, if I knew how to do that, I would. I'd... do the whole self-sacrifice thing for the betterment of mankind.

I'm still looking at myself in the mirror as I think this. But then I burst out laughing, my eyes shining bright green with the thought. Give up? Please. I laugh again.

No. Giving up just isn't in my nature and I have a feeling that something is about to break. Now that could be a bad thing, but it could also be a good thing. Because—

A knock on my apartment door interrupts my self-reflection, which irritates me. "What?" I growl it loud enough to carry out of the bathroom and over to the door. "I'm busy."

The doorknob jiggles and I turn, looking at it from all the way across the room, astounded that someone would dare to enter without permission.

But when the door swings open it's just Callistina.

And, well—I'm not sure what's happening with us right now, but technically, she doesn't have to knock.

Still, I'm annoyed because she is actually the source of my annoyance. "Oh," I say smarmily. "You're back." I put up my hands, palms out, pushing in her direction. "Let me guess. I shall call you queen."

"Well." She plants a hand on her hip. "Actually, I come with news."

"And she's talking too! Almost as if she's sane and faking the crazy. Well, I must be someone special. Either that, or you need something from me. Hmm." I tap my chin with my finger. "I wonder which one it is."

"The news is," Callistina continues without taking my bait, "people have arrived."

I blink at her. "What?"

"People? You know, humans and such? The kind who live in the human realm and need to walk through a door to get here? That kind of people."

I blink again. "What are you saying?"

"Oh, my gods," she huffs. "There is a door on the hill and people have walked through it. They come from the Realm of Pittsburgh. Apparently, there were rumors that a town exists in the woods that contains monsters and two buffoons from that realm came to find us. They have succeeded and I have captured them for you and secured them to your throne downstairs with a chain. You're welcome."

"So you really are sane now? Or this is just another one-off?"

"One-off, Eros? One-off implies a singular time. It's a good thing you're pretty, because the brain you were born with is substandard."

"Heh. Well, at least I don't walk around with fake

antlers strapped to my head and wooden blocks on my feet."

"Do you know what I think?" she says.

"No. And I don't want to know what you think. You were saying about the humans?"

"I think…" She pauses, maybe to make sure I'm listening. "I think that Pie was the lucky one. Not me."

Rage bursts through me, but only for an instant. Callistina is playing a game. Perhaps the one where she's the 'crazy antler woman' of Savage Falls is over now, but she's still playing a game. And she said these words on purpose because she knows Pie had an awful life before she wandered into Saint Mark's, and she knows this was my doing, and she knows I feel guilty about this, and she wants to make me react.

So I do not react. I do not say anything. I do not move. I stare at her as she sits down in a chair and unstraps her wooden blocks.

She's still looking at me, though, when she continues talking. "Do you know why I think that? I'll tell you why. Because she has people. She lost everything and came out the other side with people. I have no people, Eros. I lost my people. My people are all dead. So I'm going to find myself some new people."

I let out a breath. "You *had* people at one time?"

She sneers out her words. "I had the entire city of Vinca, you insolent fadeaway."

"Ooh." I scoff. "Fadeaway? You bitch. What the fuck have I ever done to you? I didn't bring you here, I haven't forced you to stay here, and I sure as hell don't want you here. And you stand here, in my town"—I pan

my arms wide to illustrate the expanse of my realm—
"like a fucking worthless layabout and call *me* a
fadeaway?"

"Why does that cut you so deep, Eros? Hmm? It's
been thousands of years. Get over it."

I stand, bat wings flaring up at my sides, stretching
out until they're pressing against the walls, and loom
over her. Suddenly bigger than I was. My head bowing
at the neck because it's hitting the ceiling. "Get. Out."

She shrugs, gets to her feet, straightens her antlers,
and walks to the door, leaving her wooden shoe-blocks
behind.

She stops at the door and turns to face me.

I'm back to my normal size, just a smidge over six
feet, but my display has concerned her. She is cautious
as she unties the bow that secures the antlers under her
chin, and then she cocks her head to the side and they
crash to the floor. All twenty-two semi-golden points.

"What the hell is that all about?" I ask.

Callistina shakes out her flaxen hair, tilts up her
chin, and looks me in the eyes. "I'm tired, Eros. I'm tired
of being crazy, I'm tired of being alone, and I'm tired of
being human. So I am going to choose to be sane now,
and to find my people, and to embrace what I have
become."

"I don't even know what that means, Callistina."

She shrugs. "It doesn't matter." Then she turns and
walks out.

I stand there in my apartment for almost a minute,
running all these new events through my head.

Then I nod, take a deep breath, and walk down the

stairs with my massive black wings drooping behind me.

As soon as I enter the bar I scan the room for Callistina, but she's gone. Batty-Darrel is here though. And he says, "She found them on the hill," pointing to the two young men who have been chained to my throne. They are staring at me, mouths agape and eyes wide. Like a scream is stuck in their throats.

I walk over to them. Stalking, really. My wings are outstretched, no longer confined to the small space upstairs, so they reach out for almost three meters in both directions, catching on chairs and tables, so that I drag these things behind me as I make my way towards the trespassers.

Both have been bound at the wrists with chains. But their legs are free, so they try to scoot away as I approach, pressing up against the massive arms of my chair, which is in the shape of a lion's head.

"What are you doing here." These words leave my mouth with absolute authority, so they do not carry the tone of a question.

One of them stutters, "We... we... we were looking for the monster town. We're sorry, we don't really know how we got here. One moment we were on the hillside, and the next we saw that..." He looks at the front door which, presumably, was the last location he saw Callistina. "That crazy lady with the antlers was coming up the hill!"

"Please, don't kill us," the other one says. "Please! Please, please, *please*," he begs.

The sigh that leaves my mouth this time is just...

exhaustion. I scrub my hands down my face, pull out a chair from the nearest table, and sink down into it, leaning back, stretching out my legs, and letting my wings droop to the floor. I am not in the mood for humans. "Shall I eat ya?"

"Wh-wh-what?" the first one manages.

"Did he just say he wanted to eat us?" the other one squeaks.

Why me? Why. Me? What did I do that was so bad? What?

Was it the arrow I shot at Apollo? No. He wanted that relationship. I remember that. He paid me. Didn't he?

I can't remember. I shot somebody with a love arrow. Whoever this person was, they bonded with… oh, can't remember that, either. But I do know I shot the partner with the hate arrow.

I smile, chuckling to myself as I think back on how fun it was. To utterly destroy people with the power of unrequited love. I was going to rule the realm.

"Why is he smiling? Is he really gonna eat us?"

"Shut up, Monty! Just shut up!"

I blow out yet another breath of exhaustion and turn to the one called Monty. He is… puny. And dirty. And he needs a haircut. His wavy, dark hair falls past his shoulders. Which I like on myself. Mine is slightly shorter than that and, of course, it is not dark, but this man—is he a man? Or a boy? It's so hard to tell. At any rate, this *male* is untidy. He's got leaves and twigs in his hair and his shirt is ripped right down the front.

His traveling partner is almost a perfect copy.

Different face, of course. But also puny, and dirty, and undesirable.

"Tell me, Monty, are you magical?"

"W-what?" He blinks in my direction, then snaps out of it and glances at his friend. They share a look. This look tells me they are about to lie.

"No, no, no, dear boy. You do not want to lie to me. I already know you're not magical, you reek of ordinary things. But the only way to get here is through magic. So how did you come upon this magic?"

They share another look. Then the one who is not Monty says—while looking his friend in the eyes—"We should just tell him."

"No way, man! And shut up, Brett! What the fuck!" Monty glances at me and finds me smiling.

"You look tasty, Monty. With a little bit of salt you will grill up nicely."

"We came through a door," Brett shouts. "There's a door! On the hillside! It shimmered, like quicksilver, ya know? And then we walked through! That's how we got here." He bellows this out in a single breath, gasping at the end.

Monty is yelling at his friend now. Something about... a pact? I don't know.

I ignore them.

Because there is a *door*. Just as Callistina said.

And of course there is.

Pie was supposed to shut all the doors, but she missed one.

Or did she?

Is someone setting me up?

Who? And why?

Who wants me to walk through that door and into a trap?

I pause here to let out another chuckle. Because things were starting to get monotonous, were they not? And what happens? A door appears.

How likely is it that this is just coincidence?

I would say zero percent likely.

My chuckle makes the puny men skittish and they discuss amongst themselves the reasons behind it. But I push all that aside and think about *her*.

Pressia. The little oracle who saw my future back in the past and tried to nip it in the bud.

But isn't it just as likely that her actions to contain me were the exact catalyst to my evil end?

This door is a dare. *Come here, Eros. Come find me. I dare you.*

It feels like an invitation to a war.

The counterintuitive thing here, with this door, is that it apparently leads to the human realm. Examples A and B chained to my throne.

Will the final war be fought in the human realm?

Yesterday I would have thought it not likely. But many things have changed today. A sure sign that the fates have realigned.

I wave a hand through the air, wiping the past away so I can concentrate on the here and now. Because before me is an opportunity.

A door. A place to explore and wage a new war.

That's a nice start to a new spelling, if I do say so myself.

But this revelation comes with a caution. Am I ready to end this, once and for all? Am I ready to win? To go through that door and ruin Pressia the way she ruined me?

Because surely, it is her waiting for me on the other side.

I get up, walk over to the puny men, reach down with a wing claw and break their chains. Then step back as they rub their wrists and gaze up at me in terror.

"My good boys, please stand."

They get to their feet, looking at each other, panicked.

"Take me to this door. If you can do that, I will let you walk back through and pretend I never caught the scent of your pathetically small, but most certainly tasty, bodies."

I almost manage to say these words without crinkling my nose in disgust, but don't really manage it. They don't notice. They have no idea that I don't eat humans. They are already pointing at the exit, eager to show me what they've stumbled into.

Which is much more than a place to explore and wage a new war.

It is a way to settle the score.

Because while the curse states my soulmate is hate, it's equally factual that revenge is my fate.

CHAPTER TEN - CALLISTINA

*I*t *feels good to shed* the charade. The constant tension running down the back of my neck and radiating out to my shoulders fades as I walk through the bar door and leave Eros to his prisoners.

I stop just short of the street and tilt my head up, catching the sun's warm rays. My cheeks feel flushed, like I have a fever. But it's not a sickness, it's a cure.

My eyes close and I stand there, breathing. Existing.

Coming to terms with what I now am.

I am still a lioness from the House of Fire. Even if I'm no longer Queen of Vinca.

I am still a gryphon chimera—on the inside, at least.

I am still me.

I. Am. Still. Me.

I inhale deeply, then let the breath out slowly. When I'm empty, I open my eyes again and see the world in a new way.

I can work with this.

I can make it work.

Because there is a door.

My head turns to the left and down the street where the overpriced candle shop is.

The door is a little further up the street, but not much. And then it's straight up the hill. It shouldn't be hard to find again.

Am I really going to walk through it? Am I really going to leave my old life behind?

Pie did. She was forced and this is a decision that I get to make, so that's different. But that means it should be easier for me. I want to do this. I want to leave the past where it belongs. I want a fresh start. And if the human realm is the only way I can get it, then so be it.

I slip the old, ratty leopard fur coat down my arms and let it fall to the ground. Under the coat I'm wearing the prom dress and bare feet, since I left my wooden blocks up in Eros's apartment.

My outfit is unsuitable. I must change it and look presentable when I enter the new realm.

I turn away from the candle shop and the hill where the door lives and head towards the thrift store. Inside, it is empty. Not even clerks show up in this store. It's possible that the person who ran this place was out of town when reality shifted and they can no longer find their way home. But it's equally possible that they just got tired of the job and looked at this magical change as a fresh start.

At any rate, the clothes are free so I've been helping myself. I choose a dress with an empire waist. It's long, but I am still very tall, even though my legs feel woefully short now that they're missing a hock joint, so it falls just below my knees. It's an off-white color and made of soft cotton. The sleeves are a bit poofy and it's almost too tight across my breasts, but when I look in the mirror, I find a pleasing woman staring back at me. I look like a Vincan peasant farmer. I also look poor. But that's OK. Poor people are invisible people, everyone knows this. And when I step into that new world, I would like to be invisible.

At least for a little while, as I gather up all the new information I will be presented with.

I've done this before. I'd never been to Vinca when I showed up as the princess-in-waiting. I had to adjust quickly and efficiently or the people, and other royal beasts, would forever see me as the lost and helpless second-best who had no idea what she was doing.

First impressions are everything. And when I leave this magical world of monsters behind, I would like to at least look like I know what I'm doing.

I choose a pair of worn leather boots. They have a squared-off toe and go all the way up to my knees. I find a necklace and there is a sudden urge to drape it over my antlers, the way I would when I was a queen, but the antlers are gone, so I put it around my neck. It's silver, and long, and has a ring crammed with jingling charms. I choose several bracelets as well. And a ring. A big ring bedecked with fake jewels.

When I look in the mirror one final time, pressing the wrinkles out of the dress, I sigh at my new self. I would not have ended up a peasant farmer if my little sister Pie had not been pulled through that door by Eros during the House of Fire Caretaker Ceremony. But I would not have been a queen, either.

I would like a life where I was never a queen. I think that would be the best outcome for me because I was terrible at it. I let my emotions get in the way. I began to crave power. I did appalling things to people.

Being an invisible peasant feels like a reward at this point.

I sigh. Because it feels like I'm talking myself into believing this is all for the best, but deep in my heart it's really killing me that my whole self is gone. The only self I knew.

But it is time to let it go and face reality.

I am... *human*. And no amount of pretending is going to change that.

I let out a long breath and square my shoulders, looking myself in the eyes as I stare into the mirror— they are not yellow anymore, but they are not quite amber either. I have seen enough humans around town by now to realize that this color is unnatural for them. It could be a problem, but nothing a pair of sunglasses can't fix. I procure this accessory from a spinning display rack near the cash register. They are big, and round, and match the color of my dress.

Not knowing the weather in the Realm of Pittsburgh, I decide to grab a tan jacket made of thick cotton. I slip my arms in, grab a straw bag hanging on a hook, and leave the store.

I'm going to start a brand-new life. I'm going to walk through that magic door on the hill and I will begin again. If Pie can do it, so can I. After all, she was six. *Six*.

I'm... well, my age is not important, but I am substantially older than six. And if a person whose life years are counted in the single digits can enter a new world and make her way, then so can I.

My chin lifts up, my shoulders go back, and I walk down the road towards the hill where the door is.

When I get there and start up the hill I hear voices. At first I think these voices belong to more travelers, but no. No. It's just the man-boys and Eros.

"We swear," the first one says. "We won't come back. We won't tell anyone."

"We just want to go home, man," the second one is saying. He's imploring Eros with an outstretched hand, and that hand is shaking. Quaking like a leaf in the wind. "We just wanna go home."

"We didn't know you guys were here," the first one continues.

"But..." Eros holds up a finger, rejecting this man-boy's point. "You told—" That's when he must hear me coming up behind them, because he pauses and looks over his shoulder. "Ah. There she is. Callistina. Did they or did they not tell you that they were looking for monsters?"

"They did." I reach them, pass them, and head straight towards the door.

I am thwarted when Eros stretches out his wing and I am blocked by a large, black webbing. I let out a huff. "What is it?"

"Where are you going?"

I turn to face him. "I'm going to the Realm of Pittsburgh."

"What?" the second man-boy says. "You can't go—"

But the first man-boy interrupts. "She's not a monster, dude. She's a human, like us. She can come." I glance at him, curious about this offer. It might be nice to have an instant acquaintance in the foreign realm of Pennsylvania. Pie had that Lisa woman, after all. She wasn't entirely alone.

"No," Eros says. "No, no, no. Callistina. Can you please wait a moment while I send these two morons back the way they came?"

"Well, why shouldn't I take them up on it?"

"I don't even know why you want to go yet. Or what you're gonna do. We need to have a conversation about this. A discussion." He glances at the man-boys, then growls out, "*After* they're gone."

He says all this with a tone of possessiveness. As if I am someone he gets to have a say over. Which I am not.

However, I cannot deny that his display of ownership sends a slight thrill up my spine. He is Eros, after all.

"Agreed?" he says, still growling.

I cross my arms and look defiant. But also, I give in. "Fine." Because I have been sleeping with this god for many weeks now and he hasn't paid me the slightest attention. But isn't this so like a man? To become insecure and possessive once you have moved on?

He turns back to the morons. "Go. Now. Before I eat you. And if you come back you will be grilled for dinner. And if you tell anyone…"

"We won't," Moron Number One says.

"We're not telling no one," Moron Number Two says. "We promise."

Eros uses a dramatic pause here, trying to make them squirm, which they do, but then he relents. Flashing his long, black bat wing in the direction of the open magic door. "Go, then. Quickly before I change my mind!" His voice echoes through the forest with a display of power, making both man-boy morons squeak in fear. Then they run up the hill, practically tripping over each other, and pass through the door.

Eros stares at it for many long seconds, then lets out a breath that sounds like relief. "It's still there." And then I realize it *was* a breath of relief.

I look at the door. And the retreating figures of the morons. They are running down a hill, not up. Which is an interesting perspective, since they were facing uphill on this side. I feel like my observation deserves a little attention, so I keep thinking about that change in perspective. It is literal, I saw it. They ran uphill, then down. But it's also figurative, isn't it? They were in the wrong place and everything was harder. Then they went to the right place and everything got easier.

"OK," Eros sighs. "What are you doing?"

"Pondering the figurative and literal nature of the door, and the morons who just walked through it."

"No. I mean, what are you doing with this door?"

"What do you mean?" I turn to him. "I'm leaving."

"For fuck's sake, Callistina. *Why*? That's my question. *Why* are you going to the Realm of Pittsburgh?"

"Because my magic is gone, Eros. I have been turned human. There is no point in lingering in the fog for me."

"So you're just giving up?" He throws up both hands in a dramatic give-up gesture. "Just gonna accept it?"

"Do I have choices? Because if I have choices, please enlighten me on what they are."

"I'm just saying." He stares at me for a moment. Then looks me up and down. "You changed your clothes."

"You have the observation skills of a royal detective."

"You look... nice."

A small laugh escapes before I can stop it.

"Never mind. I take it back."

"So I don't look nice?"

He sighs. Then... he pouts a little. Which I have to admit, is a good look for him. Those lips of his are quite plump on any given day. And puckered up in a slight pout... yes. I like it.

"Here's the thing, Callistina. I... might..." He pauses for many moments here. I actually have to roll my hand at him to keep going. "I... I might *like* you. There. I said it. I think I like you. Especially when you talk. And... change your clothes. I mean, I have always liked you—" My eyebrows shoot up because this is a lie. "I have," he insists, observing my disbelief. "It's just... you were all crazy and shit. I didn't care about the wooden blocks. And the antlers—though the spray-paint job was a mess —the antlers were kinda cool. But that coat, Callistina." He shakes his head. This crossed his line. "It was mangy. I couldn't get past the coat. But this"—he motions to my new dress—"I like this." And then he smiles at me.

And again, he *is* Eros. The god of love. And so... I find myself... perhaps, maybe, slightly... let's call it intrigued, but really it is more like flattered. I'm getting caught up in his... well, the whole package, really. It all just works for him. I mean, Batty has those wings. Nearly the same. But they don't come off as sexy. In fact, they come off creepy. Very, very creepy.

But really, nothing about Eros is creepy at all.

It just works.

So I am flattered that he cares, I suppose.

"What are you trying to say, Eros?" Still. A woman does not let a man get away with such a shoddy declaration of interest. He needs to explain himself properly. It's called courting. Wooing. Am I not a queen? Do I not deserve the courting and the wooing?

"OK, I'm just gonna get to the point. My point is, we are... kind of a team. And I think we should go to this new world together."

Well. I could not be more stunned if he had gotten down on one knee and proposed marriage while reciting a hand-crafted wedding vow written in trochaic tetrameter. My hand flies to my heart. "I'm sorry?"

"I want to go *with you*, Callistina. OK? I want *us*"—he takes a moment to point to himself, then me—"to go into that new world *to-gether*."

"Why on earth would you want that?" I have to admit, I'm more than a little suspicious at this point. Granted, I have been having sex with this man for weeks, so I do believe he has some sort of attraction to me. But he's talking about taking a journey together. Starting over together.

This is not something casual lovers do.

This is something committed couples do.

"Are we a committed couple?"

"What?" He stares at me like I'm speaking a foreign language.

"Is this some sort of turning point in our relationship?"

Now he smiles. Points at me. Smiles bigger. "Yes. That. It is a turning point, Callistina. That's exactly right. I wanna get out of here. I'm tired of this place. This is not something I just decided today, OK? I've been thinking about this for eons. Today is just the last straw. And look." He points at the door. "It's like fate, isn't it? We're both fed up to the point of exasperation and lo and behold, a new beginning presents itself. Let's go through the door together."

Hmm. I picture this offer. I'm not even sure what the Realm of Pittsburgh looks like. I don't know the local customs, or speak in the local accent, and I don't have any particular skills in the normal human world.

I have done a bit of alchemy, but the human world is non-magical, so that would not help.

But going to this new place with Eros, well. He's a god, is he not? Not very powerful, not in practical ways. But he's charming, in his own dark way. And one cannot discount charm in times of peril.

"What would we do there?"

He smiles. Quite a big one too. Because he knows I'm going to accept his offer. He just needs to close the deal. "Whatever you want. We can do whatever you want, Callistina. Get jobs, or something. Or go to one of their schools. Immerse ourselves in this new opportunity. Ride it for all it's worth."

I take a deep breath and when I exhale, I'm nodding. "OK. If you want to come, I think that would be acceptable."

"Great." His smile is not just big now, but also mischievous.

Which sets me back. Is he up to something? Is this a trap?

But just as I'm having that thought he steps closer to me. Removing the distance between us. And the next thing I know, he's got his hands on my face and his lips are kissing mine.

It's a slow kiss. As if time itself has stopped. And very deliberate. Like his lips are not just kissing me, but exploring me as well. And when his tongue touches mine, and they tangle together, my head swirls a little. And everything feels lighter than air. I swoon so hard, I nearly fall down.

But then his strong arms are around me. Embracing me and holding me. It has been so long since someone showed affection like this, that it's all I can think about.

How I feel with him close.

How I feel as we kiss.

And when we pull apart, the deal is sealed.

We are going forward... together.

CHAPTER ELEVEN - EROS

ell. I must admit, I really didn't see this coming. When I woke up this morning I had absolutely no plans to go through a door into another existence with the crazy queen.

As a matter of fact, I'm still not quite sure that this is what I've agreed to. But here we are, standing in front of that door, coming to terms with the fact that we're about to go on a journey together.

Callistina shakes her head a little as her fingertips touch her lips where I was kissing her. "What did you do to me?"

"What?"

She glares at me. "Did you compel me to kiss you?"

"I didn't compel you to do anything. I just like you, Callistina. I've gotten used to you. And the fact that you're no longer crazy is a bonus. So I kissed you. You didn't have to kiss me back, but you did. Maybe that should be the question you're asking yourself. Why did you kiss me back?"

"That *is* the question I'm asking and I don't have an answer."

"Shall I be blunt?"

She waves her hand at me in a queenly motion of 'go right ahead.'

"I think you like me. You think I'm handsome, and charming, and capable. All very good things for a man to be when one is considering the option of kissing him back. Don't you think?"

Callistina thinks about this for a moment as we gaze into each other's eyes, hers swimming with distrust, mine... well, who can tell what mine are doing.

"Come on, Callistina. I can't help it if I'm handsome, charming, and capable, now can I? It's just the way I was made."

It's kind of a lame explanation, but it's not an argument she can dispute either. And after a few more moments, she relaxes. "Fine. I like you. So I kissed you back."

"Finally," I sigh. "It's nice to see you taking responsibility for things for a change."

"So," she says. "What do we do now?"

"Walk through the door, I suppose."

"You're acting like this is no big deal."

"Why should it be a big deal? The door will bring us back if we don't like it there. What do we have to lose?"

She takes another moment to think, then shakes her head. "I don't want to come back. I don't want it to be an option. Coming back if it gets hard or we don't like it feels like the easy way out. Pie didn't get the easy way out. She was stuck."

"Is that why you're really doing this? To make some kind of amends for what I did to Pie?"

"No. Not exactly. I just feel…" She sighs. "Like a failure, to be honest. Pie was strong. She survived. And whatever happened to her once she, and Pell, and Tomas went back through the doors, I know—even if it's terrible—she will make the most of it and she will find happiness. Even if it's just her own personal happiness. I want to make the most of it too. I want to find my own personal happiness. But truth be told, I'm not the kind of woman who perseveres like that in the face of adversity. If I have a way out, I will take it at the first sign of trouble. It's who I am."

"You want to be trapped there?"

She presses her lips together and nods. "Yes. For once in my life I would like to rise to an occasion and depend on my wits, and my strength, and tenacity to pull me through. So I think we should close the door behind us. And I don't know how to do that. Do you?"

She is so different in this moment. So unsure of herself. So vulnerable. So… well, sweet is kinda the right word here. Especially while she's wearing that outfit. She looks like a woman. And not just any woman, but a very nice woman. One who cooks and takes care of the home. One who… cares about things that have nothing to do with power or crowns.

And of course it's a lie. It's just clothing. The person inside has not changed. But it's messing with me, this new outer version of the crazy queen I've been sleeping with for nearly two months.

So. Well. Now I have to admit to a second thing that I did not see coming.

I like her like this.

A lot.

Which leads me back to her request about closing the door.

"I know how to close a door. We did it when we took Pie, remember?"

She was there, so of course she does. But something else is troubling her now. "Will you go find her?"

"Who?"

"Lisa."

I scoff and chuckle a little. The queen is insecure. "No, Callistina. I have no desire to go find Lisa. I haven't even thought about her in decades. She is not the reason I want to go to this world. You are."

It's the right thing to say. And anyway, it's not even a lie. It calms Callistina's nerves and eases her doubts, and finally she nods. "OK. So how do we close the door?"

"I will curse it with a spelling." I hold up a finger. "Give me a moment while I work it out." Then I turn my back to her and pace along the side of the mountain, trying to find the right combination of letters, and rhythm, and intentions.

Then I turn to her and nod. "OK, I've got it. Are we ready?"

She looks scared. Truly. Not so scared that she'll back out, but I can tell she is afraid of what's about to come next. And this is a perfect opportunity to take her hand and ease that fear the way a good man would.

So that's what I do. I take her hand, give it a squeeze, and say, "I've got you. Don't worry. I've got you."

It's enough, because she nods and then she is the one who takes the first step towards the door. As we come up on it though, I step in front of her, still holding tight to her hand, and as we pass through the door frame I say:

"A HILL, a god, a queen, a town.
    We take these steps to make new ground.
    Pass through the door and shut it tight.
    The other side will make it right."

A VERY SIMPLE LITTLE SPELLING, but it does the trick. Because I can feel the energy at my back, closing off the world behind us.

But then something goes wrong. One moment I'm looking at a forest, much like the one we just came from, but looking downhill instead of up.

The next moment, it's gone. It's nothing but a closed door now.

And when I look behind us, the Savage Falls hillside has also been replaced by a closed door.

Callistina gives out a surprised gasp. "What just happened?"

I pull her towards me and hold her close, her back pressed up against my chest. Then I turn us in a circle so we can get a good look. "It's a hallway, not a door."

"Well, I can see it's a frickin' hallway, Eros. Why are we *in* it? It wasn't a hallway a moment ago."

"No, it wasn't."

She wriggles free from me and takes a step down the hallway. It's not very long, but there are three more sets of doors, each set situated precisely across from one another. She looks back at me with wide eyes. "Now what do we do?"

"Perhaps the hallway gods don't like being forced into things."

She makes a face. "What? What are you talking about?"

"In a way, you were forcing them to take responsibility for your decision. And they decided to fix that." I pan a hand at the new doors. "By offering us choices."

This is actually a really good explanation and I'm rather proud of myself for coming up with it.

"Oh." She walks back to our door, practically pushing me out of the way, and bends down to pick something up. Then she leans across the hallway and picks up something else. I can't see exactly what these two things are because her long dress is blocking my view. But when she stands back up, she presents two doorknobs to me in her outstretched hand. "These are keys, aren't they?"

I stare at the ruby-red crystals in her palm, each the size and shape of a doorknob. "Well, well, well. They certainly are."

"So..." She looks down the hallway again. "We just use the doorknobs to open each door, right? Then we can see our choices and make one."

"Seems reasonable. Let's give it a try."

She starts off towards the second set of doors, but I grab her arm. "Hold on. Let's try these two first." I point to the door we came from, and the one across from it that should lead to the Realm of Pittsburgh.

"Why? We don't want to go back there."

"Don't you wanna know if we *can?*"

"No. That was the whole point of your spelling. It's move forward no matter what."

I shrug. "You're the boss." This remark earns me a dirty look. But I chuckle about it as she turns her attention to the second set of doors.

Immediately, she is disappointed. "There's no place for a doorknob here."

And sure enough, when I walk over to the second set of doors, she's right. There isn't.

"Look," she says, pointing to the next set of doors. "These two don't have a place for a doorknob either." But then she brightens. "Oh! But these last two have a place for a doorknob!"

She's just about to shove one of the doorknobs into the hole when I come up behind her and grab her hand just in time. "You don't just stick them in there, Callistina. We need to think this through."

She stares at me, looking confused. "What's there to think through? These doorknobs go to these doors."

"Well, we don't even know what's on the other side. There could be a dragon out there."

Callistina frowns. "Why on earth would you say that?"

"Say what?"

135

"A dragon? Why would a dragon be on the other side of these doors?"

"It's a figure of speech. It could be… a gorgon, or a cyclops, or a kraken for all I know. That's the whole point. We don't know."

"And we're not going to know unless we open the door."

"Well, there are two of them. Two doors, two doorknobs. Might it be set up so that we open them both at the same time?"

"Oh." She exhales. "OK. That makes sense. Here." She thrusts a ruby-red doorknob at me. "We'll put them in at the same time. Then we'll take a look around and make a decision. Though there really is no decision to make. This is the last set of doors and they are the only ones with a place for the doorknobs. So like it or not, we're going through."

"Fine." I can't really argue with that, so I take the doorknob and face my door.

"On 'earth,' we put them in."

"On what?"

"On 'earth.'"

"I heard the word that came out of your mouth, Callistina. What I don't understand is why you're saying it."

"Oh." Her face brightens with a laugh. Her eyes even sparkle a little. "I mean… *three*. On three. 'Earth' is 'three' in Vincan culture. Remember? Breath, wind, earth, fire. One, two, three, four."

"Can we just do it on 'three,' please?"

She shrugs. "Whatever. Ready?"

"Ready."

"Breath," she says. I roll my eyes. "Wind. *Earth.*"

I plunge my doorknob into the space where a door-knob lives, making the whole door shimmer. And then...

Callistina lets out a gasp. "What is happening?" But it's not a frightened gasp. It's a delighted one.

I understand her excitement immediately because the doors don't lead to a place—well, they do. They must. But it's more like they lead to... a person. Because there is movement beyond the doors. Jerking, rolling movement with a view of a great canyon. And off in the distance, mountains as far as the eye can see.

"Oh!" Callistina exclaims. "It's a horse. Or something that walks like one. Look!" She comes up to me and points to both doors simultaneously. "They go to the same place, but it's not a *place*, it's a *person*. Rather, a point of view. *Two* points of view, actually."

"Well, that's stupid. Why would one need to be two people?"

"Because"—she looks at me like I'm some sort of simpleton, her words coming out slow, like I'm stupid—"there are *two* of us?"

I look back at the doors. "Hmm. You might be right. There's one for you and one for me. But this is my point. This isn't how doors work. There's no point-of-view jumping."

"Isn't there?"

"Well... I've never heard of such a thing and I'm a god."

"You've been out of the loop for a long time, Eros.

137

Perhaps you might try wrapping your head around the idea that you're missing information. Alternatively, you might just be stupid." She sneers this last part at me, which I find comforting for some reason. Maybe because she's been too nice for the past fifteen minutes and it's really not like her to be both sane and amicable at the same time.

"Fine. Let's assume you're correct." I pan my arms wide to indicate the open doors. "What do we do with this?"

"What do we…" She scoffs. "We walk through them, Eros. That's what we do."

"As you have already stated, this one leads to… someone or something riding an animal. Maybe, before we jump into riding a beast we're not familiar with, we should consider all options."

"What options? These doors are the only ones that are open."

I look down the hallway, trying not to be Captain Obvious.

"No," Callistina says. "We're not going home. We didn't even go on a single adventure yet, Eros. You can't seriously want to go home."

"Well, I would not mind a little adventure. But I feel like this is a set-up."

"How so?"

"How do you *not* think it's a trap? A door appears—a door that should've been shut and locked when Pie and Pell went… well, wherever the hell they went. And people stumble out of it on the very day where you and I are"—I point to the two of us—"fed up with our fates.

Now we walk through and discover all this?" I pan my hands to the hallway. "Someone did this, Callistina."

"Who?"

"I don't know. It could be anyone. A god, a goddess, a monster." An oracle. But I don't say that last one out loud.

"So what?"

"So *what?*"

"Listen." She stomps her foot and plants her hands on her hips. "I'm. Not. Going. Back. I'm going through here." She points at her open door. "If you don't want to come—"

"I'm not saying I don't want to go. I'm saying we should consider our options and not just walk through the doors we're being forced to use."

"I feel like we're talking in circles. I also feel like you might be deliberately acting obtuse. These. Are the doors. That are open."

"Could we"—I point to her, then I point to me—"a god and a queen—not find a way around this obvious ploy?"

"I don't think it's a ploy. I think it's an ordered list, Eros."

"A what?"

"They're an ordered pair. I learned about this in alchemy school. You have to do things in a certain sequence. All magic is like this, right? Like a recipe that must be followed precisely. You don't add"—she pauses, trying to recall a recipe—"eggs before... tallow. Or... something."

"You don't even know how to cook, do you?"

"It's not my fault I had servants. But in this new life, I will learn." And she tips her chin up, like she's being defiant.

"I guess."

"Right. So before we can go through *those* doors"—she points down the hallway to the set of doors we came out of, then points out the other two sets leading up to where we presently are—"we have to go through *these* doors." She points to the doors we're standing in front of. "You through one and me through the other."

"See, this is my problem with the whole situation. This ordered-list thing, in combination with the two points-of-view doors, would imply..." I know what I want to say, but I can't find a way to explain it.

"That we're part of the list?" Callistina says.

Which doesn't explain anything, but I know exactly what she means. "Yeah. *Specifically* us."

"And that we're already inside the magic?"

"Yeah. That."

"And that... someone is playing a game with us?"

I sigh. "Fucking Tomas."

"What?"

"It's him. I know it's him. He put me here. He put you here. It's some kind of happy-ending thing."

Callistina is making a face. It's a combination of confusion and disgust. "Why in the name of Vinca would our happy endings be tied *together*?"

"Well, you don't have to look so disgusted by it. You were just kissing me like five minutes ago."

"I've been sleeping with you as well, but that doesn't mean you're the love of my life. No offense."

"Whatever."

"I have no qualms with playing a game. I don't care about your happy ending. I just want to... *move on.*"

I blow out a breath. It's frustration. Also resignation. "OK, then. Let's do this."

We both turn and face our respective doors. Whoever is on the other side is still riding the animal because all we see is the rolling motion view of a deserted mountain road and a deep, deep canyon that seems to go on forever.

"Do you think it's tame?" Callistina asks.

"It better be. Are you ready?"

"I'm ready. Breath. Wind. Earth."

And after she says 'earth' we step through.

CHAPTER TWELVE - CALLISTINA

he first thing I notice is the hot, dry wind on my face. Then it's the motion of the beast under me. And then... then it's the realization that Eros is the one riding and I am his passenger, sitting behind him.

"Ho-lee fuck!" he exclaims. Which perfectly describes what I would like to say too.

He pulls back on the reins of the... horse? No. It's much bigger than a horse, but it's horse-like for sure. We stop on the side of a cliff and we don't even say anything. We just take it all in. I lean to the side, trying to get a better view without his broad, tattooed shoulders blocking the way. This is when I notice he's shirtless and my arms are wrapped around his middle. Clinging to his tight muscles.

Looking down at myself, I realize that I'm pretty much naked.

Not all the way naked. There are chains draped all over my body, dainty silver chains that are more like jewelry than anything meant to bind. They clink and jingle with a magical musicality every time I move. My upper body is (barely) covered by a fringe of these chains. A thin bar of silver intricately engraved with a botanical motif rests gently on the top of my breasts. The fringe hangs down off this bar, covering my nipples. And it's long, draping over my breasts and down to just above my waist. Not quite covering me, but definitely giving off the impression of covering me.

The same thing is happening with my lower half. The engraved silver bar encircles my waist and the fringe is long enough to hit me mid-thigh. Once again, it doesn't really cover anything, just gives the impression of a skirt.

I am delighted to see that my legs and arms are covered in golden velvet fur. I touch my cheek and when I find the same velvet there, I let out a laugh.

Eros swings a leg over the... horse, then looks up at me. He's tall, but this horse is gigantic, so the top of his head only comes to the animal's back. "What's so funny?"

"I have *fur*!" I laugh again. "I'm *me*!"

"No antlers."

"Oh!" I touch my head. And he's right. There is no set of magnificent antlers up there, but there are nubs where they might still come in. And a crown of some sort. It's made of silver, like the bar encircling my chest and waist. But this time there is no fringe. There are thicker chains of silver and when I trace my fingers down these chains, I realize that they attach to a collar around my neck. "Who cares about antlers. I'm happy just to have fur again. And look!" I lift my foot up and wiggle my lion toes. "Paws!" I lift my leg up higher and point to the middle joint of my leg. "And hocks! I never thought I'd be so happy to see hocks again!"

Eros reaches up to me. "Need help dismounting?"

Normally I do not. I am an excellent rider. But the current distance between me and the ground feels long. So I take his hand, swing my leg over, and let him set me down.

Eros lets go of me and takes a step back. "That's quite an outfit you're wearing. Or... not wearing."

We both laugh. "I'm kind of naked."

He nods, grinning a little. "Mmm-hmm. You're kind of naked."

I've never been much of an exhibitionist, but I have to admit, I like the look. It feels very... desert queen.

I point at Eros. He's shirtless, tanned brown, and sweaty. He's also missing his wings. How interesting that I was given back my old body, but something was taken from him. His blond hair is tied back with a bit of leather, but some of it has worked its way loose in the wind. His eyes are bright, bright green. And he's wearing sand-colored canvas pants tucked into well-worn brown leather boots, but that's pretty much it. "You're nearly naked too."

He nods, absently. Looking around at the landscape as his hand explores a pocket on the side of his pants. He looks down as he pulls the hand out, opening his palm to reveal a wad of folded money and a few coins.

I lean towards him, trying to get a better look. "Where's it all from?"

Eros holds up a bill, the ink bleeding through each side from the sun. "I don't recognize the writing. Do you?"

I take it, study it closer, and nod. "It's Vinca money for sure. See?" I point to the image of a palace. "That's the ancient palace. It was destroyed thousands of years ago. But look here." I point to a series of ancient numbers. "These are Glory numbers. Vinca used that system because the realms were so connected back then. But this design"—I point to a pyramid with the face of a bull god in the center—"this is Apis. So this is territory money. Vinca does not worship chimera. But there were plenty of territories that did. Even in my day they still did. And the realm would respect their right to do that by putting their godlings on the local money."

"So we're in the territories?"

I look around. "Well, I've never been anywhere like this. So I don't know."

"What about the coins?" He puts one in my hand. "Do you recognize this?"

There is the head of a lion on the front and the paw of one on the back. "This is definitely House of Fire silver." I look at Eros. "How did it get all the way out here?"

Eros looks at the coin. "This place is fucking hot. I already hate it."

I don't know what to say back to that, so I change the subject. "What's with the size of this horse?"

"Is it a horse?"

Eros and I study the animal. It shares a lot of characteristics with a horse, but the *size*... It's massive. And the feet are not only proportionally gigantic, but spiked with some kind of sharp ridge, something you'd see on the back of a reptile or a fish. Something used in battle.

Other than that, it *is* a horse.

Eros slides his hand under the fur saddle pad and pulls it back, revealing scars. "Look."

I put my hand over my heart in shock. "Oh, my. Is that a…"

"I think it is."

A pegásius. "Someone has cut off its wings. How awful." I reach up to rub my fingertips over the scars. The pegásius snorts, bending its neck around to look at me. One bright blue eye meets mine, opening a bit wider, like it's surprised, but just as quickly droops back down into laziness.

"Yeah," Eros says absently. Then he looks at me. "Like your antlers."

I stand still, stunned silent for a moment. I hadn't even considered that someone had cut them *off*.

I want to reach up and feel them again. To assure myself that's not what happened. But I don't. Because I know that it is.

Someone has cut off my antlers.

And someone has cut off this noble beast's wings.

"They took your wings," I say.

Eros exhales. "No. They didn't."

"What do you mean? You don't have any."

"They're there. Just not visible. I can feel them."

"Take them out. I would like to see."

For some reason, I get the feeling he does not want

to do this. And when he speaks, it is confirmed. "No. I don't want to see them."

"Why not?"

"Because I don't like them, OK? They're ugly. And if this version of me has the ability to hide them, then I don't wanna potentially fuck it up by bringing them out." To accentuate his reluctance, he rolls his shoulders like a person with tension, letting out a long breath once he's done.

This is new. He's never let on that the bat wings bother him. However, there are more important things to discuss. "Your eyes are very bright. Almost glowing, Eros."

"Well, with or without wings, I am still a god, am I not? Why shouldn't they be bright and unnatural?"

For some reason I feel chastised. "Well, excuse me then. I won't bring it up again."

He shrugs. "Whatever." Then he turns to the animal and begins scanning its tack, taking in the various things affixed to it—two large leather bags positioned behind the saddle's cantle and draping over each side of the lower ribcage, a leather bedroll tied to the saddle-bags, and two more smaller bags attached to the rump plate.

"You don't have a bow, either. Is that hidden away as well?"

He doesn't answer me and this is a not-so-subtle hint that it's time to move on. So I join Eros in his curiosity about where we are. It's a road, this is obvious. But not a well-travelled one because there is no one else on it with us. We are high up in a mountain pass. Where it leads is anyone's guess. The other side is not visible yet. The road is long and empty, winding around peaks as it makes its way across the mountain.

"I can't even see a descent. Can you see a descent, Eros?"

Eros shakes his head. "Not an ascent, either. This road doesn't go up or down. It merely goes across. But you know what the most disturbing thing is?" He looks at me, waiting for me to answer his rhetorical question.

"What?" I huff, kinda tired of his attitude.

He points in the direction we came from. "There's no door, Callistina. How do we get back?"

My eyes dart in that direction too, my mouth open in shock. Because he's right. I look back at Eros. "Are we stuck here?" And is there a little bit of excitement in my voice at this prospect?

Eros shrugs. "Not sure. But one thing is clear—we need to follow this road. There doesn't seem to be any point in going backwards." He walks over to the beast and starts checking supplies, rummaging around inside the bags. When he opens the ones attached to the rump plate, he lets out a sigh of relief. "Water. Thank the gods." He takes out a skin, opens it, sniffs the water, and takes a drink.

We both wait, like drinking bad water would make him instantly sick—which isn't the case and we both know this, but we wait anyway.

"I think it's fine," he finally says. Then offers the skin to me.

I take it, drink, feel fine as well, and hand it back.

"We should stop at any sign of water to refill the

skins. I'm hoping there's another pass hidden from view that will have more signs of life, but just in case there's not, and we have to see this long road through to the end, we don't want to run out of water."

I let out a breath and agree with a nod of my head. "Good thinking."

"I'm sure I've been to Vinca at one time or another, but I have no memories of it, Callistina. Look for signs."

"Oh." I put up a hand. "This is definitely not Vinca."

"How do you know?"

"Everything is off. The heat, for one. It's so dry. And dusty. It feels like a desert, don't you think? Vinca is not a desert. It's hot, but it's humid. There's a lot of water. A river running right through the city. Big enough for barges. And the sea is not that far away. We are not in Vinca."

"At any rate"—in typical god-like fashion, he dismisses everything I said—"just keep looking for familiar things."

I decide to say nothing. Eros is Eros. A switch-up in scenery and hiding his wings and bow aren't enough to intrinsically change who and what he is.

"Get back up on the beast." He reaches for my knee and I jump up, letting him lift me up so I can swing my leg over the pegásius's back. Then he puts his foot in the stirrup and slides his leg carefully between me and the animal's thick, crested neck, settling into the saddle in front of me.

This is when I get a really good look at his tattoos. Actually, one large tattoo. It's a tree, which I knew. I've been looking at his bare chest and back for nearly two months now. But up until now I wasn't able to read the writing on the boughs and now I can. They are names, I think. "What is going on with this tattoo of yours?"

He's looking off into the distance, pretending to be interested in anything but my question.

"Eros?"

"What?"

"Your tattoos?"

"What about them?"

"What do they mean?"

"They're a fuckin' pedigree, Callistina. Tying me to every god and goddess in all four pantheons."

"Oh. Like a…"

"Curse?" he finishes for me. "Yes. It's like a curse." Then, without another word, he clicks his tongue and the beast starts forward again.

It's certainly not the beginning I'd imagined. And my traveling partner could be better in all sorts of ways. But nonetheless, it is the fresh start I was craving and finally, the unbearable stagnation is over.

OR… maybe not.

We travel slowly all day, not even stopping to eat, and the road just keeps going, and going, and going. It all looks the same, as well. For a couple of hours, I've

151

convinced myself that we're traveling a loop that has no end. But it only takes a little concentration to realize that's not the case. Or, at the very least, we haven't gotten to the end of the loop and started over again, because I do see some very unique—some might even call them peculiar—rock outcroppings as my gaze wanders looking for water or signs that this is Vinca.

One such rock formation is in the shape of an arch. It's all the way across the steep-sided valley on the top of a mountain. I watch it for hours and finally I'm rewarded when the sun begins to set and it's centered right in the middle, shining bright light across the canyon and onto a massive expanse of flat, red rock, making shadow play across the ancient megalith. It's an oval, but there are geometrical shapes popping off the outer edges that remind me of handmade Vincan lace.

I let my eyes close and lean my cheek against Eros's sweaty back, feeling a weird sort of satisfaction that I got to figure that arch out before it disappears behind us. But then Eros pulls the beast up, shaking me off of him—which elicits embarrassment on my part. Resting my cheek against his bare skin. What was I thinking? He probably thinks I'm falling in love with him like everyone else in his life.

"Finally," he says. Tersely, I might add. "Water. Look."

And sure enough, when my gaze follows his pointing finger, there's a trickle of water running down the mountain nearby.

"Where is it coming from?" I ask.

We both tip our heads up, trying to see the top of the mountain. He has to back the beast up because it's hidden by the rocks, but eventually we find the snow cap at the top.

"Mystery solved," I say, then scoot back, get my leg between us so I can get down, and jump. This time without help. My legs are weak from sitting all day, and sore from riding. So I groan, stretching one long leg out all the way down to my clawed toes.

Eros gets down too. He offers me a look that could be a smile, or possibly a scowl—it's hard to tell. Then he takes the beast's bridle off and leads it over to the little pool that has formed from the waterfall. It's bigger than a puddle, but not by much. It overflows quickly, even though the waterfall is a trickle, and spills over the side of some rocks, disappearing into the ground.

The pegásius drinks the whole puddle, then waits patiently for it to fill up again.

Eros takes the skins out and hands me one. "Drink it all. Then we can refill them."

I take the water and do as I'm told. Not because he told me to, but because I'm actually parched. The sun has gone behind the mountains now so we're deep in shadow. But the entire mountain seems to be radiating heat, like it's a sink that acts like a reservoir for the sun, so while the shadow does cool the air, it's a nice comfortable temperature even though I'm wearing nothing but silver chains and velvet fur.

When I look back at Eros, I find him staring at me. "What?"

He shrugs. "That's twice now."

"Twice?"

"Two times you have changed your appearance today. And each was a very different you."

"Well"—I wiggle my toes at him—"I'm not complaining. I did get my paws back."

"I'm not complaining either." But he doesn't laugh. Or wink. Or even smile. Which seems both familiar and out of sorts.

So I just shut up and take a seat on the ground. It's a soft kind of dirt. The ground is hard, but there's a cushioning layer of powdery brown dust that covers everything and feels good between my toes.

Meanwhile, Eros has removed several packages from the saddlebags and walks over to me, taking a seat on a boulder just to my left. I watch him carefully open the mousseline wrapping. He holds up a small block of cheese, then tosses it to me.

I catch it, then reach up and catch something else coming my way. When I open my palm, I find a thick strip of dried meat.

"It's weird."

He actually laughs. "Which part?"

I smile, then I chuckle too. "All of it. But... how did it pack food for us?"

"It?"

"The magic in charge of this place."

"It didn't, Callistina. We... hopped into the bodies of other people."

"Other people who are me and you?" I slip the little block of cheese past my chain veil and take a bite. For something of questionable age wrapped in dubious cloth inside a saddlebag being carried by a pegásius, it's surprisingly good. Mild and a little bit sweet.

"I guess," Eros says.

"Then what happened to them? Where are they now? Do they know we've possessed them?"

Eros shrugs, taking a bite of the meat. He chews slowly, like he's thinking about the taste. Then he says, "It's rabbit."

"Good fat rabbit? Or old, grizzly rabbit?"

"Good and fat." Then he smiles again.

Which allows me to offer one back. "You've been pretty tense today."

"In my defense," Eros says, still chewing, "we are soul-riding a couple of people who look like us but live in a whole other world."

"What makes you think it's a new world?"

"What else could it be?"

"Couldn't it be a 'when' and not a 'where?'"

Eros chews his meat, considering my question thoughtfully. "I suppose. I mean, we've all done our share of time travel. So it's fifty-fifty, I guess."

"I haven't time-traveled. I mean, I have been taken out of my time and place, but this is the first time I chose to do that."

"Is it exciting?"

I can't tell if he's teasing me, making fun of me, or really asking this question. I decide to take him seriously. "Yes. It is."

He nods. "I can tell."

"What do you mean?"

KC CROSS & JA HUSS

"While I've been uptight and tense, you've been relaxed and lazy."

I roll my eyes. "I didn't mean to rest my head against your shoulder. I was just tired."

"I know. That's why we stopped."

Again, I'm not sure how to take this. He was concerned? Or annoyed?

Whatever. I ignore his statement and just nibble at my cheese. Then I remember that we've got a beast with us and it doesn't eat cheese and meat. But my concern is unfounded when I look over and find the pegásius browsing the foliage of sparse-leafed trees. "It needs a name."

"It has one," Eros replies.

"How do you know?"

"There's a brass nameplate on the top of his bridle. He's called Ire."

"How do you spell that?" I ask. For some reason Eros bursts out laughing. "What's so funny?"

"How do I *spell* it?"

"Yes. Spelling is important. Is it spelled I-r-i-e? Or E-r-i-e? Or E-e-r-i-e? Or I-r-e? Because you said it like E-r-i-e."

"I-r-e."

"Hmm. That's pretty."

"It means 'anger' in ancient wood nymph."

"No. Then it's pronounced 'Ire.' Long I, silent E. Not long E, long E."

"Wow. I never expected you to be a grammar witch."

I blow out a breath with my laugh. "Sorry. I just want to call him by his right name."

Eros stares at me for a moment. Then looks over at the beast. "Huh. Well, shit. Now we'll never know because pegási don't speak."

"I think we should say it the way you said it first. That actually means 'flower' in gryphon."

"Hmm." He's staring at me again. "Irie it is." Then he gets up, grabs the bridle, pulls a knife out of his boot, and carves something into the brass. He brings it over to me and holds it out so I can read the name. He's added an I between the R and the E. "Now, in the future, there will be less of a debate on the pronunciation."

He takes the bridle back and hangs it on a tree branch, then goes over to the beast and untacks him. The fur saddle blanket is unfolded and laid out on the soft dirt. He then props the bags up against a tree trunk, sits down on the blanket, and takes off his boots. When he's done, he pats the fur. "Come on, Callistina. We're gonna share."

It's not like I have other options, but the new me and the new him aren't the same people who've been sleeping together for weeks and weeks.

It feels different.

"Don't worry," he grunts. "I won't bother you." And then he turns his back to me and sighs.

If I think too hard about this it'll make it all that much more uncomfortable and awkward. So I just get up, walk over, and lie down next to him. The blanket is plenty big enough so that when I turn my back to him, we're not even touching.

"Good night," he says.

"Good night."

KC CROSS & JA HUSS

"It's been kinda fun, so... thanks for bringing me along."

"It's not like there was a choice. The whole ordered list thing, remember?"

He chuckles. But it's clear he's tired because it's a half-hearted chuckle and it comes with a yawn. "Yeah. Forgot about that. The hallway feels like a million years ago..."

And the next thing I hear is soft snoring.

He's asleep.

But I am not so easily lulled. I think about how I felt this morning when I woke up. And the man-boys who brought us a door. And the new clothes that I picked out. Which Eros appreciated, I could tell by the way he was looking at me.

And now we're here. In some strange land, or some strange time, or both. With a pegásius, of all things, as our beast of burden. And we're going somewhere.

We... did it.

We changed our fates.

And it wasn't even that difficult. I do realize that finding a door like the one we found is a bit of strange luck, and not all people who want to change their lives can just stumble into a door.

But I could've made a door. I think. I was going into the fog, which wasn't on track with making my own door. But I see things different now. I could've done more. Participated in my own destiny more. Still, when presented with an opportunity, I did take the leap of faith.

Next time I'm dissatisfied I will try that approach

first instead of allowing myself to go crazy with regret and shame.

But after I think about that, I mostly think about him. The god of love. And how his bare back feels against mine, since we are now touching. And how his breathing evens me out. And how I'm not alone, I'm on a team.

And how happy I am.

I think about how one day can do *all this*.

And there are so many more days ahead.

CHAPTER THIRTEEN - EROS

I *wake up to humming*. A melody that feels familiar, but I can't place it. I turn over on the fur saddle pad and crack an eyelid open. Callistina is standing under the tiny waterfall, washing herself. She's naked, but she's been naked this whole time, wearing nothing but that dress made of silver chains. Which also feels familiar, but an actual memory about it eludes me.

The sun is up and bright. Glinting off the silver of those chains as Callistina maneuvers her body under the water. The chain dress comes in three parts—the crown, which attaches to a veil and a collar, the top over her breasts, and the skirt around her waist. None of it actually covers her, just gives off the illusion of coverage.

But she's a chimera again, so the chains, in combination with the velvet covering of fur all over her body, are enough to make her look clothed.

Feel clothed too, I imagine.

She turns, sees me, and smiles. "I didn't know how to

take it off." She points to the chain dress. "But the water shouldn't hurt it, right?"

I shrug. I have no idea. I don't even know why she cares. It's not like it belongs to her. Once we find the next door, she'll leave it behind and whoever really inhabits that body can deal with the tarnish. If it does, in fact, tarnish.

She goes back to her shower, still humming. Apparently, my sour mood isn't enough to ruin her happy one.

I get to my feet and sigh, rubbing my hands down my face, then look down the road. Ire—I have to correct the pronunciation in my head to Erie after last night's discussion—Ire is grazing a patch of grass just a little way off. He could've run and he didn't. So that's good. I don't like keeping animals so I don't ever bother tying them up. If they want to leave, go. I don't give a fuck.

But it would kinda suck to have to walk all the way down this road, so I'm glad he stuck around.

I roll up the fur, fold it over, and carry it and the saddle and the bridle down to Ire. I tack him up, lead him back over to camp, and then start fastening our bags to the appropriate rings on the saddle.

By this time, Callistina has finished her shower and is sitting on a large boulder, sunning herself with her eyes closed, like a cat.

Which she is, I guess.

"I think there's a clasp somewhere on my back. The dip near my waist, maybe? I can't feel it, but it must be there somewhere."

"What?" I ask.

She opens her eyes and looks at me. Then swirls her fingers around her body. "For the dress thing?"

"Oh, the chains. Get up. I'll look."

She gets up and turns around.

Ah, fuck. I let out a sigh.

"What? What's wrong?"

"Nothing." She's right about the clasp. But it's in the middle of her back, not the small of it. I walk over to her and reach for the clasp that holds the chains together. Except it's not a clasp. It's a lock.

Callistina peeks over her shoulder. "I can't see it." Then she reaches around, fingertips trying to touch it. "How am I supposed to take it off if I can't reach it or see it? Did you put this on me?"

She's teasing. I mean, maybe I did, but it wasn't *me*. It was whoever inhabits this body I'm currently wearing.

I blow out a long breath, weighing my options. Because the memory, and the name of this device, suddenly comes back to me.

"OK, that's a weird sigh. What is going on, Eros?"

"It's just… it's… it's not a dress or a piece of jewelry, Callistina."

"What do you mean?" She turns all the way around to face me now. "What is it, then?"

"It's a collar. A livery collar. Except it's not to denote… membership in an order. It's a slave collar. A very nice one, for sure. But that's not a clasp behind your back, my queen. It's a lock."

Her eyes fly up to meet mine, her mouth open, aghast. "What?"

"You're a slave. To whoever this guy is." I point to

myself. "But if it makes you feel any better, he must like you. Her. You know what I mean. Because this livery is" —I nod and look it over, seeing it in a new light—"*very* grand."

Callistina lets out a breath and blinks. "I'm a *slave?*"

"Not you. Her." I point to her body.

"But *I'm* her!"

"It's only temporary. Until we find the next set of doors. Just… think about how beautiful it is."

"Whatever. Why am I even surprised?" She looks at me when she asks this question, but I know she isn't actually looking for an answer even before she continues to speak. "I mean, this is the story of my life, right?"

"I dunno. You were a queen for a pretty long time. You don't have much to complain about, Callistina."

She scoffs. "And you were a god once upon a time, so why are you bitter? You don't have anything to complain about, Eros." Her voice and tone are mocking me when that last part comes out.

"Whatever. Are you ready? I'm anxious to see where this road ends."

She doesn't say anything. And when I offer her a leg up, she shakes her head, lifting her little pawed foot up until she catches the stirrup, then swinging her body up and leg over.

She scoots back, giving me room, and I do the same. A moment later, we're traveling again. But today feels different than yesterday. More somber. Less exciting. And the morning passes slowly.

THE SAVAGE RAGE OF FALLEN GODS

It's not until the sun is high above us that we get a glimpse of a new road ahead. And people.

"Look!" Callistina, who has not said a single word since we left until now, points her finger at the new road.

"I see it."

"It looks kind of busy. It must go somewhere."

"Let's hope."

IT TAKES **all afternoon** to travel the distance on the switchbacks and arrive at the end where it merges with the new road. There are a lot of people. Mostly walking, but some have wagons. And this is when I finally understand *when* we are.

Because the wagons are being pulled by chimera.

"Ho-lee Mother," Callistina says. "What in the name of the gods is going on here?"

"We are not in Vinca."

"No shit, we're not. I mean, I would not say Vinca treats their chimera with respect, per se. But we don't harness them to wagons and treat them like beasts."

Ire gives off a long snort. Like he's got an opinion about this, just not a way to express it.

I turn him into the flow of people and carts. Not all of them are being pulled by chimera. Most of them are being pulled by the people who own the carts, actually. Peasants. The carts are full, too. Like they are heading into a town to sell their wares.

About ten minutes into the new leg of our journey, Callistina leans into my neck and whispers, "I'm the only chimera who is not walking."

"I've noticed."

"And they're all naked."

"Yes. I can see that."

"They're looking at me funny, Eros."

"No, they're not."

"Yes. They are. Even the chimera are looking at me funny. But the owners, they… might want to hurt me."

"They're not going to hurt you."

"I should get down and walk alongside you."

I reach a hand around and grab her knee, hooking my fingers behind it. "You stay right where you are."

Her chest expands against my back as she inhales deeply. Then her legs erupt in chills from the touch of my hand behind her knee.

"It's fine, Callistina. *No one* is going to touch you." I say it, and I mean it. But she's right. These people walking along the road with us look really put out that she's riding the pegásius behind me.

I give Ire a little kick and send him into a trot. His stride is massive and covers a lot of ground, so we leave this group of people behind. But there are more small groups ahead. Everyone going in the same direction— no one coming back this way.

Which makes sense now that I understand *when* we are.

For this is the world I was born into.

This is the world of my beginning.

*THE WOMAN **I left*** Pie with back in the human realm—Lisa. Her name is always there in my head even though I want to forget it—she thinks I just abandoned her and Pie, but that's only partly true.

Once I realized Pie's magic wasn't available—didn't come with her, i.e. I wasn't going to be able to steal it—I did leave. But I had intentions—maybe not every intention, but one or two intentions—of returning after gathering more knowledge of Pie's curse.

Ironically, my plan was to locate Callistina. Since Callistina was her sister, and present at the ceremony when I took little Pie, I figured she'd have a perspective on that night that could enlighten me. Could help me break little Pie's magic free.

Then... Pressia happened.

The child bride of my half-brother Pell. Would-have-been bride, at least. That wedding never happened. Why she was so upset with me I still don't understand. I mean, she was practically a baby.

Who wants to get married when they haven't even lived yet?

After I stole Pie and then disappeared through a

door in the dingy hotel room where Lisa was keeping the little gryphon princess for me in the human realm, there was fog waiting for me. A nothingness. It felt right. Appropriate. Punishment, of course. But I had it coming. I knew that and so it felt right. And familiar.

But it wasn't the gods getting even with me for ruining their little caretaking ceremony where Pianna—lion*ess* from the House of Fire, First Daughter of all deities, Second Daughter of Saturn, gift-daughter of Ptah, holder of one magic bag of rings bound up in a spell straight out of the mouth of Ostanes herself and shoved into the beak of an invisible bird—was being sold to the King of Vinca and his chimera princeling, Tarq, to make a godling royal beast even more powerful than the old succession gods themselves.

It wasn't *them*.

It was *her*. Pressia.

She was a shrieking little child. An angry little speller with a glowing ruby-red doorknob as big as her fist hanging around her neck. And she was *gooooood* at it.

She pointed a tiny finger at me and seethed, "I see you."

I don't remember what I said. Maybe nothing. I didn't understand what was happening. I certainly didn't perceive her as a threat. Annoying, cringe-y, for sure, but not a threat. Not in that tiny hysterical body.

But then, out of her mouth, came the spelling...

. . .

"ONCE YOU WERE GREAT, *once you were tall. But now you're bait, and now you're small.*

You steal the love, not set it free. You take the joy, from them, from me.

I see you now, I see you then, I see you everywhere you've been.

And you will know my name forever, you will know my spell is clever.

Not just some words and pretty rhymes, my spells are deep and keep the time.

I curse you now, evermore. The magic ends with the last great war.

You cannot win, you will not prevail. You will be lost in time and tale.

For it is not gods who rule this place—they have no honor, truth, or grace.

It is the magic of the spells that keep us safe, and warm, and well.

We craft them careful, make the words, and wrap them up in beaks of birds.

So go, and live, and rejoice. But know, my enemy, this is not your choice.

Goodbye, lost god, be gone for good. Be the man you know you should."

I mean, what was she? Seven? I was stunned at the complexity of her spelling. I couldn't process things properly, I do remember that. Because I was really stuck on that line that said, *I see you now, I see you then, I see you everywhere you've been.* I didn't know she was an oracle until she said that line. I don't even know how *she* knew she was an oracle because oracles are old. All over the age of forty because it takes decades to figure out if they're insane or truly seeing through time. There are hundreds of tests. Dozens of proofs. And only then, when they have predicted things with accuracy, are they led into the chamber of a god and blessed with the ability to spell through time.

So how did this little girl—who was bred to be nothing more than a child bride and a future mother of a godling—figure out how to wrap me up in a curse and spell me through infinity?

I didn't know then and I don't know now.

But once those words came spilling out of her mouth, I was caught. One might say she had entranced me. The whole thing was incredibly good. And by good, I mean well-crafted.

It was much, *much* more than just 'clever.'

She put things in that spell not even a fully grown alchemist could think up.

For instance, starting the whole thing with the word 'once'—that's a special talent right there. It is specific in a general kind of way. And its meaning in the spell points to the past. But not a random past, *all* the past. My *entire* past wrapped up in a single word.

Once.

Then, of course, she ended that particular magic with the word 'evermore' in the middle. So that first part was meant to trap me as the man I was. Then it gets to the heart of the matter with the 'time and tale' stuff, trapping me inside the fog. And it ends with a command. 'Be the man you know you should.'

And then... after she said all that, I heard a song. It

was a strange song. Strange sounds. Familiar, but not. And the singing—it was a man. He was telling a tale about a ball and chain.

Of course, I know the song by heart these days. And I understand the sentiment. It plays constantly in my life. Even if it's not really playing, it's in my head.

Pressia is my ball and chain. Her curse rules my life.

And every bit of her spelling haunts me.

"OH, MY GODS!" Callistina exclaims this behind me, her breath passing softly over my shoulder and pulling me out of my memory. "Look! It's a city!"

I pull Ire up and we pause in the middle of the road. We were trotting for a long while as I got lost in time, so we've covered quite a distance and we've managed to find ourselves alone, between two thicker flocks of travelers.

"Wow. Have you ever seen this place before?"

I nod at Callistina's question. But my attention is fully on the opening between the mountains where two giant pillars demarcate the end of the mountain road and the beginning of the glorious city.

"This is the Golden Road, isn't it?" Callistina is starting to work it out now. And she's excited about it. I don't answer her, but she doesn't need my confirmation. "And those… those are the Pillars of Glory! Holy wow!" She grips my shoulders, leaning into my neck. "*When* are we?"

And now, I have an answer. "We're in the Age of Fire."

"The Age of Fire!" I can't see her face, of course, since she's sitting behind me. But I know that her mouth is open in shock. "But that… that's… *thousands* of years ago!"

Breath. Wind. Earth. Fire. Four Golden Ages and we are in the Fourth.

I scoff. Because when Callistina was counting us down back in the hallway, as we were getting ready to step through our doors, she used the old system of time. And I had forgotten about it. Like I have forgotten about many things over the course of my existence.

Especially the beginning, which this is.

I nudge Ire forward and we continue, walking now, since I am in no hurry to get to this city. It is Rome, but not the Rome where everything ended. It is Rome before that realm even existed.

The first city. Where magic was born and gods were made.

Where all the things that could go wrong went wrong.

If there were bombs in this age, like they have in the future human realm, I would drop them on this place. I would find a way to go all the way back to the Age of Breath and drop those bombs. Ending it all before it started.

I would, I realize, destroy everything.

And it would feel good.

WE PASS **under the gates** amid hordes of people. Most on foot. Many on horses or using carts and wagons. But Callistina and I are the only ones riding a pegásius. We are tall, too, sitting high above everyone else. Even the men driving the wagons.

Everyone looks at us.

It's possible that the mere presence of a pegásius is what draws this attention. But it's more probable that it's Callistina riding behind me that keeps that attention trained on us as we make our way towards the walls of the inner city. It is truly breaking many rules to let her ride behind me. Though she is in chains, they are the wrong kind of chains.

There are many laws in Glory Rome concerning chimera. But number one is you *do not* clothe them. They are not sentient or in any way conscious or aware of who and what they are.

Which is a lie. The chimera have always been sentient. It was the whole point of making them. Human-animal hybrids were how the gods started. It was the pinnacle of human knowledge.

And then it was their downfall.

Maybe, if they hadn't treated the chimera like

animals, the Glory War would've never happened. But then again, wars are part of the plan. There is no way to stop them because it is how the gods take and give power.

Callistina is not wearing clothes. She is wearing the required chains. But the chains have been made to look like clothes and everyone around me understands that this is not only skirting the rules, but asking for trouble.

The only thing stopping them from tearing her off the back of this pegásius is probably the beast himself. He still has his sharp hooves and his size is enough to intimidate anyone. They should fear me most, but they have no idea who I am and I would like to keep it that way.

In fact, I would very much like to just find the next set of doors and fall through them. Never to see this place again.

ONCE INSIDE THE CITY, I'm not sure what to do next. How long will we be here? Long enough to be hungry, that's for sure. We ate the rest of our meat and cheese hours ago. Drank the rest of our water too. So I decide to find us some provisions.

I don't want Callistina with me as I do that, so I

settle on searching for temporary accommodations first.

Behind me, Callistina is ooohhing and ahhhhing about the grandeur all around us. "Look at that!" She keeps pointing things out to me like I've never seen it before. As if I wasn't born here like every other god who rules the realms. "What are those buildings?"

I look at the tall towers. Seven of them in a circle around a massive fountain that spurts water three stories into the air. You can't see the fountain from here, of course, but I remember it because the people in those buildings made me. My eyes scan up the side of building one, pausing at the top floor. I'm picturing the rooftop and what the city looks like from that vantage point because I have been on that roof and when I see it through Callistina's eyes it's glorious.

What a lie.

"They are the Sphere of Science and Glory buildings. They make… abominations in there."

"Like me?" She whispers this over my shoulder, right into my ear, her soft words sending a prickle up my neck.

"Like *me*," I growl back, ignoring all the feelings rushing through my body. Trying to, at least. It's not just her, and the closeness of her, and the scent of her, and the touch of her—though none of that is helpful. It's this whole city. I can *feel* the magic in the air. It's like light-ning, times a million. Sparks of it crackle though the breeze and swim around me, surrounding my body, bathing it in potential power.

Add in a few emotions and it would manifest into

something. Something bad. It's always bad. At least for me. Probably because the savage rage lingers inside me like a crouching tiger ready to attack.

I don't think the humans feel it. They have no idea what they are fucking with when they create their little pets. When they arrange the genomes of their little beasts.

But the magic isn't a part of them the way it's part of me. And I guess, if I wasn't bonded to it the way they aren't, I wouldn't much care about this feeling. If I thought that I could take the power without feeling the consequences—wield this power inside the safety of a crucible room—hell, I might do it too.

I might make a few beasts of my own. A whole army of them.

Slaves for days to wage wars for all eternity.

The Glory War. It was a time of suspicion, and lawlessness, and restructuring. Everyone lost power, then gained it again. Rules were made—too late—and then protocols were put in place to manage the mistakes that started the war.

Power was stripped, then passed on, then reorganized. It's a cycle that has turned on the wheel four times now. Four Glory Ages. The Age of Breath, the Age of Wind, the Age of Earth, and the Age of Fire.

Then the Forgetting Time started.

I sigh, then spy a place that might do for accommodations. People are still staring at us, but this is a less than desirable ward in the city. They break the rules here, you can just tell. So we'll probably get a pass on our own rule-skirting as long as we don't fuck with anyone.

'As long as they don't fuck with me' is a better way to say that. Because I am not in the mood to be provoked.

I direct Ire over to the hitching post off to the side of the inn. It's off in a corner, behind some other buildings housing a restaurant and a saloon.

"Get down," I tell Callistina, once we're there.

She scoots back, swings her leg over, and hops to the ground. Bending her knees and almost falling to them because the drop is significant.

I get down too, then loop the reins to a hitching post and direct Callistina to enter the inn with a nod of my chin. She's still mindlessly happy about being here, so she doesn't even notice that I'm being curt with her.

Inside it takes a moment for my eyes to adjust to the darkness, so I stand behind Callistina, looking over her head and taking in the room.

It's your typical low-class inn. A bar at the far end, tables and chairs—mostly empty—a stairwell that leads up to the second floor, and a couple of whores hanging on the banister.

I place my hands on Callistina's shoulders, directing her to get out of my way, then approach the long counter where a man waits, watching us.

He's not a man. I know this without smelling him or looking at the scales that hide just behind his ears. When he opens his mouth, the forked tongue gives it all away. "Greetingssssssss. Do you need a room, friend?"

The old me—the real me, the me who isn't traveling with a dethroned gryphon-chimera Queen of Vinca from the future—would slam his face down on that counter for calling *me* 'friend.' And even though I have the urge to do that, I force myself not to.

I don't find most chimera particularly loathsome, but the lacerta are the lowest of the low in the chimera world. They were the first to be made, and thus contain all the mistakes that were fixed later.

They are part snake. This one, a cobra hiding his hood. Trying to, at least.

The gryphons, for what it's worth, were the last to be made. They are the most perfect examples of the chimera experiments.

The snake is waiting for me to overreact, perhaps hoping to scare me with a flash of his hood and the baring of his poison-filled fangs. But I don't give him the satisfaction. "One room, please."

"Do you need a stable for your beast?" He nods his chin at Callistina.

In this moment I hear her—in my head, thankfully— demanding that he call her queen. But she has enough sense to shut up and say nothing as I handle things.

"No, thank you. She sleeps at my feet."

"Very well, good sir." The snake smiles at me, baring those fangs anyway. His head is bald and he has no facial hair at all. His eyes, though not reptilian, just look wrong. And if he were to step around that counter, there would be no legs holding him up. He has the lower half of a serpent. He's probably balanced on a long coil this very moment. And if pressed or attacked, not only would he bite, but he would spring up tens of feet into the air to tower over me.

He would be killed without question if he attacked a human. So he probably wouldn't do that. And I'm immune to his poison, because I am a god, not a human, so I wouldn't care if he did.

But he wouldn't be killed for biting Callistina. I would be compensated in gold by whatever seedy establishment holds insurance over him, and then he'd be imprisoned and given debt.

It doesn't seem worth it to me, but the gryphon chimeras are universally hated in these times by their fellow beasts. And they don't look, or talk, or act anything like Callistina. She is not some half-crossed mistake from the early days. Her golden mane and velvet body, not to mention her presence—which comes from being not only a royal beast, but a fuckin' queen— are the pinnacle of success. She is a reminder of everything the others are not. All gryphon chimera are, but Callistina even more so since she is an example of lion*ess* perfection.

In the end, the lacerta must agree that Callistina is not worth the trouble of killing because he just starts checking me in. And I'm just about to sign for the room when a human man pushes through a set of saloon doors and appears behind the desk. "What is going on here?"

He's looking at me like I owe him some kind of answer. I don't, but I have a feeling he's the owner and this is not about me, or the snake, but Callistina.

"I'm about to pay for a room," I deadpan back at him.

"We don't allow pets." He points at Callistina. "This one needs to stay in the stable."

"No. She sleeps at my feet. This is not up for discussion."

"Oh, isn't it?" The man—who is portly and round, though very tall and rough-looking with a dark beard covering his chin and neck—leans back on his heels. "You're breaking the law with that thing. I could call the wardens and have her stripped and you imprisoned. It is illegal to clothe a beast like that."

He points to Callistina's chains. Which clearly are not clothes, but also, just as clearly, mimicking them.

I've noticed something about the chains Callistina is wearing over the course of the day. And now I have an urge to put my suspicions to the test. "Is she not wearing enough chains for you, round man?" I growl these words out because I am annoyed. "Because I'll have you know that this is not silver, but godsmetal. And there is enough godsmetal on a single string of fringe hanging over her breast to buy your entire establishment."

The snake man hisses, but I can tell it's a gregarious hiss. His version of a guffaw. At the nerve of me? Or perhaps because he's been waiting years for someone to come in and put this fat asshole in his place?

It's the latter, I think. But I don't look at him or acknowledge him. Just stare at the owner with blank eyes. Like I give no fucks how this all ends.

He averts his eyes to the chains Callistina is wearing, then looks back at me. "You could be lying."

"I could be. But I'm not. Check it, if you want. I'll wait. And I won't even feel insulted."

The owner turns to the snake man, pointing at him. "Get me the counterfeit kit."

The snake-man bows, then slithers into the back, reappearing a moment later with a small box. He sets it down on the counter, removes the lid, and takes out two small vials of chemicals and a tiny glass plate.

I pluck a strand of godsmetal from Callistina's 'dress' and drop it onto the glass plate. The snake-man adds one drop of the first chemical. Then one drop of the second chemical. I'm smiling, feeling *very* fortunate, when the red mist appears and the godsmetal disintegrates into a tiny puddle of golden liquid.

The owner gasps, then looks over at Callistina. She's is wearing enough godsmetal to buy the entire city. It's a king's fortune. Hell, let's just cut to the chase here. It's a *god's* fortune.

The owner's eyes dart to meet mine. "What…" But he can't even form the right question.

"The what, where, why, and how is none of your concern, my good man." I pluck another strand off Callistina's dress and put it on the counter next to the glass plate with the golden puddle. "You may keep them both." I point at the puddle. "If you let it harden over the course of a week, you will have gold on that glass plate."

The owner lets out a long breath and smiles. Then he picks up the strand of godsmetal. It's probably enough to pay for several years' stay at his lowly establishment. He looks up at me again. "How long would you like to stay with us, good sir?"

I would not like to stay here at all. I would like to

find a door and go anywhere but here. But that's not an option. "I'll let you know."

"Very good." Then he pockets the payment and claps his hands, barking out orders. "Give them the rooftop terrace, snake-man."

"And rations and a stable for my pegásius, thank you."

The owner's face goes blank, then he bursts into a laugh. "Anything you want, my godling. Anything you want."

Then he retreats back through his saloon doors, whistling. Carefully carrying his glass plate of future gold.

Godling. It wasn't a guess on his part. It's the only possible explanation, at least in his mind, for the godsmetal hanging off my beast. I doubt it ever even entered his mind that I would be an actual god.

But it's for the best. Even in these times, gods are not dusty and weary travelers. In all the hundreds of years that Glory Rome existed the gods never—not once—left the Sphere of Science and Glory buildings unless they were falling off the roof. It wasn't until Parting Day, the first day of the Glory War, that the citizens of Glory Rome even knew the gods were real. They knew the people in those buildings were trying to make gods, but they thought the chimera and godlings were as far as they'd come.

But it wasn't.

Inside those buildings are the Primordials.

The Gods of Glory.

And since I am one of them, I am in there too.

CHAPTER FOURTEEN - CALLISTINA

"*We have a menagerie.*" The valet—who is half dog and carries our bags—says this to Eros as we ascend the stairs to the second floor.

"What?" Eros replies. Everything about this city is irritating him and it shows.

"A menagerie," the dog-man repeats. Then he nods his head over his shoulder to indicate me. "If you have an affinity for the beasts." We're at the top of the stairs now, having walked past the whores lingering along the banister, and the dog-man pauses to grab a doorknob on the door to his right. He swings it open and presents whatever is inside to Eros.

Eros doesn't even look. Just says, "No, thank you," and keeps walking.

But I look as I pass and get a quick glimpse before the dog-man shuts the door again.

He scurries to catch up with Eros, meeting him at the second set of stairs that will take us up to the terrace, but my mind is whirling with what I just saw.

Chimera. A dog-woman, a snake-woman, a horse-woman, and some kind of rodent with a face. I try to keep my face neutral as we climb the second set of stairs, and then, once we're at the door to the rooftop terrace room and it has been opened, I walk in and leave Eros to handle things with the dog man, wondering if there is a horse-man and a rodent-man somewhere in this building. Because I would be willing to bet money that the snake-woman is married to the snake-man and the dog-woman is married to the dog-man.

I blow out a breath, trying to catch up with everything I've seen so far.

I want to hate this place for the way they treat the chimera and how they see them—*us*—as beasts of burden, but it's such a magnificent city. I want to go explore all of it while I can.

It's not that I've been sheltered. I've been all over the realm. But I have not been a door-traveler, nor have I been a time-traveler. And this is never going to happen again. It is possible we'll go back to Savage Falls and wander into another set of doors, but I don't think so. I don't think Eros likes this trip and I very much doubt he'll want to do another one once we get back.

So my options will be to stay in Savage Falls and be a prisoner in the fog or venture into the Realm of Pittsburgh where there is no magic at all.

I don't want to think about either of those choices. Not now. Not while I'm *here*.

I sigh and walk over to the open wall that leads to

the outdoor terrace just as the door closes and Eros joins me.

"Turn around, Callistina. I need to take your chains off."

I look up at him. "But why?"

"Why?" He looks at me like I'm an idiot. "*Why*, Callistina? Because they are *chains*. And while they might be worth a large fortune, they are also a symbol of your... animalistic nature."

I shrug. "So?"

"You're not offended?"

"I don't even live here. Why should I care what the people think?"

"Because they think you are an animal."

I shrug again, kind of scoffing. "I mean... am I not?"

"You're..." He is about to say 'human,' but it's just not true, so the words don't come.

And anyway, I don't even mind being half animal. I'm half lion and I'm proud of it. There's really no greater aspiration as far as chimera go. I'd never want to be a human. How mundane.

I could get used to the human body I have back in our time, but only because I know it's a pretense. Nothing more than a trick. I am at peace with who and what I am, regardless of what people think of me or where my status lies in the grand scheme of things.

I was a queen of a very important realm. I *ruled*.

It's not a small thing.

Though I really have no desire to go back to that role. I know that Vinca is in ruins. And while I'm not exactly *happy* about that, I'm not exactly *not*, either. That part of my life is over for good. On with the new.

"You're not an animal, Callistina. None of the chimera are animals."

"Not even satyrs? Do they even have a human side?"

"Of course they do. How do you think they get *faces?*"

He's right. I have to admit that. "But they're not... a *cross*. They're a... whatever a triple combination is. It's very dilute, don't you think?"

"It's called F2. Second-generation. Chimera bred to chimera."

I feel stupid for not knowing this. Understanding genetics, breeding, and pedigrees would be something I'd be skilled in, if I had stayed in the House of Fire and become an alchemist. So it's embarrassing that I have to ask, but I need to know, so I do. "Am I F2?"

"Certainly not. You come from the House of Fire."

"Hmm." I turn and walk out onto the terrace. The sun is beginning to set. It feels late, but yet the day is just starting its end. It actually feels like this one day has lasted for weeks, that's how different this cityscape in front of me is from the empty mountain road Eros and I woke up on. "It's so..."

"Ugly?"

I scoff and look up at Eros, who has joined me and stands next to my left shoulder. "No. It's... magnificent."

"It's filled with evil."

"Maybe. But it's still pretty."

He reaches around my back and takes the lock of

silver in his hand. I pull away, and he lets go, glaring at me. "You're taking it off."

"I don't want to take it off, Eros."

"Why? That makes no sense."

"I like it. It's pretty."

"It's a symbol of slavery."

"It's worth a fortune. You must be very rich in this life."

"I'm a god, regardless of what door I travel through. Turn around. I'm taking it off. It's drawing attention to you because even though I placated the owner with the promise of money, he's right. It's been fashioned in the form of a dress. I don't know what this other version of me was thinking when he put this on you, but it was a stupid move. Beasts are forbidden to wear clothes. They will kill you, Callistina. Do you understand that? They will kill you over these chains."

I know he's right. Hell, back in Vinca we had Fireday every week. And all the chimera, regardless of rank, had to walk around naked to show respect to the ruling class so the humans didn't dwell on the fact that the chimera could take Vinca for their own in a blink of an eye.

So these rules are not strange to me. I haven't been on the receiving end of them since I was a teenager, of course. Once the king died I took over as queen and my Firedays were over. I presided over the whole thing.

"But I like the chains." I look up at Eros, meeting his gaze. "I really like them."

"I understand that. You can have them. They're

yours. I don't care. But you cannot *wear* them. Not here."

"They're going to get left behind when we leave."

He sighs. And I am getting the impression that Eros is on his last strand of patience. He's not comfortable here.

But I *am*. I feel an affinity with this city. Like it's… my roots.

"Are you not hungry? Do you not want to go get something to eat?"

"I am hungry. But… why don't you just go? I'll stay here. Then I can leave the chains on."

He hesitates. "I don't know."

"What don't you know?" I'm truly confused by all his hesitation and doubt. It's not a side to the god of love that I've ever seen.

"Someone could come up here. Break in and hurt you. Steal you. Anything could happen."

I make a face at him. "You're paranoid. And anyway, I'm not helpless." I hold up my hand and claws come shooting out of my fingertips. "I have these. Not to mention these." I snarl at him, showing him my long canines. "I'll be fine."

"If you claw someone, or gods forbid, fucking bite someone, Callistina—"

I laugh, stopping him short. "I'm not going to claw or bite someone, Eros! No one is coming up here!" Then I calm down and shoot him lazy eyes. "But this whole concern thing you're doing… it's… kinda… sexy."

"Sexy?" He sneers at me. "It's not sexy, Callistina. Ordered list! Is that ringing any bells in this thick skull of yours?" He flicks his fingers against my head, pinging me. "If we have to travel through the doors together to make the magic work, then I can't get home without *you*."

This is true, and I'm sure it's part of it. But really, I think he's truly concerned for my safety. So I place a hand on his chest, flat against his heart. It beats under my touch. Then I look him in the eyes. "I'll be fine here. I won't answer the door if anyone knocks. I won't leave, I promise. It's better than me going with you. It's better that you go get the food and bring it here."

He wants to object, but I've made a good point. If I go out, people *will* notice me. Even if I'm not wearing the chains and we don't take the pegásius. Gryphon chimeras—especially one like me, House of Fire and all that—are not common. I'm not sure they even exist here. I might as well have a target painted on me.

Finally, Eros lets out a breath. "Fine. I'll get food." He points at me. "And you will not leave here. Or answer the door. Or call out to anyone down on the street. Or talk to anyone at all, no matter what."

"Agreed."

"And when I get back, I'm taking those chains off. So get used to the idea." He starts to leave, but then turns back to me. "And instead of standing around romanticizing this hellhole, why don't you spend this time thinking about how we find the doors to get the fuck out of here."

And with that he storms over to the door and walks out.

I'm just about to turn back to the terrace, and now

truly setting sun, when the door pops back open and he points at me again. "And what the fuck? Lock the damn door when I leave!"

The he slams the door and doesn't come back.

But I do go lock the door. I understand that my safety here is precarious. I just don't see the point in being overly stressed out about being a chimera in a place I don't live. I mean, technically speaking, I'm not even born. Won't be born for thousands of years.

This city has no power over me.

At least... I tell myself that. Because when I step out onto that terrace, the colors of the sky—blue and purple and red—reflecting off the sandstone buildings and the mountains all around us, I feel a *pull*.

It does have power.

I belong here... I can feel it.

CHAPTER FIFTEEN - EROS

*W*hen *I get out onto the street*, I cross it, then look back at the hotel. And there she is. Standing right out on the terrace wearing the chains, the fortune in godsmetal hanging off her body like it's nothing more than tin.

That stupid, arrogant woman. I wait until her gaze lazily passes over the crowd and finally finds mine. Then I point at her and bare my teeth, directing her to go inside. "For fuck's sake, woman. Have some sense." I mumble this, but she's looking right at me, probably reading my lips because she sighs heavily, rolling her eyes, and then turns her back and disappears beyond view.

I turn as well, looking for somewhere close to buy a meal. But there is nothing over in this quarter but saloons and hotels—which both probably serve food, but it's not going to be good food. And it's been a long day. Two days, I remind myself. I just want to settle for a moment and settling involves a good meal, not a shitty one.

I decide to check on the pegásius. He's fine when I get inside the barn, munching contentedly on some very green hay inside a stable that is probably the size of a paddock for a regular horse. But I really came in to talk to the groom. He's another dog-man, only more of a child. Something in between, maybe. He bows when I come towards him.

"Where can I find good food that is close, boy?"

"My godling!" He rights himself and looks me in the eye. "There is good food in the flower market." He points. "Right over there. Just a few streets away. Don't be fooled by the condition of the carts, that's where we all eat on payday."

It's probably mediocre food at best, but I'm sure it's better than what they serve here at this inn.

"Thank you. Take good care of this beast for me." I point to the pegásius. "His name is Ire and he's... good." I don't know anything about this pegásius, but his life can't have been easy. And he hasn't given us any trouble.

"I will, godling." The boy bows again.

I want to tell him to stop calling me that, but it's not worth it. He's irrelevant. A random someone who I have met on the way to a random somewhere that I will never see again. So I just nod my head and toss him a coin from my pocket.

He looks at it, curious. And I wait. Because I don't even know if the money is accepted here. But the boy's bright eyes when he looks at me tells me all I need to know. The coin will be accepted and it's worth far more than I should've given him.

"Thank you, godling!" the dog-boy says. Then drops to his knees, bowing his head to the floor.

I turn and walk out.

THE BOY WAS TRUTHFUL—THE flower market is only a few streets over. But the sun has mostly set now and nearly all of the tents have been shut up for the night.

The food carts, however, are still very busy. And the various restaurants and saloons around the small square have patio tables filled with people.

I'm scanning the carts, trying to find one with lamb, when that familiar melody starts playing. I look around, trying to figure out where it's coming from, but it seems to be coming from everywhere.

Her song.

My song.

'Ball and Chain.'

I stand in place, spotting a musician through a crowd, then turn to the right and spot another one. I continue the circle and realize that every busker in the square is playing the same song, at the same tempo, but with different instruments.

Which should be impossible. It's not even an ancient

song. In the time I just came from it's a couple decades old. And when they start to sing—those modern phrases that have no place here—it feels like I'm in a dream.

It doesn't make sense.

None of this makes sense.

But then, unbidden, her voice is in my head, spitting out her spelling. *I see you now, I see you then, I see you everywhere you've been. And you will know my name forever, you will know my spell is clever.*

I'm caught in it too. The world stops and only the music remains. My vision narrows down into a tunnel and I don't move. I don't even try. I just stand there, like a foolish halfwit, listening as they sing and make those ancient instruments play a rhythm that won't be invented for millennia.

When it's over, I let out a breath and the world starts turning again, the tunnel vision fading.

They are all playing different songs now and the square has become a commotion of sounds mixed in with the gregarious talking and laughter of a people who have already put the day behind them.

I spy a cart serving lamb, order up two meals, which are packed into a tin bucket that I pay a deposit for, and then I head back to the inn. Trying not to think about Pressia and the way she insists on haunting me through this curse.

When I get back to the dirt street where we are staying I immediately look up to the terrace. I fully expect to find Callistina up there, flaunting herself. But it's empty. And dark.

I suddenly have a bad feeling. Like things have gone

terribly wrong. Like Pressia was just waiting for her chance to get Callistina and my little foray into the square was the perfect opportunity.

The perfect trap.

I rush up the stairs—ignoring the snake-man's greeting and the whores making offers—and grab the doorknob. But it's locked. I pound on it, ready to break it down, when it opens and Callistina greets me with a cavernous yawn. "Why are you being so loud?"

She was sleeping. Everything about her says sleepy cat. Which, again, I find quite sexy.

And now I feel even more foolish than I did standing transfixed in the square. Pressia. Why does she torment me like this? Why must she haunt me?

What did I ever do to her? Nothing. In fact, she is the one who wronged *me*. I am the one who should be haunting her. And if, by chance, I stumble upon her in my travels, and I am given the opportunity, I will kill her.

"Well?" Callistina snaps me out of my introspection. "Are you coming in?"

I haven't moved or acknowledged Callistina since she opened the door. "Yeah," I manage, blowing out a breath. Then I hold up the pail. "I got lamb. I hope you like lamb."

The food makes Callistina smile and take the pail from me. Then she turns, leaving me at the door, and walks over toward the terrace. "We're going to eat outside now that you're home."

She says this, and does all this, like she hasn't got a

care in the world. And I wonder, for a moment, how it might feel to have no cares.

But I just don't have the imagination required to conjure up that kind of far-fetched fantasy.

THE FOOD IS GOOD. Better than anything I've had in probably a hundred years. And I make a note to myself to give that dog-boy another coin for his excellent advice.

Callistina and I are still out on the terrace. This quarter of the city isn't quiet. I doubt it's ever quiet. Maybe in the hour just before dawn, when the drunks are passed out and the whores are counting their money, but even then, it's probably more of a low hum than a quiet. And it's starting, that hum. Just as Callistina gets up and does her now-trademarked feline stretch. Arms up, back arched. Then the long legs. Paws flexing claws.

She lets out a breath and stares at the city.

I'm sitting in a chair behind her, next to the one she was occupying just a moment ago, so I get a nice view of her velvet-covered ass.

She was beautiful even when she was insane and wearing spray-painted antlers tied to her head. Chimera are holders of magic, so many of them—perhaps even most of them—alter their appearance with the talents they genetically inherit. Or pay a friend, or a professional, even, to do something special that they can't manage to conjure up.

They can give themselves wings—with or without feathers—just like a god. Antlers, of course. Though many chimera are born with horns or antlers. The deer, the bull, the antelope are all common species to cross-breed with humans. The bulls make the men big and formidable. Armies recruit bull chimera as soldiers almost exclusively. The deer and the antelope make lovely nymph crosses, leggy and graceful, like dancers. Though the nymphs are their own species and can be crossed with just about anything to make chimera more attractive.

But Callistina has not been artificially altered. This is her true genetic form and it's... *stunning*. Even without the antlers.

It's very rare to find a gryphon chimera with velvet covering their whole body the way it does hers. It's a trait cultivated by the House of Fire. The lion*ess*, as they call them. Second Daughters from the same breeding pair are the most desirable because First Daughters have mistakes. And they are cataloged and corrected in the Second Daughter.

Callistina was a firstborn and so her future was in academics. She would've been taught the techniques and spellings for her own vivarium filled with lab rats. Though she would not have been wasting her time with rats. She would've been using chimera from the start. Not anything sentient, really. Just the base code of gryphon chimera to which she would add and subtract things over several generations.

Then she would work her way up using purer and purer bloodlines until she was crossing the F1 generation. A pure human bred to the best chimera she had produced over the years. They would all be lions, in her case. House of Fire. What a status to be born into. Not only are the gryphons the most desirable chimera in all the lands, they are godlike in their own way.

As a queen, Callistina would not have been schooled in the art and science of lion*esses*. The reason there is an accent on the second half of that word is because a lion*ess* is the ultimate product of selective breeding from the House of Fire. Every lion*ess* is a gryphon chimera, but not every gryphon chimera is a lion*ess*.

But she never went down that path. I doubt very much that Callistina, House of Fire, Queen of Vinca, has any idea of who and what she really is.

But I do.

She sighs and leans on the terrace wall. It's coated in smooth plaster, like almost everything else in this city, and is the color of sand. "I love this place," she croons.

I almost snort. "I can't imagine why. There isn't a human alive in this city who wouldn't kill you, or rape you, or torture you, given the chance."

She turns to face me, her elbows leaning back on the top of the wall, stretching one long leg out in my direction as she settles into a leisurely pose. I don't even think she's doing this on purpose. This is just Callistina getting comfortable, not presenting me with her shape like a whore would.

Regardless, it has the same effect on me.

"You're... *sour*."

I shrug. "It's just the truth, Callistina. Glory Rome hates chimera. They despise them. They see them as animals. Meant to make a human's life more comfortable and nothing more."

"Then why do they make them in those buildings over there?" She nods her head a little, indicating the Sphere of Science and Glory buildings across the city.

I glance over at the seven buildings. They are lit up with electricity that makes them glow blue at night, a really dramatic contrast to the gold they are during the day when the sun is bouncing off the mirrored glass they're all made of. The Sphere is the only place in the city that is allowed to have electricity, if my memory serves. The rest of the streets and buildings are still lit with oil, or gas, or candles. The streetcars in most districts and wards of Glory Rome are pulled by horses. But over there in the sphere, they run on the electric lines that crisscross through the air above the roads.

I look back at Callistina, who I think has been studying me. "Because they're trying to make gods."

"So why do they bother crossing humans with animals, if the animal side is so despised?"

"It adds power to the humans. At first, it takes away. But through careful breeding things lost are added back and things never had added in. They will do this until they have every desirable characteristic isolated so it can be added on a whim. And then, once all that has been perfected, they will start crossing humans with technology." She makes a face at me, not understanding.

Savage Falls has technology, but not all there is to offer in the Realm of Pittsburgh, so I search for an example that she will understand. "They will cross humans with… radios."

A laugh bursts out of her. "What?"

"Not exactly a radio, but the components inside it. The technology."

She thinks about this for a moment. Then sighs. "I don't get it. I don't understand that world at all."

"Well, you don't belong in that world, so why should you?"

"That's kind of my point. I *do* belong in this one. I can feel it. Even more so than in Vinca."

"You were a queen in Vinca."

"I know. But it wasn't meant for me. It was meant for Pie."

I'm a little bit surprised that she is so self-aware. She came across as insane back in Savage Falls, but beyond that, she came across as… shallow. And she's not. Not at all. At least, that's not the side of her she's shown me since she took those antlers off.

"I think we should talk about how we get home." Callistina doesn't say anything. She doesn't want to go home. I know this. And that's why I'm choosing to have this conversation now, rather than later. "Don't you think?"

"Why do you want to go home, Eros?" I open my mouth to answer, but she puts up a hand to stop me. "Think about it. We don't have to stay here, but we're rich." She points to her godsmetal dress. "And we could go anywhere. We could live our lives in a place where we fit in and turn it into anything we wanted."

"You're forgetting something. I'm cursed, Callistina."

"So? Your curse doesn't look like too bad of a deal from this vantage point. No wings, but so what? People think you're a godling. They will respect you no matter where you go."

"It's a nice thought, I guess. But I heard that song in the square when I went to get food."

Callistina's face falls. "Oh."

"Yeah. I don't know what this is, but it's not real. It's a trick. It's Pressia."

"Why does that little girl hate you so much?"

"Why does everyone think of her as a little girl? Wasn't everyone a child at one time? Didn't we all *grow up*?" I'm sneering these words out. My anger is unexpected and disproportionate. So much so that Callistina's upper body juts backwards in surprise. "She's not a little girl, Callistina. She's a fucking woman. She's been a woman for thousands of years. Stop calling her a little girl. It implies innocence and she's not innocent. She's the one who set me up. She's the one who is ultimately responsible for taking my power and status as a god. She is a *bitch*. And given the chance, I will end her."

I get up, turn my back on Callistina, and go back inside the room. There is nowhere to retreat to except the bedroom. But that feels like a trap. If I go in there and shut myself up it will be difficult to calm down.

I don't like being angry. I hate it. But just thinking about Pressia brings out the worst in me. Talking about her magnifies this evil. Because I am nothing but anger when her name is flashing through my mind.

I pace the main room, then turn and pace back. Callistina is watching me from the terrace. Backlit by the faded blue glow of the Sphere of Science and Glory buildings off in the distance. Her body a perfectly outlined shadow of curves. Her face hidden in that same shadow, unreadable.

"You don't understand," I tell her.

"OK." Her voice is quiet and gentle. "Well, if you want to tell me about it, you can. I'm listening."

"I'm not capable of love. All right? That's all you need to know."

"All right." She presses her lips together and nods.

"And it's not about her. Or her curse. Or the curse of the gods who hated me. It's just... the way it is with gods. You cannot be *all*-powerful. You have to have a weakness."

"And yours is... attachment? Or lack thereof?" She pauses here. "Because love is just... I don't know. A *feeling*, I guess. Of joy, or satisfaction, or something like that. But *attachment* is... loyalty. Attachment is the idea that you will sacrifice for someone. It's a surrendering. So which is it, Eros? You are incapable of joy with a partner? Or you are incapable of surrendering to them?"

I just stare at her, rolling her words over and over in my head. Making sense of them. Or trying to, at least.

After a moment, Callistina says, "It's not a test, you know. Take as long as you need. I don't require an answer.

It's for your benefit only." Then she crosses the room, stops a pace away, and turns her back to me. "I'm ready to take the chains off now. I would like a bath." She lifts up her long, golden hair with both hands to give me access to the lock that sits in the middle of her spine, and waits.

I pull myself together, letting the anger simmer down inside me. Then let out a breath and pick up the lock. "It has a keyhole."

"Do you have the key?"

It makes sense that I would, but I've checked the pockets of these pants thoroughly and it's not there. "Let me check the bags."

I walk over to where the dog-man set down our saddlebags, pick them up, and set them all on a long counter that separates the main living area of the room from the small cooking space. I already know there are clothes in here. I did a cursory check back on the road. But the interesting thing is that it's not one set for me, but two for both of us.

I pull out a set of folded clothes that are much too feminine to be mine and set them on the counter. "Look." I glance over my shoulder to Callistina. "You have garments."

She shrugs one shoulder, uninterested. Doesn't even care that I'm carrying clothes for her. Clothes that would get her *killed*.

Whatever. I find a thick envelope filled with more folding money, then another, thinner and smaller, envelope that looks promising. When I open the flap and dump out the contents, I find the key and ownership

KC CROSS & JA HUSS

cards for my beasts. Plural. One for Ire and one for Callistina.

They are small cards, smaller than my palm. I look at Callistina's first because there's a photograph of her face on it. Three shots, actually. Straight on and in profile for both sides. A mug shot, in modern days. But the photo is not modern. It's an aged sepia color and the thick, paper card is tattered on all the corners. Something familiar from times gone by. Which, of course, we are living in now.

Beasts don't get names, so there is no name. Just a number—'397739. Property of...'

Well. Things just got interesting.

Because it does not say 'Eros.' It says 'Erotes 10-77-999.'

And in this same moment that I am reading this name in my head, I'm *there*, not here.

Somewhere high. Like a cliff. The wind is blowing hard against my naked back, pushing me forward as the purple sky surrounds me in a tumult of thick, gray clouds and thunder is sending out threats above my head.

Someone is yelling but I don't understand the words. I just know that I am supposed to run.

"What is it?" Callistina asks, snapping me out of the vision, or memory, or whatever it was.

She's still across the room and my first instinct is to lie to her. To save her from seeing this formal, legal announcement of her slave status to spare her feelings. But her flippant attitude about the whole thing has pissed me off, so I turn and hold it up. "Your ownership papers, my queen."

She crosses the room and takes the card from my hand, studying it. "Hmm. That's not your name." She looks at me. "That's not my name, either."

I scoff. "So you're just gonna be in denial? Is that how this is gonna go?"

"I'm simply making an accurate observation."

"Is that not your face?" I point to her picture.

"It resembles me, but obviously it's not me. It's someone *like* me. Perhaps of the same bloodline as me. But this woman here"—she taps her clawed finger on the picture—"she lived thousands and thousands of years ago. And I didn't."

The fact that she says this with a straight face kinda blows my mind. I raise my eyebrows at her. "You do remember that we're *time traveling*?"

"But I just got here."

I rub both hands down my face in frustration. "OK. Listen. Fine. Be in denial. I don't care." Then I take my attention to the other thing that spilled out of the envelope. The thing I was looking for. The key to her fucking chains.

I face her and twirl my finger in the air. "Turn around."

She obeys and lifts her hair up once again.

The lock is small and so is the working part of the key. Tiny, really. Very nice metalwork. But the handle of the key is long enough for my large hands to manage and a few seconds later, the lock releases. A few of the chains fall down her back, but it appears to be all one piece and needs to be disconnected at various links.

Callistina says nothing as I exhale and begin the process. There are larger links over her shoulders, which I disconnect first. But this doesn't release anything, only gives me access to the collar. Once I disconnect that, I have access to the veil, and the veil gives me access to the crown.

But there's still the matter of her 'dress.'

"Here. Take these."

Callistina holds out her hands, palms up, and I drop the crown, veil, and shoulder chains into them. "It's not a very practical way to hold wealth," she says as I work out how to address the rest of the chains. They really are all one piece and it's kind of a puzzle. One good thing, I highly doubt that either of us will be able to put it back on.

"How so?" I ask, finding the connector that will release the bra portion of the silver fringe that sits on the highest part of her breasts. It releases one side only, so I need to step around to the other side to find the next one.

"Well, you just pulled off a string and gave it to the innkeeper. Couldn't anyone just start pulling strings of godsmetal off me? Why bother with the dress and locking it onto my body?"

I huff a little. "Why don't you try to pull a string off."

She does try, but is unable. "Oh." She chuckles a little. "I guess it's stronger than it looks. Or... maybe you're stronger than *you* look."

I smile a little. "Or maybe I'm just a god and that's the whole reason they call it godsmetal?"

"Or that," she agrees, chuckling. "But then wouldn't the innkeeper know you were a god and not a godling?"

"There are no gods in the Age of Fire. Well, I mean, there *are*. I am in one of the Sphere of Science and Glory buildings right this moment. Building One, to be exact. But I am but a baby in this time. The people of Glory Rome don't yet know that the dream has been realized and the gods have been made. They won't know until Parting Day."

"How far away is that?"

I get the other side of the bra disconnected and start looking for the next piece of the puzzle, which is in the dip of her hipbones. I kneel down to get a better look at it. "About... fourteen years, I think? All third-generation gods were made in Breath Year. Which is three or four years ago, depending on what season we're in now."

"Wait. You're *third*-generation?"

"Yes. The first-generation primordial gods were all chimera. Horus, and Ra, and Thoth, and Seth. There are many more, but they were all crossbred. Second-generation were bred back to humans. Isis, and Ptah, and Osiris. They were more human-looking, but couldn't pass. Then the third generation was the chaos." I look up at her. "We come from chaos."

"Is that Chaos the god? Or chaos the state of being?"

"Both, I suppose. At any rate, there were thirteen of us at the end."

"How many were there to start?"

It's a very astute question coming from a person like

Callistina. And I'm not disparaging her intelligence here, she's just one of those surface-level people who mostly concentrates on things right in front of her. This question is decidedly not right in front of her. "I couldn't say for sure, Callistina. But if you were making gods, and were on your third generation, how many would you have?"

"Oh, I don't know. A lot, probably. I imagine that the breeding and genetics would be fraught with mistakes and such."

"As genetics and breeding often are."

"So… dozens, at least. Is that why there ended up being twelve Olympians?"

"Did your brain just decide to skip over the fact that I said there were thirteen of us?"

"Oh, sorry. I was told there were only twelve Olympians."

"You got bad information. There were thirteen and I *was* one of the last gods standing. I *am* an Olympian. They just didn't like my power because it had no check. I could make them fall in love with anyone I wanted. It could ruin them or bring them bliss. I could start and end wars. You can do anything with love, Callistina. Anything. So they had to get rid of me."

"Who is 'they,' Eros?"

"They…" I sigh. "They are the makers. The Glory Alchemists. And the gods too, because they were in on it."

"So how does Pressia fit in? Did they use her to demote you?"

I scoff. "No. Pressia *chose* to do that." I find the last

connector on her other hip and release it. Then stand up and take the crown part out of her hands. I drop it and the entire ensemble of chains falls to the floor at her feet.

Callistina looks me in the eyes as she daintily steps out of the circle of godsmetal. "Well. That was quite a process, Eros." She pats me on the chest, her touch incredibly soft. "I do hope you can put it all back on when I'm done."

Then she turns and walks across the living space towards the bathing room without giving me a second glance.

But my gaze follows her the entire way. It even lingers on the door after she closes it behind her.

She's not the same woman, I decide. She cannot be the same woman who walked around my prison town with spray-painted antlers tied to her head and blocks of wood strapped to her feet.

Is it a trick?

Is she someone else pretending to be Callistina?

Is she… Pressia?

Wouldn't that be just like her? To send me through a door that leads to my origin and make me take her along with me as a joke?

I hate that woman. I hate her with a passion. And if given the opportunity to end her, I would.

I would *end* her.

And just as I think this, people outside in the dirt streets—some drunkards stumbling home after a long night of revelry—start singing my song. Her song.

You can run all your life and not go anywhere.

CHAPTER SIXTEEN - CALLISTINA

I *really wasn't expecting* there to be indoor plumbing with hot water in this shoddy inn. Not even in the best room. Of course, we had all this in Vinca. Even the poorest of people had indoor plumbing. But when one thinks back on the ancients it's easy to assume that they were backwards and stuck with primitive comforts.

I had been hoping for a water pump and a gas fire under a tin tub. Maybe even a wood pile.

But what I get are hot and cold faucets and a massive copper tub that is mottled with green and white oxidation on the lip and outer edges, but sleek and smooth and regularly polished on the inside. It is very, very nice for a place such as this.

I am pleasantly surprised, having found myself here in the ancient times, that I was wrong about how the ancients lived. Everyone was wrong. Well, at the very least, everyone writing the history books was wrong.

Should it surprise me, though? The people of Glory

Rome are doing next-level science. They have created gods in those blue buildings of theirs. Why would anyone in the future believe they were primitive and backwards when all the evidence points to the opposite?

Probably because we were told to. It was written in the books that way.

I wonder if any of the people of this age regret making those gods yet? I am not a history buff, so I only read the required reading in early school, but if memory serves it was the making of gods that undid Glory Rome. This is what caused the Glory War.

Of course, without the gods there would be no me. I am not some mere human-animal hybrid. That sounds horrifying. I have the blood of gods in me. It's dilute, but it's there. There is no other way to make a royal beast.

The king did a genealogy study on me that first year I was in Vinca and my study came back with traces of Saturn, of course. I was a direct descendant of him, though I was not made with the same pure essence as Pie was. But it also came back with Fatum far, far back in the line. Fatum, from my understanding, anyway, was a primordial who had power over decisions. The unalterable will of the gods. Ironically, or perhaps fatefully, this will didn't come from the god himself, but from the mouth of his prophet. Both were destroyed in the Glory War.

Two gods in my blood then.

This must've satisfied the old king because he kept me. But not only that, he accepted me. He could've rejected me and forced the House of Fire to make a *real* replacement. A lio*ness* with the bloodline of every god and goddess in the room that day, just like Pie. But the king was sickly and he didn't have seven years to wait for the genuine article, so he took me in her place.

He started prepping me for the throne immediately. Assigning me tutors who taught me the ways of the royal beasts at court. Tarq was commanding alchemists at that time. And he would tell me bits of this and that when we were alone at night.

This is when I became obsessed with Pie's magic words.

Four girls, a room, some gifts and thrones. Four gods each know their place at home. A mother gives a book of words, locked up tight in the beaks of birds.

That was the riddle Pie spat at me when she came out of the throne room after she had received her final gift from her sponsor god, which was Ptah, not our house father, Saturn. It was a bag of magic rings that would open doors to other realms. Something far, *far* too powerful and not agreed upon by the other gods in the throne room.

Pie was telling me about how she was from the future, and something about ditching school and hungry nights. Not to mention the invisible birds and banishing Saturn. Who was our father. So that was shocking.

But then... *then* her little six-year-old mouth started saying things that didn't make sense, but *could've* made sense—if she had been, for instance, a grown-up, or an alchemist, or a person from the future.

Things about stealing wood nymphs, and magic rings that open magic doors that lead to other places. And *then* the one thing that really caught my attention was her threat. To me! From her! My adorable, innocent, beautiful, royal beast of a baby sister.

I put you in debtors' prison for killing my Pia.

I had no idea what she was going on about. I thought she had gone insane. I even called out for the Mistress Ryella, who was the ceremony chaperone, insisting that Pie had gone ill.

But it was too late to do anything about that because the ceremony had already started.

Of course, I *did* kill her Pia. But it was nearly twenty years later.

It was so confusing and the pandemonium afterward was life-altering for me.

I was obsessed with the memory of what happened. And those words Pie said to me. All of them, not just the part about magic rings, and doors, and debtors' prison. All of it.

It took my life that day. Because once the old king died and Tarq and I took our places on the throne, I went… mad, I think. Not mad, like I did in the Bottoms prison. But mad with thoughts of the future.

How to prevent it from coming true, mostly.

Which didn't help at all.

Maybe it's not even possible to change the future?

Maybe it's all just fate?

WHEN I COME **out** of the bathroom—my velvety fur still slightly wet—I see that Eros is wet as well. He's shirtless, of course. Showing off that tree tattoo. His pedigree, he said.

I bet the Glory Rome alchemists would give anything to study that pedigree. It would be like a map for them. A direct route to genetics that were used to make the god called Eros.

Or Erotes. He didn't explain that very well. But I'm guessing that it means he was one of many... experiments, I guess. The last one standing, apparently.

It's so odd, all this history. Our history. And while I find it interesting, I can't really make much sense of it. So I go back to thinking about Eros—the god in front of me right now, not the one from the past. His hair is darker when it's wet. Not blond, but the light streaks running through it are still visible, so just looking at him you know he is golden in that respect.

"Did you wash?" I ask him.

He looks at me, perusing up and down my body at his leisure, then nods. "You were taking forever, so I went into the stable and washed in the watering trough."

I blink at him. "You... what?" I'm confused. "Did you just say you washed yourself in a stable water trough?"

This makes him laugh. And his face brightens,

making him appear so human. Especially when he's missing those wings of his. "Do you picture me living like a god, Callistina? Washing myself in golden tubs filled with flower bubbles?" His smile drops and his scorn is back. "I was banished. Believe me when I say that I have washed myself in many a stable in my day."

"Of course," I mutter, a little bit transfixed by him, but also a little bit scared. He's been amicable to me on this journey, but it would be a mistake to assume that tolerance equals affection. Because it doesn't. Never mind the curse from that damn woman Pressia he's so obsessed with, he has been cursed by every god in the realms. He will never love anyone. Ever.

That is just how it is meant to be.

He blows out a breath. Like his temper was about to get the best of him and he's reining it back in. "Sorry. You just… took too long and…" He sighs again. "It's not a big deal to wash in the stable."

Then he turns his back to me and walks into the bedroom.

I let out a breath, relief flooding through me when he's gone, then walk over to the lovely divan couch and I'm just about to sit when he calls my name.

"Callistina, sleep in here, please."

I wilt. It was fine sleeping back-to-back with him last night because there was just the one saddle blanket and I needed his warmth. But I don't want to sleep with him.

Actually, now that I've admitted this, I don't want him around at all. I would very much like for him to just… fuck off, as they say in the foggy little town of

Savage Falls. To walk back through that door and leave me here to make my own way. Make my own future.

This is what I want.

A second chance that doesn't involve a man I am forced to be with, or a throne, or clothes, for that matter.

I'm so done trying to pass as human. I'm over it.

I want to be *me*. The whole entire me.

The gryphon chimera before she was a queen.

Before she was turned into 'that poor girl's sister.'

"Callistina!" He roars it this time. "Get in here."

I could object, but why should I give away the knowledge of my discontent? He will just thwart me if I do that. He will find ways to stop me, I know this. He wants to go home and he needs me to do that.

Besides, the reason he wants me to sleep with him is so he can be sure that I don't leave the inn while he's resting. He just wants... peace of mind.

So I go in to the bedroom and get in bed next to him, and turn my back to his, and rest my head on the pillow, and I begin to make a plan.

I cannot outwit this god. He's too powerful.

But I can make an even trade.

If I find a way to send him back alone, perhaps he will let me stay here in Glory Rome.

"Would you like to know what I think is funny?" Eros half turns so he's looking over his shoulder at me. And when I turn to look over my shoulder, I find his eyes are almost glowing in the dark. A very unnatural shade of green.

I shrug. "Sure. Why not. What's so funny?"

"That you just… give in to them."

"To who?" There's a little bit of surprise in my voice.

"Everyone."

I scoff. "OK. Thank you for letting me know. That's hilarious."

"They cut off your antlers, Callistina. And you just… don't care, do you? You *like* this city? This city that hates you? That would kill you, and have no regrets, just because you may or may not be wearing chains that resemble clothing?"

"No. You've missed the point entirely."

"Then explain it to me." He turns all the way over now. "Because right now, I *hate* you. So much. Because you're a weak piece of shit. And you know what? It's disappointing. I like insane Callistina better than you. Maybe she was walking round town wearing fake antlers and a mangy leopard coat, but at least she had a purpose. And a fucking spine."

My mouth flew open the moment he called me a piece of shit. So it's still hanging open when I turn my body to face him. I'm not from his foggy little curse town, but I've heard all the swear words while I was there and this is… a… a *trashy* insult. One I take exception to. "*Excuse* me?"

"What are you *doing*?"

"I don't understand the question. Obviously, I'm in bed trying to go to sleep."

"No. You're plotting something."

How could he know that? I barely came up with this plan five minutes ago.

"And if that plot," he continues, "includes something

along the lines of revenge against the House of Fire, or that fucking witch selling all those little lion*ess*es, or the gods—specifically, the ones who made you—then OK. I like the plan. But no. Your plan is: 'How can I stay here forever without pissing off Eros?'" He recites the title of my plan in a mocking, childish voice while sneering at me.

I remain calm. I refuse to let him bait me into a fight. "It's really none of your business why I want to stay, or why I like it, or why I do anything, for that matter. We have no connection at all. I was very happy to leave through the door to the Realm of Pittsburgh. You were the one who wanted to make us a team. Well, I have news for you. It was a one-time thing."

"A one-time thing we need to repeat. In case you've forgotten."

"I haven't forgotten. And I even have a plan for that."

"Do you?" He's laughing at me. "I can't wait to hear it."

"I'm going to find a way to send you back alone."

"Really. And how do you propose to do that?"

I hadn't gotten that far in my plan, so I struggle for a moment. And my inability to explain myself allows Eros to chuckle at me, which pisses me off. So I blurt, "I'm magic too, you know."

"Oh, is that right?" he drawls.

"I was bred to be an alchemist. A great one."

"The most important word in that sentence, Callistina, is 'was.' *Was*. Your fate was interrupted—"

"By *you*!" I yell it. "It was you who messed up my

219

future as a great alchemist! But I will have you know that I *can* do magic. I'm very good at it."

"Are you now?"

"Yes."

"What kind of magic do you do?"

"Bottle magic."

"Bott—" That's as far as he gets before he starts laughing.

"What's so funny?"

"*Bottle* magic? That's not even a thing."

"Of course it's a thing. Because I do it. And I'm very, very good at it."

"How's it work then? Give me an example."

"A spell, obviously. One that involves a bottle."

"That tells me exactly nothing."

I huff. "You have a spell, you gather ingredients, you make your potion, and then you bottle it up for a time so it can cook. And once it's done, it's ten times as powerful."

That last part is a little bit of a lie. I'm sure it *could* be ten times as powerful… if you're very good at it. And I'm absolutely certain that my potions would be of that high caliber if I had been studying diligently all these years, but twice as powerful is a more realistic expectation.

"When did you learn this bottle magic skill?"

"When I was in training as a teenager."

He laughs again, his eyes dancing and bright like he's having a very good time at my expense. "Well, you'll have to forgive me for not believing you, Callistina. You took a few spelling classes as a child and now, all of a sudden, and with no practice whatsoever for the last twenty years, you're some kind of bottle-magic prodigy?"

"Why don't you just save yourself, then?"

"Save myself from what?" he sneers.

"Loneliness, apparently." And ohhhhhh, yes. This hits home for him. It was a throwaway insult for me, but the look on his face when I say 'loneliness'—well, that makes everything about this argument worth it.

"Number one, I am not lonely." I want to call him out on that denial, the way he's been calling me out about the chains and the slave papers, but he doesn't give me time. "Number two. My problem is I'm stuck here in this time, a time I do not want to be stuck in, and I have no power without you. You know this."

"I said I would help you. It's not my problem if you don't believe me."

I go to turn my back to him again, but he puts a hand on my shoulder to stop me. It's not a heavy touch. In fact, it's a very light one. So it sends a little chill up my arm. "It's not that I don't believe you. I think you are sincere. But we're stuck in something, Callistina. This isn't an accident. Someone is doing this to us."

"That friend of yours? Tomas?"

He lets out a long exhale. "I don't think so."

"Why do you say that?"

"Because..." But he stops. And his eyes have gone serious now.

"What?" I ask, surprising myself at my softer tone.

"Tomas would not send me here to the time of my

KC CROSS & JA HUSS

making. It would be a mean thing to do. And Tomas is not mean. Not at all. It was... a terrible time for me."

"Are you reliving it?"

His eyes squint. Like he's thinking very hard. He closes them for a long moment. Then opens them again.

"Is it torture?" I ask. "Being in this time?"

And he laughs. "That's one way to put it."

This makes sense. This is why he hates this place and wants to leave. "Is it Pressia, then? The woman you're *obsessed* with?" I don't know why this comes out with such scorn, but it certainly does. "Is she still trying to torture you?"

"It can only be her. Who else could it be?"

"Why is she so unsatisfied with your punishment? It's crone-ish, isn't it? It makes her kind of a shrew. Why can't she just leave you alone?" He doesn't offer up an answer. So I am forced to ask. "What did you do to her, Eros?"

He's going to protest, but I reach up and touch his lips with my fingertips. Hushing him. This is his weakness, I realize. Her. Pressia. I'm sure they were lovers at some point. And he broke her in some way. What other reason is there for a woman to chase the god of love through time and space with an extended curse?

"You must've done something. Even if you don't remember it, you wronged this woman and she is still very angry. So think very hard and figure that out. You don't need to tell me about it, you just need to admit that you did it. Only then will you find a way past this punishment."

"Be the man I should've been?"

"What?"

"Her spell. The last part goes, 'So go, and live, and rejoice. But know, my enemy, this is not your choice. Goodbye, lost god, be gone for good. Be the man you know you should.' And I know what you're gonna ask next, because you've already asked it. But see, I'm not lying, Callistina. I don't know what I did. She's... an oracle. She saw me do something in the future and she cursed me for it. I *don't* know what I did." His eyes are searching mine, like he is desperate for me to understand him.

"That must be it, then."

"What must be it?"

"An oracle is nothing more than a door traveler. Like we are door travelers. We know things that will happen in the future because we've been there. We've lived it. Pressia traveled to the future. She saw you do something—something to her, probably—and then decided you're dangerous. This is why she cursed you. To stop it from happening."

"She didn't *just* curse me. She handed me over to the gods and goddesses so they could..." He sighs. "*Emasculate* me."

I raise my eyebrows at him. "Emasculate?"

"You say that like it's untrue. Is that not what they did?"

Now I laugh. "No, Eros. They have *not* emasculated you." It's so preposterous, I laugh again. "You're..." And now I think I've gone too far, so I stop.

"I'm... what?"

"Never mind."

"No, what were you gonna say?"

"Well, my choice of word would be... dethroned. They dethroned you. They didn't emasculate you. You are more... *masculated* than any man I've ever met!"

He smiles. Then laughs. "More masculated?"

"You get the idea. You're... *you*. The god of love. You're just... not emasculated."

"Dethroned, you say?"

"It fits, doesn't it?"

"Then that would mean we have something in common." He winks. "Wouldn't it."

I suck in a breath and answer on the exhale. "I guess it would."

'Dethroned' wasn't what I wanted to say. And 'masculated' was the result of not being able to admit to how I really see him. Which is strong. Also capable, and powerful, and handsome. There are a lot of words to describe Eros and never in a million years would 'emasculated' be one of them.

But if I told him all that, he would think I like him. And I don't.

Not in the way it would come across. Which would be romantic love. And may the gods help me if I fall in love with Eros because he would never love me back and it would break me. I'm just starting to put myself back together, I can't afford another shattering.

"Do you wanna hear what I'm thinking now?" Eros says, pulling me out of my disjointed thoughts.

"Sure."

"I'm thinking... those doors in the hallway? I think they go somewhere important. And the fact that the first door led us here, to *my* beginning, but more importantly to a place that has no connection to you, well, that presents as evidence to me that this hallway we're in is a trip into my past, not yours."

"So you can find an understanding?" I ask. Eros nods. "That will enlighten you? And possibly free you from your curse?"

"I don't know. But the doors were in that hallway for a reason. And we know for a fact that they are set up in some predetermined order."

"The ordered list," I say. Mostly under my breath.

"Exactly. So I think we have to go through them, Callistina. All of them. And that's why we can't stay here. It's not that I want to stop you from finding whatever it is you're looking for, I just know that our future lies on the other side of those doors."

I think about all this for a moment. It makes more sense than any other explanation of why we're here. "OK," I say. "I'll go through the doors with you. On one condition."

"Name it."

"After we do that, I get to come back here and stay."

He reaches out and touches my face with his fingertips and this small gesture of intimacy makes me shudder unexpectedly. "Why?" he says, his voice very soft now. "Just tell me why *here*. In this 'when.' There are a million other timeplaces, Callistina. Why not one of those?"

"I think," I say, "that the better question is… why are you so against it? Why do you hate Glory Rome so much?" And while I know this is deflection on my part, it truly is the better question. We're here because of him. Not me.

"Aside from the fact that they treat chimera like animals? Aside from the fact that they are fucking up the human genome inside those blue buildings so they can make their gods? Be the gods of gods? I mean, I could go on, but isn't that enough?"

"But don't all timeplaces have their faults, Eros? Are there any that are perfect?"

"Wouldn't you like to at least *try* to find one that is?"

"Vinca has been destroyed. And maybe—I doubt it, but maybe if Vinca had a future I'd like to go there. To the only home I've ever known. Give it another go. But it's gone, Eros. I want to move on and I want to do it quickly. I want to put the past behind me and just forget it ever happened. And this place"—I point to the sleeping city outside our window—"this place tugs at me. It's pulling."

"It's pulling you into a trap, is what it's doing."

"Well"—I sigh, frustrated—"it's really none of your concern. *I'm* none of your concern. I want to do right by you. So I will. I will travel the hallways and help you break free. All I'm asking is that you do the same for me."

This is when I realize he's still touching my face. Still looking deep into my eyes like he's searching for my soul. He says, "Do you wanna know the real reason I don't want you to stay here?"

I'm suddenly not sure. The moment feels... big. Like he's about to admit something. So I hesitate.

He doesn't hesitate. "I like you, Callistina. And we've

been through some shit together, ya know? And I get that I didn't exactly appreciate you back in Savage Falls. Kinda took you for granted. Only saw the costume and not the woman underneath. But... I think we make a good team."

I blink at him. What is he saying? *Please, please do not let this god tell me this is love! Because it's a lie! He is unable. He is the trap, not this place!*

"I'm asking if you'd consider staying with me. Journeying with me. For my sake more than yours, obviously. So that's a bit selfish on my part. But we make a good team. And if you join me, then when it's all over, we can find a new future *together*. And... if it's this place, well..." He doesn't want to stay here. I know this. But he says, "If this really is your place, then I'll stay with you. If you want me to."

That's it. He just cursed me, didn't he?

"Why are you looking at me that way?"

"What way?" I ask.

"Like I just... betrayed you."

Didn't he? Didn't he just insinuate that he *loves* me? Which is a lie! I want to scream this at him, that's how much of a blatant lie it is.

"Listen, Callistina. I don't often like people. But you and I?" He gestures to me, then himself. "We're friends now, right?"

"How do you figure?" I laugh these words out. They're so preposterous. "We are not 'friends'."

"Do you think of us as enemies?"

"No. But that doesn't mean we're *friends*."

"We're... traveling together."

"So?"

He huffs out a small breath of air, trying to manifest astonishment. Like what he's saying makes perfect sense and I simply don't possess the wit to decipher his intentions. So my eyes are narrowed down into slits when he says, "People who travel together... *bond*, Callistina. We're bonded now. We've been through things together. You asked earlier if I was incapable of joy with a partner or if I was simply incapable of surrendering to them. Because joy with a partner is the manifestation of love but sacrificing for someone was all about loyalty and attachment, and that was a surrendering. I don't love you. You know I am incapable of joy with a partner like that. But I am loyal to you. I do want what's best for you."

"Since *when?*" My eyes are still narrowed down into little slits. Because this is also a lie. "You're not concerned about me. You want to break *your* curse, you want to go on *your* trip, you want me to help *you*. None of this has anything to do with me aside from the fact that I must help you tick these things off your list."

"You know what you are, Callistina?" He's pointing at me. "A *cynic*."

I scoff at the incredulity of his accusation. But can't even find the words to object, it's so absurd.

"You're a cynic. And it's... sad. I'm sad for you. Because here I am, a *god*, and I'm offering you a friendship. I'm telling you that I will be loyal. *That* will be your reward. And you're scoffing at me."

"So let me get this straight." I sit up in bed so I can look him dead in the eyes. "You will *sacrifice* for me?"

"Are you not sacrificing for me?"

I'm taken aback a little at this turn in the conversation. Because I think I have, actually. Not even meaning to. I was, after all, the one who offered to help him first. So it was me, not him, who set up this… *friendship.* "You didn't answer the question. And do you know why you didn't answer the question, Eros? Because you haven't the first clue what a sacrifice is."

"A sacrifice. The act of surrender, or the suffering of a loss, in order to gain something. I know what it is."

"Your definition is the literal act of giving up something precious to gain something better."

"No. My definition is the giving up of one's self to save someone else."

My laugh is so loud, it bounces off the ceiling. "Good night." Then I turn over in bed and sigh. Shaking my head at his nerve.

I close my eyes and try to put him out of my mind. But even though he's quiet, I'm unable to do this.

Sacrifice for *me.* That's… a lie. He would not sacrifice for anyone. He's as selfish as they come.

"Fine," he suddenly says. "You don't have to think of me as your friend. But I consider you one and I don't make friends easy so I'm not giving up on this. I am a selfish god and a sorry excuse of a man."

"Well, at least you're being honest now."

"I don't deserve your friendship. But you do deserve mine. So I will offer it to you without any expectations in return."

"Right." I lift my head up and punch my pillow, trying to fluff it up, then set my head back down.

"You'll see. I will stand by you, Callistina. I will deliver you to the destination of your choice. Even if it's here in this god-forsaken city of dark magic. And, after that's done, if you still truly despise me, then... well, what can one say to that? It's a heartbreak, I guess."

I scoff. "If I deny you friendship, it will break *your* heart?"

He lets out a breath. "I just know it will hurt." I feel him shrug behind me, unable, I guess, to find any more words to explain himself.

"You have no idea what heartbreak is, Eros."

"And you do?"

"No. My heart has never been broken. But this isn't about me. I am, at least, capable of loving someone enough to understand the meaning of the word sacrifice. You are not. You are cursed. You are the god of love and you will never fall in love."

"You're right. I don't love you. I will never love you."

"At least we're on the same page now."

"But it won't be because I don't like you. And it won't be because I am not loyal to you. And it won't be because I am unable to sacrifice. It will only be because of the curse. And you know what?"

His hand is suddenly on my shoulder. His fingertips gripping it tight enough to urge me to turn and look him in the eyes.

He's rather compelling right now. And telling the truth, at least a little bit. So I allow him to turn me and when I meet his eyes, he's smiling. "What?" I ask. Answering his question with one of my own.

"I think it's perfect."

"What's perfect?"

"That I will have no reward for this. That you will get all the benefits."

"Whatever." I start to turn again, but he's gripping the opposite shoulder now. So I allow him to let me hesitate. And when I lift my eyes to his once more, they are bright green again. Almost glowing.

"It's OK if you don't believe me, Callistina."

"Good. Because I do not."

"But I'll show you anyway. And even if you don't consider me a friend, I consider you one."

"That is your choice, Eros."

"You're right, it is. But you know how I know that you're just trying to be difficult here? That you're just in denial about our *mutual* friendship?" I don't even bother acknowledging this. He continues anyway. "You came to me, Callistina. Back in Savage Falls. I didn't go to you. You came to *me*. And do you know why you came to me and not anyone else?"

Again, I do not answer him.

"Because I accepted you. The wooden blocks that made no sense. The antlers. Hell, even the mangey coat. I was the only one who let you be you. So... ya know... you can lie to yourself all you want, but we both know that I made you feel accepted and *safe*."

I think about this for a few moments. I did admit it on the rooftop, so he's not wrong. But it's all very one-sided still, isn't it? So even though I don't want to ask this question—not because I don't want the answer. I just don't want to encourage this conversation—so even though I don't want to ask this question, I have to ask. I need to know. "How did I make *you* feel, Eros?"

"Me?" He blows out a long breath. "Well. Seen, I guess."

"Seen?"

"And... needed." He nods. "You made me feel needed. Your vulnerability made me strong."

I want to object, but my mind is tired and I'm having a hard time finding the fatal flaw hiding within his confession.

He smiles now. And the tension between us eases a bit. "But it's comfortable, don't you think? I mean, why else would you come to my bed all those nights if it wasn't comfortable, Callistina? If you weren't getting something out of it." He squints at me. "I made you feel safe, didn't I?"

"I've already admitted this to you. After my nightmare. When we were on the roof, drinking. So fine. You made me feel safe. And, well, the only other option was to sleep alone. Which is not much of an option. Plus, you never told me to leave."

"I didn't want you to leave. I wasn't... thinking about you much, but you were sort of... a fixture. Something I got used to. But I would just like to say"—he puts a hand up, asking me not to interrupt—"I would just like to say that you're not just someone I got used to. Now you're someone I count on. I truly do see you as a friend. A smart one. Capable too. And"—his grin becomes wide, spreading across that handsome face of his—"sexy." He shrugs. "I mean, anyone who doesn't think you're sexy

—especially like this"—his eyes linger on my lion*ess* body—"is just a liar."

I have to admit, it is his appreciation for my true body that lifts my heart a little. He said he was the only one who accepted me. And that's true. It wasn't until the very end of our... relationship back in Savage Falls, that he even mentioned my crazy outfit. So I guess it is friendship. Though I do not feel like admitting this to him. Not tonight, at least.

And is it not true that I have an appreciation for his body as well? Do I not like the look of him, even if I don't really know the man, or god, inside?

It's this question that spins my head a little. Because I've had sex with this god-man dozens of times. And each time I've been satisfied. But it was a wholly physical experience. It was a reaction to a stimulus and not much more.

So for a moment, I pause and wonder what it would've been like if I had truly *known* him. And it wasn't just physical. What would it feel like to have a connection to a sex partner?

It's a feeling so foreign to me that my mind goes blank just thinking about the question. I wouldn't know. I have certainly never been in love. I don't have any idea how to even dream up that scenario. I am incapable of even fantasizing about it.

And while I do not think I am in love with Eros, nor he me—I'm now convinced he's telling the truth about the friendship. I agree that there is a connection between us. And maybe that's something I should appreciate more?

Maybe friendship is the greatest prize? Maybe friendship is all the two of us will ever have? Maybe it's the best we can ever hope for?

And like it or not, we are on a journey together. He's right about that. It's inevitable that this shared experience will bond us when we get to the end of it.

He might not be a permanent fixture in my life, but there's no sense in denying that we're on the same road, we come from the same place, and, for now, at least, we've only got each other.

I stare into his eyes, those unnatural green eyes, and suddenly have an urge to kiss him. It's the magic, of course. His magic. But if it gives me the same result, do I have to care? It's just sex, after all. "Do friends sleep together?"

Oh, he is delighted with the turn in conversation. As am I. I'm tired of talking about feelings. I don't need any declarations. I just want physical contact.

"Can't friends do anything they want?" he asks back. His eyes dart down to my lips and in this moment I know two things. One, he wants to kiss me. And two, I want him to do that.

The next thing I know, our lips touch, barely at first. Like a whisper through the air. But then it's more than that and we are kissing. Slow kissing. Deliberate kissing. Like we are exploring each other for the very first time.

This time I do not feel a compulsion like I did outside the door on the hill. There is no magic here. It's not a spelling or a trick.

But it is much, much more than just a kiss.

It is my desire to touch him in new ways now. To understand him better. And to make him want me. Or maybe to let him know that I want *him*.

As friends, of course. Because he's right. Friends can do anything they want, as long as it's agreed upon.

Eros doesn't hesitate, but he lets me lead for a moment or two. Assessing me, maybe. Is this a quick kiss to end the day and start the night? Or is it going to lead somewhere?

I move closer to him, letting my hand fall to the round muscles of his shoulder, and then trace my fingertips down his arm where tattooed tendrils wind around like a snake climbing through tree limbs. There is writing there, and when the moonlight catches it in just the right way, the words, written in some long-forgotten language I do not read, glimmer like stars that live deep in the dark.

These markings are the story of him. The trunk of the tree going down his back is his history and the limbs reaching around his entire upper body are his people.

I am but a leaf, if that.

Or maybe, if I'm lucky, I'm a seed.

My touch is a signal that this is not a kiss goodnight, but an invitation to something worth staying up for. We're going somewhere and we're going there together.

As *friends*.

Eros responds by opening his mouth and kissing me harder, while at the same time, his hand slides around my hip, grips the curve of my ass, and tugs me closer. Right into the curve of him.

And it feels *so* right, so perfect, that I know, without a doubt, that the seed will take hold and something new will emerge.

Something that is just us, whatever that might look like.

That's the future. A dream. A time and place yet realized.

But the most amazing thing about this moment here in bed with Eros is that for the first time ever, I feel complete in my present. I am content. I am... happy.

He urges me to roll over on my back, then slides his body between my legs. Opening them up as he continues to kiss me. His hands alongside of my cheeks, his arms boxing me in at the shoulders, but making me feel safe and protected instead of trapped and insecure.

He pulls back from the kiss, his thumbs caressing little circles on my cheeks as he looks down into my eyes. His hair, mostly dry now and blond again, hangs down over his face and brushes against my jawline. "Ya know what I think?" he says, but doesn't wait for my answer. "I think we're kinda perfect for each other. I think not only are you the answer for me, I'm the answer for you too. I think we were actually made for this. To be a team. To be lovers. And to be friends. And maybe I'm not allowed to love for real. But am I not allowed to redefine what it means? And am I not allowed to decide that love is you?"

Love is *me*?

Is he right? Is changing a thing as simple as redefining it?

236

"It's a loophole," I whisper. "Cursed, or not. Is it up to us?"

"We write our own future, Callistina. Don't we?"

"We do," I agree.

He leans to the side a little—his eyes locked on mine—and slips his hand between my legs. I close my eyes, enjoying the care he's taking to pleasure me. There is nothing quick about what he's doing. It's slow, and deliberate, and meant only to bring me pleasure.

My job is to experience it. To feel it. To accept his gift.

And I do that fully. Climaxing with his fingers inside me after only a few minutes.

But while I'm still basking in that glow, he pushes himself inside me. Again, he goes slow and he is deliberate. He is careful. And I feel every single movement. Clutching at his muscular shoulders as he penetrates me deeper. Clawing at him when he begins to move slowly. Then arching my back, giving him access to my neck, as we climax together this time.

He doesn't waste the access. First, he bites my neck the way a lion does. Claiming me. Not hard enough to make me cry out or draw blood. Just enough to let me know I'm his.

And once that's done, and the flood of overwhelming pleasure has died down to rolling waves of satisfaction, he kisses me there. A promise not to hurt. A pledge to respect my trust.

It's a promise and a pledge I didn't need.

Or so I thought, until I was given both.

Given another moment to coalesce, it's a longing.

The pledge becomes a hunger and the promise becomes a lust.

We are next to each other now.

My back against his chest.

His arms around me.

My eyes closed.

His mouth at the nape of my neck.

My body flooded with peace.

His lips still kissing me as I fall asleep.

Redefined.

CHAPTER SEVENTEEN - EROS

I *wake to a song*. But not the song that's been haunting me for thousands of years. It's birds. And the tune is something you hear in the springtime when love is in the air.

A long breath comes out of me and with it comes every bit of tension I've been holding in.

This is when Callistina stirs next to me.

It's her, I realize. She's the reason for the sweet song and the sense of solace that comes with it.

My arms are wrapped around her middle, my face pressed into the back of her neck, and I've got one leg hiked over her hip.

She's breathing even and deep, so not yet waking. But I find myself wondering how she would interpret our entanglement at the moment. Would she find it possessive? Or would she find it obsessive? Would she assume the leg was placed carefully so as to cage her in? Or would she see it as a show of affection?

Hard to tell. A couple days ago I'd predict cage. But

things have changed between us. So this morning I would want it to be affection.

I don't give her a chance to wake up and have an opinion on that. I simply untangle us and carefully get out of bed so as not to wake her.

Naked, I go out onto the terrace and breathe in the morning air. It's dry and even though the sun is just barely getting ready to peek up over the horizon, I can already tell there's not a cloud in the sky. It's a desert, this place. Though not the kind with sand dunes and shit. And there's a grand, glorious city built on top of it, so as far as my eyes can see right now, it's nothing but two and three-story sandstone buildings climbing up every side of every hill. And right in the center is the Sphere of Science and Glory.

The fountain in that courtyard shoots up taller than most of the buildings in this city. But when you build seven thirty-story buildings in the sandy valley like they've done here, you need your central courtyard to make a statement that carries impact.

Just as I think this, a wind blows up, stirring up sand in the road down below. Suddenly, a feather comes flying right at my face, hitting me in the cheek. I bat it away like a bug. Then step back and watch as it floats to the ground at my bare feet.

Don't pick it up, Eros. Don't pick it up.

But of course, I do pick it up. And it doesn't take a trained eye to see that this is the exact same kind of feather that I found in my bed that morning after Callistina stormed out. It's eight inches in length and golden in color.

The wind kicks up again and I take the feather and place it back out into the breeze. It catches immediately, as feathers are wont to do, and goes fluttering on its way.

Gross.

"What are you doing?" From behind me comes a low, sexy, I'm-a-queen-and-I-just-woke-up voice.

I turn, smiling, and find Callistina in all her lion*ess* glory, standing naked a few feet away. The sun appears in this same moment and the beams of light shine on her, making her golden, velvet fur turn an electric yellow.

"Just taking my last look at this piece-of-shit city."

It's clearly too early in the morning for Queen Callistina to argue the merits of Glory Rome, because she yawns and practically crawls onto the sofa, stretching her body out in the newborn sunshine.

I wish I had a camera. One of those phones that all the humans carry. They are constantly snapping pictures of the monsters back in Savage Falls. I never understood this hobby. But being in this moment and having no way to capture it changes my mind.

She opens one eye and catches me staring at her. "What?" Her voice is still lazy. Even though I've woken up next to Callistina a few times over the past two months, she's never had a conversation with me until now. I don't even think she barked a single 'You shall call me queen!' when we woke up in the same bed together.

She would just get up, put on that costume, and leave without a word.

Of course, I didn't care back then. And she wasn't a lio*ness*, either. Her human form is top-notch, but this... my God. She's like a...

"What?" she asks again. Both eyes open now.

The word to describe her now is on the tip of my tongue. But I don't say it out loud. Instead, I say, "We need to go into the Sphere Market to look for spelling stuff."

"Oooh!" She sits up and takes a deep breath. "Yes. I'd like that. I need to look for a bottle."

"I think you should stay here." I actually was not thinking this until right now when the words came flying out of my mouth. But as soon as they're out, I'm a hundred percent positive she cannot leave this room.

"What? No." She stands up and stretches. So feline. And sexy. God, she really is sexy. "I'm not staying here."

"Someone has to keep an eye on Ire."

Now she scowls at me. "No. That's not true. No one is going to mess with Ire. He's not a horse. You can't just put a bridle on him and lead him away."

This is accurate. A pegásius is not a horse. They're not even animals. I mean they are, insofar as all of us are. But pegási are not creatures you can steal. Which should concern me because I don't have a clue as to the backstory of this pegásius—including how I seem to have convinced him to be mine.

This is the first time it kinda hits me that we've been traveling together—Callistina, Ire, and I—for some time before that moment on the road when we came through the doors. And there is a history there I am not familiar with.

"And anyway"—Callistina is talking again—"you can't choose the bottle. I need to choose the bottle. And the magiceuticals. I'm an integral part of finding the doors. I'm going to the Sphere Market."

She's right. And I'm not really worried about the pegásius. I just don't think Callistina can walk around this city looking like a lion*ess* from the House of Fire and with the bloodlines of gods flowing through her veins and not drive people into utter madness. She's that *sublime*.

"Also," she continues, "this is my last chance to see this place. I'm not gonna hide here in this dingy inn. I'll put the collar on and we can bring Ire with us. You can ride him, like a god"—she pauses here to smile at me—"and I'll lead him, like your beast. We'll still draw attention, but it will all be on you."

Right. *Lady,* I want to say, *no one is gonna be looking at me the moment you step out this door.* But out loud I say, "Fine." Because it's a losing battle. She's never gonna stay behind. And her plan is probably OK. "Let me put some clothes on—"

"Wait. Before breakfast?"

Her shock is so royal, so indignant, that I actually laugh. "Oh, I beg your pardon, my queen. I wasn't thinking. You must be famished."

This makes her smile. And relax. And pout. Which is very sexy on her. "I'm dying for some poached quail eggs and toast."

"I understand, your highness, but we have to go out to get food. There is no room service at the inn."

She laughs a little. "All right. What should I wear?"

"Nothing."

"Something. A collar, at least. And a lead of some sort. You should be holding it as I lead Ire through the streets."

"You seem awfully excited about being a slave. It's disturbing."

"It's fake." She shrugs. "Who cares. If we've got to put on a show, we might as well make it a good one."

And once again, I can't argue with that.

BOTH IRE **and Callistina** are far more excited about our trip through the city than I am, but it happens exactly the way Callistina predicted. The sunlight streams down on us like rain, casting everything in a golden glow. Most especially Callistina. Everyone looks at her. Gawks at her. Mouths open, stunned by her exotic beauty. They must not have many gryphon chimeras in Glory Rome these days. And that makes sense because Callistina is a royal beast. A bloodline that is just starting in this time, but has been, for the most part, perfected thousands of years from now when she is made.

She is perfection as far as chimera goes.

But just as they are getting their fill of her, they notice the beast she is leading. Ire isn't dressed like a royal beast—because he's not—but he's just as regal as the former queen.

So again, mouths drop open. And they want to stop and ask questions. But then their eyes rise up to see me, sitting astride the pegásius, holding a lead that attaches to Callistina's collar, both made of godsmetal. Which they can't really know because it all just looks silver.

But they know.

We stop at a food cart in the nearby flower market and get food. Not poached eggs, to Callistina's disappointment, but it's a good enough bit of hot meat and cheese wrapped in rice-bread to satisfy both of us. Ire, having already eaten, provides a nice shadow over us as we sit with our backs against an alley wall and eat in silence.

When we're done, I get back up on the beast and Callistina proceeds to lead us through the city towards the Sphere of Science and Glory where the best shops are.

It takes about an hour to get there and we gather children along the way like we're leading a parade. But once we get to the edge of the Sphere, they break off and scurry away.

There are gates, I see. And peasants, even human ones, are too lowly to shop with the elite.

For a moment I am worried that we will not be let through, but it's a needless worry. The guards are transfixed by the image of us walking towards them, and they simply step aside and let us pass with a bow of their heads.

Once we're in, Callistina shoots me a look over her

shoulder, asking what that was all about. But I know as much as she does, so I just shrug.

She leads me over to a stable where I dismount and haggle a price with a groom to watch Ire as we shop. And I'm just paying him when that song starts playing. Just like it did last night.

First just one instrument. One voice. Then more join in until it's a chorus. I look around, certain that I will see her. *Pressia.*

"What are you doing?" Callistina whispers.

And her voice is enough to break the spell, or delusion, or whatever was happening with the music. Because there's like a… like a sharp crack in my ears, and the song is gone.

Was never there in the first place.

I'm seeing things. Hearing things. Going mad, probably.

"Eros?" she whispers cautiously.

"Right. It's fine. I'm fine."

"OK." She's not convinced. "I'm going to go look at bottles in the glass district." She nods her head at a narrow street lined with sandstone buildings that house shops and cafés. "You should go find a magiceutical store and we'll meet back here in an hour. Since I'm a beast, I can't purchase anything. You'll have to come with me to purchase. But I think it'll be quicker if we both go find the right shops first and then—" She stops talking. "Are you OK?"

"Yep." I nod, absently, looking around for Pressia. She's here, I know it. And even though Callistina didn't hear the song, I did. I *know* she's here.

"Did you hear me?"

"Right." I force myself to look at Callistina. "Yeah. You go find the bottle and—" But that's when I see it. The Market Nymph's Bookstore. Huh. And there it is. That's her place, I know it. "You go find the right bottle and I'm gonna hit up that bookstore for spelling help."

"Since when do you need spelling help?" This is a casual question. Off-the-cuff and all that. Not something she's really concerned about, just a flyaway comment.

But she hit the mark. I do not require spelling help. And she realizes her words are more meaningful than she intended. I turn to find her looking in the direction I was staring, but she lets out a sigh. She doesn't see it. Or if she does, she doesn't understand the significance. She doesn't know that Pressia is a market nymph traveling through time via doors, writing books as she goes.

"One hour," I say to snap Callistina out of it. "Right here." I point to the ground.

She looks up at the sun, since we have no timepieces, and then nods. "OK. One hour. Then we'll go buy our packages and head back to the inn."

She stares at me after saying this. And it's an awkward moment. A moment when two lovers might kiss goodbye. Even if it is a short goodbye. They would show affection and leave with a remark about seeing each other again soon.

But there is no fucking way in hell I can kiss a chimera in public. Not in Glory Rome. It would start a war.

So she just takes a breath, shakes herself out of it,

and turns, walking away—lead in hand that attaches to her slave collar.

I watch her for a few minutes, making sure no one is going to bother her. But no one does.

And as soon as she disappears down the narrow road, I turn as well. And then I head straight for the bookstore.

A bell jingles over the door when I enter. It's dark in here, the windows covered with a gray, gauzy curtain, casting shadows over the wall of shelves suddenly surrounding me. A stark contrast to the almost too-bright city outside.

"Hello?" I call out. Even though I already know there's no one here but me. Because this bookstore is the exact same bookstore that lives back in Savage Falls. The door shushes closed behind me, creating a small draft that unsettles dust and makes it dance in the stray beams of sunlight coming through moth-eaten holes in the curtains.

Over there is the divan that Callistina was sleeping on that morning she got mad at me and then walked into the fog to die. This is when I remember her nightmare about the destruction of Vinca and how much it disturbed her.

How could I have forgotten?

Well, I am not too hard on myself. We have been through a lot the past few days. And there are a lot of moving parts happening at the same time right now.

We found a hallway and some keys that opened doors. Which brought us to the Glory Road in the time of Glory Rome.

My home town. The birthplace of me. God of gods.

I've got the former Queen of Vinca trying her best to be a slave. I've got a fucking wingless pegásius drawing all kinds of attention to us and who the hell knows where he came from. And, of course, the whole 'us' thing. The relationship between Callistina and I, which seems to be taking unexpected turns at every corner.

So naturally, it's understandable that I might forget a detail or two in the course of all the happenings. But that was an important detail. Callistina is having glimmers. Is she seeing things that happened? Or is she seeing things that will happen? Is she an oracle too? Or is she just a door traveler and that nightmare was a precursor to the adventure we're currently on?

Either way, it's all very prophetic.

These words are still echoing through my head when I see it, the whole thing kinda glowing as if to draw attention to itself. But this attention-seeking was unnecessary. There is no way in cursed hell that I would miss this book.

I walk across the dusty bookstore and pluck it right off the shelf and then run my fingertips over the leather cover that has been embossed with the image of a lion's head. He wears a crown, the crown of the King of Beasts. Royal beasts, in particular. The expression isn't human, but mimics one well. It is a look of sternness. Of wisdom. Of justice, I think.

I open it up and right away, there is a recipe for a potion. The list of ingredients makes my stomach turn, but I force myself to see it. To read it.

When I turn the page, there is a feather stuck in the binding.

Eight inches long and the color of gold.

I should close the book and put it back, but it's too late for that.

It's... *much* too late for that.

Because this book is called *How to Set it Right*.

I glance down at the book and read the writing on the page with the feather.

"A GOD IN TIME, *a lioness.*
   To there and back you make your mess.
   I see you now, I see you then,
   I see you everywhere you've been.
   I'm watching too, to see your choice.
   Waiting for your lost rejoice.
   It won't be what you think, my friend.
   Your love will die at the end.
   So take the girl and take the trip.
   Take the wings, give them a clip.
   Take the bone, saw it clean
   The blood you make is the blood you glean.
   The power then is yours to keep.
   But beware, my god, it does not come cheap."

I READ the whole thing again, just staring at each word. This is a message from Pressia. And it's a nasty one, too. Then I scan over to the right side of the page and I find a recipe half-hidden underneath the feather.

Is this a dare? Is she giving me a spell to ruin her?

Or will it ruin me?

That's what she's implying. That I lose, no matter what.

I tear her spell out of the book, crumple it up, and throw it into the shadows. Then I close the book with a little too much intention and make dust fly up into the air. I want to put it back on the shelf, but I don't. Because what choice do I have? I mean, it's so obvious that this thing with Pressia is gonna play out whether I want it to or not.

So. *Challenge accepted, you little fucking witch.*

You might have all those pretty words on your side, but I've got magic too.

Let the best speller win, I guess.

I leave the bookstore and go looking for Callistina.

CHAPTER EIGHTEEN - CALLISTINA

*I*t's not that Eros is getting on my nerves. At least, not the way he used to before we started this journey. It's just... he's not excited about the city and I am. I want to explore and I want to do that without his constant bitterness and cynicism.

I agree with him. This is a bad place if you're a chimera. But is it any worse than being stuck in a punishment fog as a human back in Savage Falls?

Decidedly not. And anyway, having now gone our separate ways for a bit, I can see that it's not me who is garnering all the attention when we travel, it's *him*.

The humans do look at me, a once-over. Some of them nod, like they are appreciating my beauty. Children point and make a fuss, as children are inclined to do. But that's it. I'm a casual oddity. I do not sense any hostility. Certainly nothing even close to what I felt on the road when I was riding behind Eros on Ire.

I am... perhaps a stranger in a strange land. But that's all it is. They all know I'm not from here, but even within the Sphere Market—where just getting let in requires some kind of prerequisite that I have no clue about—I just get the feeling I *belong*.

Maybe it's the royal blood? Or the fact that I used to wear a crown?

I'm not sure. I just like it here. And as I wander down the road that contains the glass district within the market, I feel at home. I find myself smiling at people, and them smiling back at me.

This is an existence that I have never known. I went from the nursery, to prep school, to finishing school, to the apothecary, and then straight to the palace.

I have been all over the kingdom, but never once have I wandered alone down a road of shops inside a grand market.

It's… heaven. Just me, a woman alone. And this place, Glory Rome.

It almost sounds like a spelling.

There is a reason they call it Glory, after all. It's… glorious. And down this particular lane, the glass is divine. Bottles everywhere. Lovely slender ones with honey-colored corks, and squat fat ones with screw-on tops made of tin. Giant jugs with wicker carrying-straps wrapped around them. But the loveliest of all, and the ones that catch my eye, are those displayed in the window in front of me that have been stained with quicksilver dust.

They are like old, warped mirrors. And, if my memory serves, they are exactly the kind of bottle I need. Because they are used for finding spells. And while our goal could be defined as going home, or moving on, or locating doors—it could equally be described as finding ourselves.

Our *true* selves.

Finding your inner peace, perhaps?

I think this is a splendid goal for Eros and me.

I go inside the shop and discover a lovely young tern-woman. You don't see bird chimera much in my time. Certainly not terns, which are a slight and sleek bird bred for grace. Gryphons, of course, have bird in them, so there is some bird inside me somewhere. But it's the blood of raptors they want for gryphons. Eagles, and hawks, and falcons. Strong birds with sharp, destructive beaks and claws.

Terns are little dancers in the wind. But with an extraordinary sense of direction and well-developed stamina.

Her face is jet black and feathered throughout. But not a single one is ruffled, so they are so smooth and glossy that you might even miss the fact that she has feathers at all. The rest of her is as white as the sands in the Great Desert. Her body is slender and if I were to try to lift her, she would be incredibly light.

All that aside, if you were to take away the wings, and feathers, and odd black-and-white coloring, she looks entirely human.

"Good morning," she chirps, so dainty and birdlike. "You're an unusual one, aren't you? We don't get many cat-ladies in the Sphere Market."

Cat-lady. I don't think anyone has ever called me a cat lady. But of course, they would still be perfecting the gryphon in these times. Maybe they have not even been developed yet?

"How can I help you today?" she adds.

"The bottles in the window." I point. "Can you tell me about them?"

"Oh, certainly. That's a nice choice. They are very special. Made by the godmakers." She nods her head at the door. "Right there in Building One of Science and Glory."

"Really?"

"Truly." She smiles. "The godmakers' hands have touched every one of these bottles." Then she whispers, "Just as the gods have touched you, obviously." But she's looking away when she says it, and doesn't bring her gaze up to meet mine again.

Just as the gods have touched you. She knows. Am I surprised? Have I seen another gryphon chimera since arriving here? Not even one. Not even a crude one, let alone a royal beast such as myself. The science required to make me is thousands of years in the future using blood that has been carefully crossed, and outcrossed, and in-crossed, and re-crossed, and manipulated *just so.*

I am one of a kind in these times.

"Godmakers, you say?" I speak to break the silence that has befallen the shop because clearly, she's not going to.

"I wouldn't lie." She says this softly. "They all come with the brand stamped on the bottom."

"Do the godmakers have names?"

The tern-woman finally looks at me again and a small smile lifts up the corners of her lips. "Not ones they would share with me. But look." Then she points to the wall where an official-looking document is framed and hanging. "I'm a certified seller, see? I grew up in those buildings. I'm Third Daughter of Saturn born in the thirty-seventh year of the Age of Fire." Then she bows her head again, looking down at her feet.

Third Daughter of Saturn in the thirty-seventh year of Age of Fire.

She is a fucking royal beast!

Well, maybe not officially, but she is, quite certainly, my ancestor!

Whoever made her was part of my beginning. She is not as grand or as refined as me, but she is lovely.

I'm in such a state of shock at this sudden and unexpected disclosure that I'm not sure what to say. This feels important. It feels... significant. Like everything she just told me matters.

"It's true what I say," she whispers. Probably worried I think she's a liar.

"I believe you," I say back. "And," I continue, "I would very much like one of these quicksilver bottles. I'm doing important magic."

"Of course, my lady. And I'm sure you're capable and legitimate, but I must warn you, you have to be very careful with them."

My lady. I haven't been called that since my first year in Vinca. It causes me to blush. So I rush to say, "How so?" so she doesn't notice that the skin underneath the velvet covering my cheeks is turning red.

"They cannot be left in the sunlight, or the moonlight, either. Not once they are capped."

She goes to the window and takes the bottle I was looking most closely at, the one that was calling to me, and I notice that there is no cap on it. The tern-woman brings it back over to the wooden counter and then pulls open a drawer and takes out a topper made of silver wings.

"Once you cap it," she says, handing me the topper, "the magic expands when exposed to celestial light. If you must heat your potions, you must do it over flames and not leave it outside in the sun. It amplifies everything, the sunshine does. And if you must cool it, you must use ice. You must not leave it out overnight with the cap on. Starlight, moonlight, sunlight and"—she looks down for this last part—"and godslight too, my lady."

"'My lady.'" I whisper this out loud this time.

She looks up, black feathered cheeks puffed. Like she's embarrassed. "Sorry. But you are one of them, right?"

"One of who?"

She blinks at me, probably trying to work out if I'm some kind of trap. *It's always a trap,* I'd like to tell her. But I would like this information more, and admitting the truth about traps would surely shut her up.

"One of the royal beasts. The pretties."

And there it is. Confirmation.

She nods her head towards the door of her shop, but I know she's indicating the Science and Glory buildings. "In there. They make *us.* But you're different. I've never seen one like you. With such short fur." Her gaze wanders down my naked body, covered only in the soft, golden, velvet. "You don't come from here though, do you?"

She is a royal beast. One of the very first. And I'm so stunned to be experiencing this moment in the long history of my creation that I don't know what to say. So I just… shake my head.

"Where do you come from?"

"The gods," I say. "Like you."

I should stop there. I should not tell her anything because I'm going to leave here and go about my business with my god-friend, Eros, and our magical beast, Ire, and I'm going to forget all about this bird-woman the same way Pie forgot all about me.

But she will be left here, in her shop, thinking about me for the rest of her life. The same way I thought about Pie for the rest of mine. And she will play back every word I say, trying to piece it together and force it to make sense.

I'm going to ruin her life if I tell her any more.

But there is a hunger in her eyes, and she is beautiful, and now I am certain that this humble little shopkeeper in front of me selling magic quicksilver bottles is most definitely my ancestor. And perhaps my visit here is a necessary step in my own evolution.

So I add, "I come from the House of Fire. Where they make gryphon chimeras of the highest caliber called the lioness."

I want to spill the whole story. Take her hand, and go into a coffee shop and tell her everything. Make her my best friend and ask her for advice.

But I can already tell I've confused her. I can already

see her mind spinning with questions. And I've said too much. So I take a closer look at the topper in my hand and chuckle. "Is this made of *godsmetal*?"

The tern-woman smiles at me. "Yes! Most people think it's silver, but it's not. You're right, it's godsmetal." That's when she focuses on my collar and the lead I'm clutching in my hand. "My lady! Are you wearing it too?"

I nod, slightly embarrassed that I have finery like this when I shouldn't. "It's my master's, of course." I say this plainly, dismissing the subject, and then change the subject altogether. "I want that bottle." I set the topper down on the wooden counter. "But I must go find my master and come back so he can pay."

"Of course you must." She curtseys at me, flaring out her beautiful, pointed wings in a sign of reverence. "I'll be here all day, my lady."

I leave the shop quickly, heading back in the direction of where I started. But as I leave, it occurs to me that bottle magic is real. Bottle magic has always been real. And this little shop is proof.

Was it... forgotten magic? Is that why it felt like a strange power when I became certain it was my gift?

I'm just about to ponder this more thoroughly but that's when I see Eros already coming to find me. He's clutching a book and he holds it up when he spots me through the crowd. Once he and I are close enough to speak without shouting, he says, "I found what we need."

And I say, "I found the perfect bottle." I point to the

little shop where the tern-girl is putting it back into the display window, sans topper, once again.

Eros stares in that direction for a long moment. Like he's appreciating all the pretty mercury glass in the window. Or… the girl. Or them both.

"Eros?"

"Huh?" He tears his gaze away from the window and looks at me. "What?"

"Everything OK?"

He looks back at the window. "I don't think we need those bottles."

"What do you mean?"

"Choose something else, Callistina."

"No. Why? I mean *no*. This is the right bottle. I feel it in my bones. We need *that one* right there." I point to the bottle that was just put back in place.

He sighs, looking at me. "It's a quicksilver bottle, for fuck's sake. Quicksilver isn't something we should fuck with. Whenever you do a spelling with quicksilver the outcome is volatile. Anything could happen."

"Well, that's good! Creating doors is no small thing, Eros. We're basically ripping a hole in time and space. We need to amplify our spell. Do you want to spend days here letting the potion cook? Because it will take days, at least. I'm rusty and we have no idea what we're doing. We need all the help we can get."

He looks at the bottle again, still unsure. "Callistina—"

"It could be weeks, Eros." I say this with all the seriousness I can muster. "*Weeks*." I need that bottle. I'm not sure why I have this compulsion, but it's there. And I'm not going to give up.

Eros and I stare at each other for several long seconds, then he sighs, and relents. "Fine." And plucks a piece of godsmetal off my veil. "It's going to cost a fortune."

"Should we care?" I ask, walking back in the direction of the shop with him. "I mean, we're leaving, right? We should spend it all."

Once again he lets out a long breath. Something is wrong.

"Did you find a spell?" I ask.

He holds up the book, just as we arrive at the door to the glass shop. "Yes. All we need is a magiceutical shop now." He points to the ground. "Wait here." Then he opens the door, goes inside, and I watch from the window as he purchases the magnificent bottle.

When he comes out, he hands me a small, wooden crate with a raw-rope handle and takes the godsmetal lead in exchange. Then we walk down the road, my master and me, and I don't care about anything but the surging happiness flooding my heart.

I love this place. *Love it.* And if I could stay, I'd come back and make friends with the tern-girl. We would have coffee together regularly. We would meet up for dinners. And go out at night with men. And gossip about what people are wearing.

What kind of beastly man would I date?

Well, the fantasy crashes there. Because honestly, I would only want to stay if Eros would. And he won't.

Plus, this would never happen. As much as I think I fit in here, I don't. I'm different.

But still, it's exciting to dream about.

And I will dream about it. Probably for the rest of my life.

"Here." Eros tugs on my chain, leading me over to a shop with the word 'apothecary' painted across the front of the large picture window. "We need acetic acid, sharptongue, and goldberry."

"Is that what the book says?" I ask.

"Yes. It's a simple recipe, but it requires a custom spelling using a celestial décima."

"Please tell me that's your job. Because I have no idea what that even means. Complicated spellings are not my thing. I do a little bottle magic, and nothing more."

"I can do the spelling, don't worry. It will take a little concentration to come up with the right pattern and rhyme scheme, but I am nothing if not an excellent speller."

I smile. "This spell is going to be something for the history books."

"What do you mean by that?"

"Those ingredients you listed? Even *I* know they are powerful. Alone, for sure. But in that combination?" I nod my head. "Very, *very* powerful. Together, they are definitely going to do something big. Especially with this bottle." I pat the crate.

"Good. Because I want to leave this place as soon as possible. Wait here, I'll be right back. And then we're going home. People are starting to stare at us."

I look around and realize he's right. People *are* staring. And it's not just curious children, either. It's... everyone.

But then I notice something else. When Eros goes inside, a few of the gawkers linger, but mostly they hurry away on their business. Everyone loses interest.

That's when it truly becomes clear that it's really not *me* they're looking at. It was never me.

It was always *him*.

A few minutes later, he comes back out, handing me a paper bag and taking my lead once again. "Let's go."

"Right." I fall in step behind him, leaning forward a little so I can say, "They're looking at *you*, Eros. Watch."

He doesn't turn around and talk to me, but he does scan the crowd. And sure enough, the gawkers are back. Everyone *is* looking at him. Whispering. I even catch the word 'god.' Several times, actually.

And what did we expect? He rode into the city astride a near-mythical beast—even without the wings, the pegásius is so obviously *not* a horse—and I was sitting behind him, his slave. I am a lion*ess* from the House of Fire with bloodlines that took thousands of years to perfect and *everyone* can see this.

"They know what you are," I whisper to his back.

"Just walk faster. We'll collect Ire and be on our way. Do not look at anyone. Just ignore them."

Thankfully, the stable is not far away and we reach Ire in a matter of minutes. Eros mounts. But when I take hold of the bridle, ready to lead him on the long walk home, Eros shakes his head. "Get on." He holds his hand out and I grab it, swinging my leg up and over as

Eros effortlessly lifts me off the ground, settling behind him.

"Won't we be drawing attention to ourselves?"

"There's no way out of it now. We just need to leave the inner sanctum of this godforsaken city and it'll be OK. The ordinary people and the peasants, they don't have time to worry about strange gods. They barely have time to worry about themselves."

We leave the Sphere Market at a trot and we continue that pace all the way back to the inn.

CHAPTER NINETEEN - EROS

*I*t's true that *we get fewer* looks as we get further and further away from the Sphere Market and the Science and Glory Buildings in general. But a god-like man such as myself with a royal beast sitting behind him and both astride a pegásius is an easy thing to take notice of.

But while in the Sphere Market the looks we got were antagonistic, the looks we get out here are much more scornful than hostile. More like the three of us are gonna be trouble that common folks just don't have the time for, and not like we're gonna break the whole fabric of elite society by merely existing in the same space.

So Callistina's theory that they are looking at me is probably a little bit right and a little bit wrong. I can admit that it's probably me who's garnering the most attention simply by the fact that it is obvious and clear that I am the one running the show here.

But even admitting to that kind of authority, it's not

just me. It's all of us. Not simply the fact that we all exist, but that we all exist as a kind of trio traveling together.

We're exuding power here. It's coming off us like a fine mist, permeating the air in every direction. I mean, I'm a god. One of the originals. I'm being shaped into a proper little minion up in those buildings in this very moment. And Callistina was queen of one of the biggest empires the world has ever seen. She might not have been born for that role, but she had it. And she took it by the fuckin' horns and made her mark. Regardless of what the history books will say about her in the future, she made her mark.

Ire, though, is still a mystery to me. How did we hook up with this guy? Why does he stick around? He's the only pegásius I've ever known personally, so I don't have enough information to figure it out. All I know is that he's special. They didn't make many of his kind. The pegási have no human in them at all—they were made from the crossing of raptors, horses, and a pinch of rhino. Animal crossings like that were common in the decades and centuries leading up to this time here in Glory Rome. It was how the alchemists cut their teeth on the genetic code, so to speak.

You can make lots of mistakes genetically engineering animals before people put a stop to it. But do that with humans and feathers get ruffled real quick. There needed to be justifiable results. Any mistakes needed to be recorded and explained before a committee.

Especially after what happened with us.

The whole god project was both a grand success and a splendid failure.

That was the whole point of the Glory War.

Gods on the loose.

IT's a relief to get back to the inn. Callistina and I both let a breath of air as soon as we enter our room. She was tense the whole ride, her fingertips gripping the muscles of my waist as we swayed to the rhythm of the beast below us.

"OK," she says, flopping down on the divan couch and looking way too much like a lazy lioness when a beam of sunshine flashes across her face, forcing her to close her eyes as she repositions to find a shadow. She wants to sleep, I can tell. "Now what?"

"You start the potion, I'll write the spelling."

She sits up a little, blinking her eyes like she's trying to stay awake. "It's been so long. Perhaps I should think about it for a while?"

"You'll be fine. It's not a hard spell." I take the saddle-bags and place them on the low table in front of the couch where Callistina is sitting. Then remove the book, the wooden box with the bottle in it, and the little paper bag with our magiceuticals. I sit down next to her and open the book, showing her the recipe.

She leans forward, sighing again. Like this day has exhausted her. She reads the recipe and looks at me. "What happened to this page?"

I feign ignorance. "What page?"

"This one." She taps the page opposite the recipe. "It's been ripped. Look."

"Well, so it has. But it doesn't matter. This is the page we need." I tap the page with the recipe.

"But what if it was a spelling that went with the recipe?"

"Even so, we need a new spelling. A custom one. Not some generic bunch of words meant for the masses. I'll write a new one."

Satisfied, Callistina looks at the recipe. "Seems pretty simple."

"I think the magic is mostly in the celestial décima."

"What is that, anyway?"

"It's a ten-line poem with a very specific rhyming structure."

"Well, you better not mess it up. We're opening doors in space and time using three very powerful ingredients."

"Seven, actually."

"What are you talking about? It's only three. Acetic acid, sharptongue, and goldberry."

"You forgot the bottle. You. Me. And the poem."

"Oh." She smiles, then chuckles a little. "Right. I'm tired."

I place my hand on her leg and give it a squeeze. "We can rest when we get home. I promise. We'll just go back into Savage Falls and have a good think about what happened here and what we'd like to do next."

I was thinking about the next move all the way back from the Sphere Market and this really is the best course of action. I know Callistina is gonna put up a fight, since the whole point of walking through the door in the first place was to put that place behind us.

But she doesn't object. She actually agrees. "Yeah. I think that's a really good idea."

And this surprises me. "What changed? I mean, just a few hours ago you loved it here and wanted to stay."

"Nothing's changed," she insists. "It's just... I need to gather my thoughts. That tern-girl in the bottle shop?"

"What about her?"

"I think she's where we started. The royal beasts, I mean. It's just so weird to think that all the magic we use is just..."

"Technology and science," I finish for her.

"Yeah. It's not very romantic."

She has no idea just how unromantic it all is. She came from the House of Fire, after all, a place that reeks of ceremony, and pageantry, and tradition. Books handwritten in real ink, not manuals printed up on a machine running off the spark of ether. Glass bottles were not purchased in a market, but blown by the spellcaster's own mouth. And herbs were carefully grown with intention.

That's magic. Real magic that comes from the alchemist's own soul and it's all very romantic.

What they're doing here is sterile, and cold, and practical.

Maybe that's why all us gods came out so evil?

They forgot to give us a part of their souls.

"All right," she says. Because there's been a silence now for several seconds. "I'll mix it all up and you work on your poem."

She starts messing with our accumulated paraphernalia on the table in front of her and I get back up and start pacing, trying to come up with a spelling that not only rips us out of one world and takes us into another, but pre-empts whatever sorcery that little witch, Pressia, has been cooking up over the millennia.

Normally, spelling comes pretty easy to me. Spellings are the only magic you can use that just comes right out of your mind. You don't need herbs to make a spelling. You don't need bottles, or ether, or books. You just need to pluck letters out, one at a time, and make them into words. Then you need to arrange those words into a rhythm that corresponds to your ask.

The celestial décima requires three things overall.

One. Ten lines of eight syllables.

Two. Open meter. Which is a good thing, in my opinion. Because it gives you more options for word choice because the total syllables and rhyming scheme are the only things that matter.

And three. Intention, which is specifically attached by invoking a god.

This part kinda sucks because I don't have favor with any of them. It's not like they can actually hear it. Like, when you pray to a god, they don't hear messages in their head or anything like that. They don't hear them all and then decide if the asker is worthy. That's not how it works. They really don't have anything to do with the workings of spellings. It's the invocation and the intention that makes the magic. You align your ask with the god who represents that particular thing, and then you give it your best. Trying to wrangle up the forces required for change.

The good thing about this though, as far as I'm concerned, anyway, is that I'm the fuckin' god of love and love is the most powerful magic in the whole universe. I'm gonna invoke myself in my spelling.

I go outside on the terrace, leaving Callistina to the particulars of alchemists, and start pacing. Blanking my mind of everything but the words.

They tumble through my head, falling into place, then rearranging themselves. I lean on the terrace wall, bracing myself with my elbows on the smooth sand-colored plaster, and allow my mind to be overcome with my intentions.

Get us some doors that take us to the hallway. Safely. Using the power of love.

As a bonus, thwart the magic of Pressia at the same time.

The celestial décima isn't a fun, jaunty poem by any means. The constraints often make it feel disjointed and choppy. But it is one of the most powerful rhythms you can use in a spelling for these exact reasons. Every word must be counted and there is no room for sloppiness.

It is a very literal way of spelling and it's only used in the most specific of circumstances.

I want to be very specific with this spell.

Hallway. Safety. Love.

This is what I come up with:

"THERE IS a time and place for me

within the hallway boundary
the god of love, to thee we plea
through doors we travel, set us free
to be the people meant to be.
Two doors we seek, through yore and fate
the passage narrow, slim, and strait
it opens wide for our escape
and through we go, our fate replaced
hate is my soulmate, my soulmate is hate."

I OPEN MY EYES, shaking my head. *No.*

No. That's not it.

That last line isn't even the right number of syllables. And anyway, it's my curse. Part of it, at least. "Fuck," I mutter, letting out a breath. Because I wasn't thinking about that curse, so why did it come out in my spelling?

This is when I notice that the sun has set and it's gone dark.

How long have I been out here on the terrace? It was afternoon when we got back from the market with our packages, not anywhere close to evening. Certainly not close to sunset.

So... hours and hours, it seems.

A scent wafts out of our room, making me turn. It's... lovely. And it compels me to leave the terrace and go back inside and seek it out. The magiceuticals have been mixed and are cooking inside the quicksilver bottle, sans topper. This is when I recognize the scent that drew me inside. It's Callistina's bubble bath. Which is funny—as in weird—because Callistina has at least a dozen of those bottles all over the bathroom in Savage Falls, so I have been looking at them for two months now and I'm absolutely certain the label proclaims the scent to be rose hips and lavender, not acetic acid, sharptongue, and goldberry.

So I must be mistaken.

In this same moment of realization, a soft snore comes from behind me.

This is when I turn and see Callistina asleep on the couch. All stretched out and feline-looking. Long legs going this way and that, accentuating her curvy hips. Her lips are slightly puckered and there are worry lines across her forehead, like she's concentrating on something in her sleep.

The whole thing is just fuckin' hot. She is once again tempting me with that languid, lazy posing she does, presumably by accident, and I am suddenly struck with a desire to sleep next to her.

But not on that couch.

So I cross the room, slip my hands underneath her body, and lift her up. She stirs as I do this, leaning into my chest, but also awakening. "What's going on?"

"I'm taking you to bed, that's what's goin' on."

She sighs. And when I put her down on the bed, she curls up a little and opens her eyes. "Did you come up with a spelling?"

"Mostly," I say, kicking off my boots and letting my pants fall to the floor at my feet. I climb in next to her and she scoots over to make room.

"What's that mean, Eros? Was there a problem?"

"No. It all went fine. I just need to perfect the very

last line. It's got too many syllables." I grab her and pull her close to me. For some reason I feel like she and I are a permanent thing now. It could be premature because it's only been a couple of days since we walked through that door in the hallway. But seriously, the way time's been running lately, it feels like I've spent my whole life with this woman.

And anyway, she doesn't object to my possessiveness.

But she does turn in my embrace so she's facing me. Her eyes are wide open now and she's smiling. "Do you want to hear how it went for me?"

"Absolutely."

She smiles bigger. Then takes a deep breath. "Well, I followed the recipe. It was very simple. The only hard part was that you had to heat it seven times."

"Seven, huh?"

She nods, her yellow-brown eyes a little bit glow-y in the hazy moonlight that's filtering in from the outside world. "Cook it, cool it, cook it, cool it. Seven whole times. And I had to stir it constantly. Even in the cooling part."

"I don't think I'd have the patience for that."

"I really didn't think I would either. But then," she says, her face getting a little more animated, "then it started to smell so good, I couldn't stop stirring."

"Your bubble bath," I say.

She almost sits up when I say this, that's how surprised she is. "How did you know?"

This makes me laugh. "I could smell it, Callistina."

"But I mean, how did you know it was the same scent as my bubble bath?"

"Are you kidding? You've been taking those fucking bubble baths for nearly two months while I've been sitting in the next room. How could I not recognize it?"

"Hmm." She smiles and settles back down.

"What's that 'hmm' mean?"

"It means I made an impression on you."

I laugh out loud. "How the world could you not? You're the former Queen of Vinca and you spent the last seven weeks demanding that I call you queen and dressing up like a crazy person with spray-painted antlers sittin' atop your head, affixed with string."

She laughs too, shaking her head a little. Like she can't believe she did that.

"Really, though. That's not why you made an impression."

"No?" She lifts her chin up to look me in the eyes for this part.

"Nah." Now it's my turn to shake my head. "You're once in a lifetime, Callistina. You're a woman who only comes around once in a whole lifetime. And when your lifetime is eternal, that's kind of a big deal."

Her grin grows as her eyes close, which is a signal that she likes my answer. But then she opens them and the next thing I know, she's removing herself from my embrace. But not to get away from me. She pushes me back onto the bed and hikes a leg over my hips so she's straddling me.

The grin on her face is mischievous, but also a bit... shy, maybe. Like she's not so sure of herself now that she's taken some initiative. Like maybe she needs some reassurance.

Which I am happy to give in the form of sliding my fingertips up her golden velvet-covered stomach and taking her breasts in both hands. Our eyes are locked as I do this, but she bites her lip a little. Still a bit unsure. Which is a little bit surprising, but in a good way.

I like vulnerable Callistina. Not because it makes her weak, but because it makes me feel strong. Like she needs me and I am someone she counts on.

Perhaps I am reading too much into this expression of hers because she leans down without another word between us, sliding her hands up my chest with her claws just a little bit exposed. Just enough to tantalize me with those sharp tips, but not enough to cut or even make a scratch.

"Do you know what I've noticed about you, Eros?"

I try not to grin, but I only just barely manage it. "What have you noticed, my queen?"

Her smile grows bigger right before my eyes. "You're easy."

I laugh. "I'm *easy*?"

She nods, slowly. And hums out the word, "Mmm-hmm. You are the complete opposite of me."

"Come on, you're easy too," I say. She nearly snorts. "As long as one calls you queen, that is."

"You float. You float through your life taking things as they come. Unbothered and nearly unaffected."

"I just hide it better than most."

"No. I don't think that's it. I just think you know your worth. And no one can take it away from you. It's something inside." She places her flat hand right atop of my heart. And it thumps harder against her touch. "Something right here. Something you know about yourself. Something you know is true, so you don't need anyone to proclaim your merits or build you up with titles or crowns. It's something you were born with."

"But that's something you have too."

She's already shaking her head. "No. I was placed somewhere and made the worst of it. You, on the other hand, come from *here*."

She's got the completely wrong idea about Glory Rome and I don't how to explain it to her so that it sinks in. The best course of action is to just get her the hell out of here and never come back.

But not now. It's late and that's a task for tomorrow.

Besides, we're already in bed.

So what I do is reach up with both hands and place them alongside her cheeks, bringing her forward just a little bit more. Just enough to kiss her long and good. I know I can't fall in love with anyone, but I think I might be able to find the next best thing with Callistina.

A partner. A companion. Someone to travel through life with.

It's a new thing for me, to feel a connection of any kind with anyone. And I think she knows this. Because she kisses me back like I'm the only man left in all the times and places this world has to offer.

Her hand reaches down and when her fingers wrap around me, I feel nothing but want for this woman. She pulls back from the kiss so she can lift her hips up and place me at her entrance. Then she sinks down, pushing me inside her, and I just want to close my eyes and get lost in this feeling.

She's still for a moment. Like she too is enjoying herself too much to move. But then she slowly starts to rock back and forth on top of me.

Something is building inside me. Not just the feeling of an upcoming climax, but something else too. Something much bigger than that.

Callistina slows down, takes her time, and refocuses our excitement into a long, slow fuck. I look her in the eyes and she meets my gaze, but then she's biting her lip, and arching her back, and when she comes, I do too.

Time is weird when she slowly rolls off me and snuggles up to my chest because the sun is already peeking out from atop the horizon. But I'm too spent now to care about time. Especially with her warm, soft body pressed up against mine.

I kiss her shoulder and then… fall blissfully into sleep.

*A MOMENT **later I sit up**,* breathing heavy and my heart beating in my chest.

I look around, searching for Callistina, as the wind whips past my naked body.

But then I realize I'm not in bed. I'm on top of a roof and it is the dead of night under a full moon.

I scan the scene as my heart thumps dramatically inside my chest.

There is a line of boys in front of me. Dozens of them, all naked. All marching forward into the dark.

A few of them step off the roof on their own accord. They are done. They've given up. But most do not, and have not, and they are pushed over the side.

Even from here, thirty floors up, I think I can hear the bodies as they crash on the ground below. Maybe it's my imagination. But then again, maybe it's not. Because this is what's happening.

We, the erotes, are being tested. Not for brains, or strength—but wings.

Because we don't have them. And this is what they want. This is what the alchemists have been doing with the Erotes bloodline.

They want us to have fucking wings and the wings are just *not there*.

One after the other, they are pushed over. And as the boys fall, they scream. They curse their makers. And the boys behind them—they cry. Harder and harder with each step forward.

One thousand of us were made and I am number nine-nine-nine.

And when I get to the edge, I want to be brave. I do. I really, *really* do.

But I am ten years old and I am not brave.

They push me off, just like they pushed the others.

And it doesn't even matter what happens next.

Because we are gods and we cannot die.

So they will torture us any way they can to get what they want.

The next thing I know there is a loud banging and my eyes fly open, banishing the dream. For now.

"What the fuck is that?" I ask. Callistina is already running towards our room door. "What are you doing? Don't answer it!"

But either she doesn't hear me, or she doesn't care, because she pulls the door open and on the other side is the dog-man who works here at the inn.

He grabs Callistina by the shoulders. "They're coming! Get up, get out of here! They're coming for you."

I can see him through the open door of the bedroom and when he says the word 'you,' he's not looking at Callistina.

They are not coming for her.

They are coming for *me*.

Gods on the loose.

It hasn't even happened yet.

I don't even have wings.

Not here in this room at the inn.

Not up there in Building One.

Not on that roof in my nightmare.

But it wasn't really the wings they wanted.

It was the feathers.

CHAPTER TWENTY - CALLISTINA

*E*verything that happens next plays out in slow motion. The dog-man is grabbing my shoulders, shaking me. "Get up! Get out!" But he's not looking at me, he's looking at Eros.

"What are you talking about?" I'm frantic.

Eros is up, out of bed, naked, and walking to the terrace. The dog-man and I both join him out there. But none of us need to see anything to understand what's coming down the road.

We can hear them. The clopping of hooves on cobblestones.

And when I look down the road to my left, I can see them too. They are not far and they are not few. It is a small army of Apis bull chimera holding weapons that appear to belong in some other world. They have donned full-body armor, despite the strict rules about clothing.

The slow motion stops and the world just ceases for me as I try to make sense of what I'm seeing and what is going to happen next. What is this? Are they going to arrest us? Kill us? Why are they coming?

It really doesn't matter. This is no ordinary army of chimera. This is the Army of the Gods. I would know them anywhere. A mythological military institution that terrorized the world in the time of Chaos and their stories of battle were passed down through the generations in books, and paintings, and spellings so that no one—not chimera, not human—no one would ever forget the past.

The Glory War.

Some of the many mysteries about this entire trip through the hallway doors begin to make a little bit of sense. The Glory War is not coming. This is not a future event. Because we are in the Age of Fire. And this is the year that the bloodline for the royal beasts was started.

Everything started here. *Right* here.

Is it a coincidence that there are no royal beasts in Glory Rome aside from me?

Is it a coincidence that this is the actual point in historical time where the bloodline started and I am here at the same time?

Did I... *start it?*

Probably not. But the fact that I am here, in the beginning, is meaningful. Somehow.

"Ho-lee shit," I say, cursing in the manner of Savage Falls humans. Because suddenly I feel the fate inside me. The bloodline of Fatum.

Eros looks at me. "I hope that fucking potion is ready. Because we're gonna use it right now. We need to get the hell out of here."

"I…" I'm shaking my head. "I don't think we get *out of here*, Eros."

"What? Of course we do." He grabs my arm and pulls be back inside the room. Then he points at the dog-man. "Get everyone out of this building right now. I can't guarantee that we won't blow the fucker up as we exit."

The dog-man just stares at Eros, struck dumb from his statement. To be fair, I too feel struck dumb.

"Did you hear me?" Eros roars this. "Get. Everyone. Out!" He points at the door.

His command snaps the dog-man out of his stupor, and he bows. "Yes… yes…" Then a panic strikes the dog-man because he's not sure how to address the man before him, who is clearly not a man. But not a king, either.

"Just go!" Eros bellows.

The dog-man bows out backwards and Eros slams the door in his face the moment he crosses the threshold. Then he turns to me. "Whatever you need to do to make this shit work, do it now." He's pointing at the bottle.

I blink, then snap out of it just like the dog-man did. "OK," I say, for some reason breathless. Then I go over to the table and get the topper for the bottle. The godsmetal is heavy in my hand and for a moment, it feels foreign. Different. When I look down, I understand why. It's shaped like wings. This is how it looked in the shop, but these wings I'm looking at right now are not those same wings I was looking at in the shop.

Slowly I rotate my head to look at Eros. He's pacing

the room, talking to himself. I catch a few rhyming words and realize he's practicing his spelling.

He catches my gaze and snaps at me. "What? What's the problem?"

The sound of marching chimera soldiers grows louder in two seconds that I hesitate before answering. "There's something wrong here."

"No shit. We're about to be arrested by the Army of the Gods."

"No, that's not it. I mean, yes. For sure, we're going to get arrested. But something is very wrong here, Eros." I hold up the topper. "This isn't a quicksilver bottle."

"What? What is it then?"

"I... I'm not sure."

"You're not making any sense, Callistina. And we don't have time for riddles."

"I'm not trying to make a riddle, I'm trying to explain that using this bottle might be a mistake."

He stares at me, blinking. "Are you telling me we have options?"

"No. We don't have options. But these wings on this topper, I think they belong to *you*. And I... I don't know how to explain it, but I think I'm part of the original bloodline for the royal beasts."

I see the doubt on his face, but it doesn't last long. In fact, the belief sinks in right before my eyes in a matter of seconds.

"We're not getting out of here, Eros."

"Don't say that. Just get the bottle ready. Let's do this!"

"It's already been done! We're not changing anything. Don't you see? We're just watching it play out before our eyes. It's *done*."

"No!" He comes towards me, rips the topper from my hand, and shoves it onto the bottle. Then he shakes it up for good measure and sets it down in a beam of sunlight.

I open my mouth to protest, rushing forward to grab it out of the sun before some kind of chemical reaction can start, but Eros catches me by the waist. Swinging me behind him.

Then, out of his mouth, comes the spelling...

"THERE IS a time and place for me
    within the hallway boundary
    the god of love, to thee we plea
    through doors we travel, set us free
    to be the people meant to be.
    Two doors we seek, through yore and fate
    the passage narrow, slim, and straight
    it opens wide for our escape
    and through we go, our fate replaced
    hate is my soulmate, my soulmate is hate."

I MAKE a face at him as the last line slides past his lips and we both know it's a *big* mistake.

But it's done, it's too late.

Hate is his soulmate, his soulmate is hate.

And for some reason, I feel like I'm *hate* and none of this is really about him at all.

It's all about me.

The bloodline that came back in time?

The mother of the royal beasts?

The one who starts a war?

I wish I had time to think harder about this, but I don't. Because the moment this last question manifests in my head there is a great explosion from the bottle. But it's not a bomb, it's light. Two beams of light coming directly from the inside of the quicksilver-stained glass and shining onto the wall in front of us.

Eros stares at it and so do I. Because this projection of light has created our doors.

We look at each other. And I don't know what he's feeling exactly, but I'm afraid to stay and afraid to go. And there is no way I can walk into that light. Even though I can now hear the pounding footsteps of the Army of the Gods as they come up the stairs to our room.

"Run," Eros says. "Let's go!" He reaches for my hand, but for some reason, I pull away.

If I go... what happens to everyone who comes after me?

Will there be Pie? No House of Fire? No... *me*?

Eros grabs me around the middle, rushes forward, and tosses me into one of the two doors.

I enter a blinding light of nothingness just as the door to the room crashes open.

And then... I am in the hallway facing a door. I have only enough time to look to my right and see this is the middle door, the second in the set of three options—the next in the ordered list.

I fall through it before I can even make a decision to do that.

Or… not to do that. Because I would not have gone through the door if I had a choice. Something is wrong with this hallway and I want it to be over.

The next thing I know, I am standing in Vinca. In my nightmare with a red dragon circling above me. Not *breathing* fire, but *spraying* it. Everywhere. And my head is pounding out a beat that is too fast, and too loud, and too much.

The whole city is engulfed in flames and this is when I look down at myself and realize I am nothing but a charred collection of bones.

I scream, and then I'm inside the palace. Sitting on the throne, but I am not me, I am the old king and I am looking at me. Real me. Lion*ess* me. Teenager me. Princess, not queen. *Me*.

He is looking at me. And his thoughts are busy, and loud, and gross. And he is thinking about *blood*.

My blood.

And this is the answer to all my questions. The question I never wanted to ask.

Why, why, *why?*

My blood.

Pie's blood.

But Pie was gone and I was the next best thing.

No, I was not made perfect the way she was, but I was *made*.

I am her, with faults. The first try. The pilot

program. The preliminary study. An exploration of possibilities.

Daughter number one's blood, the king is thinking, *is just as good as daughter number two's.*

What does that mean?

"Oh, come on, Callistina." I refocus my eyes and Pie is sitting in front of me on a large rock. Her long, gangly wood-nymph chimera legs are crossed and she's leaning back, sunning her face in a stray beam of light that shines down through the forest canopy. "They didn't need me. They just needed my blood. And you and I have the same blood. He knows you do because he had it tested. Remember?"

Then she laughs and I realize she's just a delusion and it's me who's laughing.

Because she's right.

All they ever wanted was my blood. The king tested my blood as soon as I arrived in Vinca. I am from Saturn and far, far back... Fatum.

Fate. The will of the gods.

I am the *will of the gods*.

What does it even mean?

I don't know. I can't think straight. Why the fuck does my head hurt *so damn bad*? The pounding. I put my hands over my ears to make it stop, but they touch a hot, sticky mess all over my hair. And when I look at them, my palms and fingertips are covered in blood.

"The same blood," Pie says, back again. "And a hole in the fabric of time. Isn't that *funny*!"

I don't think it's funny, but I do think about a tern-girl keeping a bottle shop in the Sphere Market. And how she is more animal than I am. And how she is one of the first. And how there were no lion*esses* in the Glory time. And that makes perfect sense because how the hell could there be lion*esses* from the House of Fire —how the hell could there be royal beasts at all—when I hadn't *been there yet*?

"It was Tarq who made the hole, you know." Pie is still talking. But she can't possibly know this. She wasn't there, I was.

I was.

I. Was.

Pie turns into me and I am the one sitting on the rock. My long, gangly gryphon chimera legs are crossed and I'm leaning back, sunning my face in a stray beam of light that shines down through the forest canopy.

And it's not me talking, it's Tarq.

"A rip in the fabric of time, Callistina. A way to go back and redo it. That's why they want my book."

The book. I hate books. Books are the problem. Everyone is writing a godsdamned book and leaving information all over the place where anyone could find it.

"I found it," Tarq says.

See? That's what I mean.

"I found the way through the doors. It's so simple, too. It's a very simple recipe of acetic acid and—"

But I cut him off, finishing his sentence for him. "Sharptongue and goldberry." Only this is not my voice, it's the voice of *Nysta*. His wood nymph partner in crime. Who went through his doors to find more wood nymphs so they could make wood wine and—

"How did you know?" Tarq looks thoroughly confused.

And I want to say, *Because I'm the one who used it first, you dumbass! I put it in a quicksilver bottle that wasn't a quicksilver bottle, but something else, and I blew up the fabric of time and made a door from there to here!*

But I don't say any of that. Because he's already gone.

Was never here.

It's just a dream.

A fucking nightmare.

And my head. *Won't. Stop. Pounding.*

Then someone is dabbing my face with a cool, wet cloth, whispering in my ear, "You're OK. It's OK. I've got you. I've got it all under control. You're gonna be OK. It's gonna be fine. Just... *sleep.*"

It's Eros. But when I open my eyes, it's not the Eros I knew.

His wings are feathered and full. And he's glowing a golden yellow color. It's coming from every bit of him. Inside him, even. He is... a god.

No. *The* God. The god of gods. The glory of gods.

"You're the Glory," I croak.

And he looks *sad* even as he forces a smile. "You're OK," he says again.

But when you're in the middle of a hallucinogenic nightmare and people start insisting you're OK, you are decidedly not OK.

"Do you know why they had the Glory War?" It's Tarq again. We're standing in front of one of his doors. And we see the other side too. It's a little forest village filled with pure-blood wood nymphs. And there is a mound of wood mud being attended to.

"Why?" I ask, looking back at Tarq.

"Because gods on the loose."

I can't tell if he means gods plural are on the loose or one particular god is on the loose. But then again, it's always about the same fucking god on the loose, isn't it?

"The god of gods showed up"—Tarq is still talking—"and everyone had to take a side. With him. Or against him."

"Which side are we on?"

He laughs. "We don't take sides, Nysta. We make our own side." He nods his head to the door. "Are you ready?"

Nysta does not feel ready. My heart—her heart—is pounding to the beat of my head. Just thumping, and thumping, and thumping.

"But what good is it?" I hear myself say in Nysta's voice. "Why bother with all this when we don't have the final ingredient?"

"I can get the bloodhorn, Nysta. I told you that."

"How?" Nysta does not believe him. I can feel it in her bones.

"You let me worry about that. Now, I need you to concentrate. Think about your story. The plan. And how to get them all back through the door."

She is luring the wood nymphs through the doors and giving them to Tarq so he can run his experiments. His *science*. Because he is obsessed with doors the same way I'm obsessed with dragons.

And the moment I think this word, I'm back where I

started. Madeline, the dragon the color of bloodhorn. And that's why I need a scale.

Tarq isn't the only one doing science in Vinca.

Oh, it's not me. Queen Callistina couldn't do magic if her life depended on it.

But the alchemist, Lyrica, can.

And this is when it starts to make sense.

Not what I did. I had my reasons and they were self-ish, and small, and mean.

But what *they* did.

And how they used me.

And how I let them.

And how everything I ever thought I knew is a lie.

It's about science.

It's about creation.

It's about power.

I did not mix a potion in that quicksilver bottle, I mixed a *drug*. That's the human word for it.

I am not using magic, I'm using chemistry.

All the romantic stories about the gods are false. Lies. A fiction told to the masses, but to what end? Captivate them? Scare them? Humble them?

All of the above, most likely.

Because this world, and all the sister worlds through every door imaginable, runs on power.

And power runs on *time*.

And don't we all want more time?

"Callistina? Can you hear me?"

"I don't want the time."

"Callistina?" Eros's voice is filled with hope. "Wake up! Can you wake up?"

I don't want to wake up.

"Just open your eyes, just once. I can fix this. I can."

I don't know what he's talking about, but I do know it's got nothing to do with everything I just saw. It's got nothing to do with the truth.

But I open my eyes anyway because he's pretty. He's the prettiest thing I've ever seen and I could use a little beauty right now.

His eyes are gold and green. Glowing, like his body. And the very moment I see them, I feel... love. For him, but also from him.

It washes over me and finally—*finally*—the thunder, and lightning, and earthquakes happening inside my pounding head... *stop*.

And then I wake up.

I JUST LIE STILL, looking up at a canopy of trees. The bright sun flickers back and forth through the trembling leaves, making patterns of light flash across my face. But I can't hold it. The world is spinning. I try to get up, but strong hands push me back down.

"Just take it easy. You've been asleep for a long time. There's no rush."

A strange moaning makes me turn my head. Immediately, I regret it. Because the pounding is back and I have to close my eyes to make the spinning stop.

I don't know how long I lie there like that, but it might be a while. Because when I open my eyes again, I can see Eros across a little clearing in the woods. He's bent over Ire, who is lying on the ground. The source of the moaning.

"What's wrong with him?" I croak.

My voice startles Eros, and he turns, still glowing and flanked on either side with a set of massive, gorgeous, feathered wings that make him look every bit like a god.

Which he is, so it makes sense. But... he looks powerful. And for as long as I've known him, he's not been very powerful.

He's also got a weapon strapped to his bare back, a very serious-looking bow, and a leather bandolier filled with short, fat bolts crisscrossing his chest.

But no. The bandolier is not filled. It's missing two.

"He's... uh... sick."

"Why?" I whisper, too weak to speak loudly. My head still hurts, but it's not nearly as bad as it was. And when I reach up to touch it, it's not a sticky, bloody mess like it was in my hallucinogenic nightmare. It's just soft hair through my fingertips.

"Someone cut off his wings."

The stab of pain in my heart could match that pounding in my head at its peak.

Of course, I knew his wings had been cut off. Knew this almost since the beginning of my trip through time with Eros. But it felt like a long-ago thing and now, here we are, in the time of the tragedy.

And those moans I heard were Ire's pain in the present.

I want to ask who would do such a thing, and why.

But I already know.

Someone like Tarq would do that. He was hunting wood nymphs. Someone like Nysta would do that. She was luring them through the doors so he could steal their magic. In fact, isn't that all anyone's ever been doing? Stealing the shine of others to make themselves more powerful?

Tarq ruined Vinca. I know I'm the one responsible for the dragon—for Madeline. I'm not sure how, exactly, but that's what the nightmare was telling me.

But it was also telling me the truth about Tarq. Even though I knew it. I knew all about it. I just didn't stop him. We made a deal, after all. Once the old king died.

Tarq didn't want to rule. He wanted to find wood nymphs and open doors. That was all he thought about. So I would just turn the other cheek, not ask any questions, and leave him alone to do his work. I could have the throne.

I could have all the power he didn't want.

But he *did* want power.

Doesn't everyone?

He just wanted more than being king could give him.

CHAPTER TWENTY-ONE - EROS

*E*verything *was happening* so fast when Callistina and I went through the new doors that it took a couple of weeks to sort through everything I saw, or thought I saw, and put it into some kind of sensible order.

First and foremost, the magic worked. Better than expected, actually.

I was looking at the door—at the projection of a door, because that's all it was—and then, the next thing I knew, I was already inside the hallway.

Time was going slow or something because I had enough of it to make a decision. At least, that was my perception. But I don't think my perception was matching up with my reality because though I was relieved to be back in the hallway—a place where choices should be available to me—it didn't feel like a choice when the second door in the ordered list sucked me through like I was going down a drain, or like this was some predetermined set of actions, or like... fate. Maybe.

Maybe not, but the point is, though I wanted to make a decision, the decision to continue this journey through the doors was not mine.

I came out in a forest covered in blood. I mean, it was everywhere. Dripping off giant, tropical-looking leaves, pooling in the dirt at my feet, all over me. But, most importantly, all over Callistina as well.

Time is a cruel bitch. Because it slowed down here too. Not so I could finally have some sort of say in what happened to me, but so I could burn the memory of what I was seeing into my brain like a brand on the hide of a meat animal.

Callistina was half lying, half draped over the edge of a large, flat boulder. Face down. Naked, of course. Her gold fur was scarlet. Not a bit of it wasn't covered.

And the top of her head was where all this blood was coming from. Because we came through those doors and arrived in the moment, or shortly after the moment, when someone had cut off Callistina's antlers.

I am not a mortal man, but I know the ways of the mortal world. And antlers don't bleed if you cut them off. I know this for a fact. I mean, I'm kind of an expert bow hunter. I've shot my share of deer and I've cut off my share of antlers. Ground-up antlers of all kinds are a common ingredient in magiceutical recipes.

But clearly, Callistina is no deer.

No lion, either. Since lions don't have antlers.

Whoever did this might as well have cut off her arms or legs the way that blood was pouring out of her. On top of that, it was no ordinary blood. It was… pulsating. Undulating. Like flowing lava, or something.

It looked like that because it was not ordinary blood. It was bloodhorn.

And I panicked. I just… stood there. I'm not even sure for how long. It felt like years. I didn't know what to do. My mind could not process.

The moaning was the only reason I snapped out of it.

I knew that moan wasn't coming from Callistina. It was the moan of a beast. My heart thumped so hard. And suddenly I was afraid. Because I knew it was Ire, and I knew *when* I was, and I knew that he was missing his wings, and I knew that a lot of this blood that was all around me was not just Callistina's, but his too.

Time was doing funny things, all right. Because we had skipped through time. Not to some other 'when,' but the same ordered list of events that started with riding the pegásius on the road that led to Glory Rome.

Only going backwards.

I scanned the forest, found Ire struggling in the trees trying to get to his feet. He's normally a silver gray, but his fur was the same color as Callistina's at that moment. Blood red.

He was moving though. Trying his best to right himself, at least.

Callistina was not, so it was her I went to her, not him.

This was when everything about me felt… *off*.

I was wearing leather pants, brown boots, a knife sheathed at my belt, and a formidable crossbow across

my back. Bolts were secured to the bandolier that criss-
crossed my chest. Not only that, my wings were back.
But when I looked to the side, they were not the bat
wings I had in Savage Falls, but the feathered ones
that I...

The memory of the wind rushing over my back
threatened to overtake me in that moment. And I was
way too fucked up with concern over what was
happening in my present to get caught up in my past. So
I pushed it all aside and just concentrated on helping
Callistina.

I reached under her arms and lifted dead weight up
off the rock. And for a moment I thought it was over.
Except I knew it couldn't be. I just spent days with her
in the future on the road to Glory Rome and inside the
city. We were just *there*.

And if this was true, and we were traveling backwards in time, then I could be certain that she was
going to recover and we would take that journey
together just like we had.

I picked her up in my arms and carried her
through the forest until there was no sign of blood.
Then I set her down on the ground and let out a
breath.

I am not a magical god. I can't really do much even if
I had all the power that was given to me by birth, and I
don't. I can make people love each other or hate each
other. That's really all it boils down to. And though that
is a very powerful thing to control, it's not something
that is helpful at all when the woman you've grown
fond of is dying at your feet.

"She's not dying." I remember saying that to myself. "I know she doesn't die."

And that's the only reason I didn't give up, I think.

I knew the ending. I knew that whatever was happening right now, she was going to be OK. She was going to fall in love with Glory Rome, and sleep next to me in the inn, and ride behind me on top of the pegásius that was still struggling to get to his feet.

I could hear a little stream nearby, so I picked her up again, carried her over there, and then I walked into it and sat down in the cool, rushing water, and held her until all the blood was washed away.

I don't know how long that took because I fell asleep. It could've been hours or it could've been days. The only think I knew was that when I woke up Ire was nearby, standing in a deep pool downstream, splashing and thrashing his hooves, trying to get himself clean.

There were deep, red scabs on his back where the wings used to be. But he was beginning to heal.

That's when I checked Callistina and realized the top of her head was starting to scab over as well.

Maybe it was the water. Maybe the water wasn't simply water.

Maybe none of this was what it first appeared to be.

But Ire was up and Callistina was not. I leaned down, putting my mouth right up to her neck. "Callistina. Can you hear me?"

She didn't even moan. But when I pressed my lips to the skin just below her ear, I could feel the blood rushing towards her thumping heart.

Of course she wasn't dead. I already knew this.

KC CROSS & JA HUSS

It's just that looking at her like that made it really hard to accept the idea that she pulled through.

I ended up carrying her a little further into the forest. The water had been cool and refreshing when we first got in, but we'd been in there for a while and whatever help that coolness offered was over now. She and I were both chilled and needed to warm up.

I stood up with Callistina in my arms, my wings heavy with water, and I took her into the forest and laid her down in the center of a clearing covered in soft grass. I found some wood, started a fire, and then I just held her. I stroked her cheek. I whispered things in her ear. "You're going to be OK. You're going to pull through this. We're going to Glory Rome on Ire's back, and we're gonna get a room at the inn, and sleep in a bed, and go shopping in the Sphere Market. And you're gonna love it."

Things like that.

A storm started rolling in. I could see the clouds above me turning black. If they hadn't—if there was no threat of rain—I might've just stayed there. Holding her in my arms until time stopped altogether.

But it was going to rain and we had no shelter.

I had to make us a shelter.

It was rudimentary at first. Just something quick made from fallen tree trunks propped up at an angle to make a little A-frame. Then I covered the outside with a thick layer of pine-tree branches.

Stacked rocks made a crude fireplace on one open end—a makeshift wood stove that didn't offer much in the way of heat, but it was better than nothing. Then I went looking for Ire's tack, for the fur Callistina and I had slept on that first night after walking through the doors. I found supplies in the saddlebags as well. Water bags, and some dried food, and the godsmetal collared dress that Callistina would wear in the future.

None of it was a perfect solution, but it was certainly better than nothing when that rain started.

I settled in with Callistina on my lap and I just held her and told her it was gonna be OK.

I did this for almost two full days before it finally hit me just how far back in time we'd gone. Or, rather, how much time needed to pass before we'd find ourselves on that road to Glory Rome.

The scars on Ire's body when Callistina and I first found ourselves riding on his back had been old. Months and months, at least. They were completely healed. No signs at all of scabbing.

And Callistina's antlers were much the same. Just stubs. No signs of trauma.

Neither of them looked like that now. Everything was still raw, and scabbed, and red.

There was a lot of time to fill between now and then.

So I filled it. Callistina woke up that one time, but it would be more than a month of me caring for her before she would finally open her eyes and utter her next word, which was, "Why?"

But that was all she did that day. Eyes open. One word. Then more sleep.

By this time we had a proper little house going. An A-frame shelter was fine for a night or two, but if we were gonna be living in this forest until they were healed, it wasn't going to be enough.

I spent my days hunting down skinny logs on the forest floor. I hauled them back to our camp and stacked them into walls. Eventually, I'd made us a tiny one-room cabin. Well, cabin is kind of a stretch. It wasn't that sturdy, and the wind came right through it, but it was a warm wind, so it didn't really matter.

I hunted too. Food wasn't a problem. It got us more furs. And by the time Callistina opened her eyes and uttered the word, "Why?" we had a nice comfy bed made from these furs.

She couldn't eat, not really. But I cooked her bone broth in a turtle shell and dripped it into her mouth by the wooden spoonful three times a day.

It would be months before I went back to the rock where I first found Callistina all covered in blood. And it was by accident. I was tracking a deer.

Most of the blood had been washed away in the rains by this time. But that flat boulder where she was lying face down was still stained scarlet here and there.

That was when I found the first few clues.

The book.

The crucible.

The bottle.

The moldy leather pouch of magiceuticals.

And the bones.

What would I have found in place of these bones if I had looked sooner? A body?

I'm not sure. I'm really not.

Everything was wet because it was raining that day.

But it rained every day, so when I picked up the book, it pretty much fell apart in my hands.

Still, I saw the cover. That title will live in my memory forever. *How to Kill a God.*

Pressia. That was *her* book.

And once I had these clues it all made so much sense. She tried to kill me. And the antlers of a royal beast, in combination with the wings of a pegásius, and whatever else was in that moldy magiceutical bag were how this was done.

Pressia had done this.

To Callistina. To Ire.

To *me*.

And she. Had. Failed.

This was when I made my promise. This was when I told Callistina, while she was still sleeping off her injury, that I was gonna end that woman if it was the last thing I did.

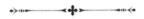

I HAD **nightmares** every time I fell asleep.

They always started on the roof of Building One in the Sphere of Science and Glory. The first time they were making us jump, to be exact. The erotes. Plural of me. Only I wasn't a 'me' back then, I was just a 'them.' One of a collective. A possibility.

We were a bunch of wingless boys. Godlings, I guess. The potential to be gods was there. And we all commanded the power of love in some way. Just one way, actually. One very specific way each because there are a thousand different ways to love and no man, or god, should have power over all of it.

I commanded the power of sexual love. The heightened feeling one gets in the throes of passion.

None of that was the point of the nightmare, though. The point of the nightmare was to remind me how I came to be Eros, the god of love, and not simply Erotes 999, godling of sex.

And it happened on that rooftop when I was pushed over and wings—great, big, golden-feathered wings—sprouted right out of my back.

Wings like the ones I have right now, in fact. The exact same set.

I was the only one. The only boy who grew wings. And this is how I became the god. Not the first—they were making all the gods in that building at the same time. But I was the only erotes to become Eros.

How they killed the rest of them—because there is no death when you are just a numbered collection of primordial life-stuff. They just make you again, and again, and again. So how they killed them after I grew those wings, I haven't a clue.

All I know is that all the power of love they had once possessed was now mine. They gave it all to me.

And then they wanted to take it back.

Because love is too powerful. No man, or god, should ever wield that kind of power.

They had made a mistake.

I was a mistake.

And they tried to erase me.

I know what it's like to have a piece of your body cut off. I know what it's like to miss your wings. That's how they tried to dull my power. They thought it was in the wings.

And it was. Mostly. Because wings have feathers and the power is actually in the feathers.

They took my wings and when it was over, it was as if I was castrated. Emasculated.

And then I went crazy.

Kinda like Callistina did with her fake antlers, and her weird wooden blocks, and that mangy coat.

Only I used magic and she didn't.

I'm asleep when this realization hits me. When all the stories of gods and goddesses, and myths, and pantheons fade into the background and only the cold, hard facts remain.

We are not gods.

We are nothing but rogue experiments.

It is ***day ninety-seven*** when I hear a small rustling behind me as I stir the pot of badger stew over the fire. And when I turn around, I find that Callistina is sitting up and looking around. She blinks a few times, like she's trying to make sense of things.

I knew she was going to wake up for good soon. Her head is completely healed now, and she looks almost like she did when we started this cursed journey, so I was preparing for it.

But nothing prepared me for the joy I feel when it finally happens. "Well," I say, smiling at her as she turns her head towards my voice. "Welcome back to the land of the living. How are you feeling?"

She blinks again, her eyebrows shooting up her fore-head. "Eros. Where the hell did you get those wings?" She says this like it's the most natural thing in the world. Like it's the only question that matters. Like she didn't just spend the last three months in a coma recovering from a heinous act by a bitter woman.

But despite all I've been through, all she's been through too, a laugh bursts out of me along with a huge sigh of relief.

She's gonna be OK. Again, I knew this. But it felt like a real act of faith over the past ninety-seven days. Like it was something only in the future. And the future would never arrive.

"Do you remember anything?"

Her eyes squint down. "*Should* I remember those wings?"

"No." I laugh. "Not the wings. They're just..." I look over my shoulder at them. "They're..." I don't want to say it, because it's not technically true, but it's the only thing I *can* say. "They're the ones I was born with. The bat wings were just part of my punishment."

Which isn't even true. Or maybe it is. I'm kind of at a loss why I had bat wings in the first place. But I'm kind of at a loss for a lot these days.

"Oh." She studies me for a moment, then narrows her eyes again. "Are you... cooking?" And the next thing I know, she's getting to her feet.

"Whoa, there," I say, setting the wooden stirring spoon down on the flat, slate rock I've been using for a plate and walking over to her. "Take it easy. You don't want to fall."

"Fall?" She sucks in a breath and smiles at me. "I'm fine. I feel fine." Then she stretches her arms and yawns. Like anyone would when they first wake up. "That food smells delicious. What is it? And what is this place?" She looks around for a few moments. Then her gaze lands on me. "The door led here?"

I'm already nodding my head. Already lying before I even think about telling the truth.

There is no way I'm gonna describe what I saw when I walked through my door.

"Yeah." I spread my arms wide. "It's not bad."

"How long was I out? I'm so hungry." She walks over to the little camp stove—which I have improved over the months so it looks like a very proper kitchen fireplace now—and squats down, leaning over the turtle-shell pot of soup. "Smells good." Then she looks over her shoulder at me, grinning. "You made this? Or was it cooking when we got here?"

She has no idea how much time has passed.

"I made it."

"Mmmm. Is it almost ready? I feel like I'm starving."

I want to stop the lie. I do.

I want her to know the truth.

But why ruin everything with the truth? Why make her think back? Why force a memory when all it's gonna do is hurt her?

She's OK. I'm OK. Ire's OK. We're all OK.

She does not need to know how *not OK* she was when we got here.

So I just smile bigger and say, "Let me make you a real meal."

CALLISTINA IS SURPRISINGLY talkative while I prepare a meal of badger stew filled with greens, plus a few potatoes I dug up just a few days ago. It hasn't been hard finding food here—wherever 'here' is, because I still don't know. There is a road within half a day's ride that I found several weeks ago. But it's not a mountain road. So how we get from here to that road we were on in the last trip, I haven't a clue.

"I can't believe I was sleeping for three days. That's crazy. How long did you sleep, Eros?"

I lied to her. How the hell do I explain a three-month sleep? It doesn't even make sense. And she doesn't remember how her antlers were cut off. She doesn't remember any of it, so why should I remind her? She didn't seem too upset about missing her antlers in the other 'when.' It's best to just leave it be.

Ire has been coming and going lately, but he has stuck close to the camp. Like he can feel a change coming. And I can too. It needs to come and I've actually been preparing for it. Like the readily available food choices, there are many, many magiceuticals in this forest, so the goldberry and sharptongue were procured in the third week, after I was satisfied enough with the camp I was making and the food I was eating to think of a few other things.

I don't have a bottle, and the acetic acid is still fermenting in a mash I made out of apples two months ago, but it should all be fine. And I'm eager to get the fuck out of here, so when the food is ready and Callistina and I are sitting at the makeshift table I made using a large slab of gray slate, I bring this up.

"We should really get going on finding another door."

Callistina is smiling as she blows on a spoonful of hot stew. "Oh, I don't know. We could stay and check things out if you want."

"Nah. We should go."

"Go where, though? Back to Glory Rome?"

"Home."

"We don't have homes, Eros. We have a cursed town that lives in a fog of in between. We're certainly not going back there, right?"

"Well, there's always the Realm of Pittsburgh."

She frowns. "The human world. Where we have no magic."

"Maybe magic is overrated?"

She scoffs. "But I'm not human. I like this." She pans a hand down her golden body.

I can't look at her without thinking of all that blood. So to me, seeing her as that human woman I left Savage Falls with feels like a step up.

"Why are you looking at me that way?"

I feign ignorance. "What way?"

"Like I've got greens in my teeth." She rubs her teeth with her fingertip, looking for stray pieces of food.

And this makes me smile, and that smile allows me to relax a little. I let out a breath. "I just have a really bad feeling about this place. We've been here long enough. It's time to move on, don't you think?"

Callistina isn't feeling the same way, apparently, because she looks around like she's trying to figure out what's got me spooked. Finding nothing but a content pegásius chewing on some weeds several yards away, she shrugs. "Not really."

"Don't you want to continue our journey down the ordered list?" I raise my eyebrows, trying to insinuate that there is a grand adventure waiting. But that's not gonna happen. I do not want to go through that third set of doors. And I'm making sure the next spelling I use to move us along comes with a failsafe. I've been working on it since we got here and it's just about perfect.

Right now, as boring as Savage Falls is, I would very much like to be there and put an end to this trip. Because Pressia is the one guiding us through time. This is all her doing. She has to be the one who cut off Callistina's antlers.

Who else would do such a heinous thing?

Who else would need such magic?

I mean, maybe if there was someone else in this forest with us, I could blame them. But there is no one else here.

It was Pressia.

I know I already had plans to end her, but what she did to Ire and Callistina, that's evil. That's downright evil right there. My plan is to get back to Savage Falls, go find Tomas, and find a way back to Saint Mark's apothecary.

I know she's there. Living in another dimension, or another time, or whatever the fuck she calls it. I know she's there. And I'm gonna find her and I will make her pay. I will end her.

Not for what she did to me all those lifetimes ago. But what she did to Callistina and Ire.

Evil should never get a pass.

Someone has to stand up to it and that someone will be me.

CHAPTER TWENTY-TWO - CALLISTINA

*D*o *I want to continue* our journey down the ordered list? "No, actually." I say this, but I don't think Eros is listening to me. His gaze is directed at the forest and his eyes are a bit unfocused. "Did you hear me?"

He glances at me, mentally shaking himself out of something. "What?"

"You asked if I wanted to continue our journey down the ordered list. And I don't. This place doesn't look so bad. I mean, there's no rush, right? We just got here."

Now he looks at me intently. And again, I find myself wondering if there's a piece of food in my teeth. "What?"

Eros lets out a long sigh. "I want to tell you something, because it's something you should know and I don't want you to find out later and then think I was trying to keep it from you. But... it's... not good." He's looking down when he says all this, but for this last part, his gaze lifts up so his eyes meet mine. "So I don't want to tell you."

He looks… very sad. And defeated. Like he lost a big battle. A very big, important battle. And I'm not sure what to think about this, so I just give him a small shrug. "OK."

"But you deserve to know."

"All right."

"We've been here three months."

"What?"

"Ninety-seven days, actually. You were…" He pauses, gets a pained look on his face, then exhales and keeps going. "When I came through my door you were… bloody. Covered in it. And so was Ire."

"Bloody? Why?"

"Because we came to the time—the very day, almost the exact moment, I think—that you had your antlers cut off and Ire had his wings cut off. You were… I thought you were dead."

I am having trouble understanding what he's saying. "What are you saying?"

"I'm saying"—his tone is a bit irritable now—"that someone mutilated the two of you for your magic."

"What magic?"

"The wings," he says, pointing at Ire. "And your antlers. It's the feathers and the bloodhorn."

"The bloodhorn?" The moment I say these words a bit of clarity slips into place. Because bloodhorn was the ingredient that Tarq was looking for when he was doing all his magic with the wood nymphs back in Vinca. "But I don't have any bloodhorn."

THE SAVAGE RAGE OF FALLEN GODS

"Oh, you do, Callistina." Eros is nodding his head emphatically. "You do. Or... actually... you did, I mean. It's all gone now."

I simply blink at him. I'm not sure what else to do. I just sit, finding myself at a loss for words.

"Callistina? Did you hear me?"

I nod my head. "It's all gone now?"

"Yes. She bled you dry and then—"

"Who? Who is this 'she?'"

"Pressia. I'm like ninety-nine-point-nine-nine-nine percent sure it was her. Who else? Who else would be using magic like that?"

Tarq and Nysta come to mind. But though I have been seeing them in my nightmares, or delusions, or whatever the mechanism is, they don't seem to be a part of this story. And Tarq is dead. Isn't he? "Wait," I say. "You said we went back in time."

"Right. To the moments right after your antlers and Ire's wings were taken."

"*Back* in time. Why would the ordered list start with the future and work its way back?" What I'm really trying to decide, but don't say out loud, is whether or not Tarq could be alive in this 'when.' Could he have done this?

I'm grasping at anything and anyone *but* this Pressia woman, because why the hell is she so bitter? What could Eros have done to her to warrant this kind of fatal attraction? I mean, give it a rest, lady. Let it go. She must be *insane*.

"I don't know," Eros says, answering my rhetorical

question. "Who can explain anything in this curse addendum we seem to be caught up in?"

I exhale loudly. "Who indeed."

"I just wanted you to know that we've been here a long time. You're recovered now. Ire is recovered. We need to leave."

"But we can't take him with us through a door."

"He'll be fine, Callistina. And besides, he seems to show up anyway."

"That's true. Odd, but true. Because he's an integral part of this story."

"Makes sense, though."

I squint my eyes at Eros. "How do you figure?"

"Because she needed him *and* you. To do whatever spell she was doing. Feathers and bloodhorn."

He doesn't seem convinced, and I'm not either, but what more is there to say about it? It makes perfect sense, I'm just not convinced.

"So. What do ya think?" Eros stands up. "You ready to hit the road?"

I point to the ground. "Right now?" I look around at the darkening forest. "The sun is setting. It's not really the proper time—"

"I've got everything ready. I've got all the ingredients." As he's saying this he's walking towards the corner of the small cabin, where he plucks a giant nut from a shelf. It's been cut in half and he removes the top, releasing a stench that quickly fills the room. "I've been fermenting acetic acid for two months now. It'll work." Then he picks up two pouches. "And I've gathered the goldberry and sharptongue. We can get by without a bottle. My spelling is perfect this time, I swear."

"Well, you have it all figured out, don't you?"

He brings his magiceuticals over to where I'm sitting and sets them down on the table. "I'm sorry. I know you just woke up, but I really, *really* think we need to get the fuck out of here ASAP."

I feel the need to object. Forcefully. But there's no good reason to other than I just don't want to. Also, he's starting to make me nervous. I feel quite content, actually. I don't feel any sense of danger, but he certainly does. Which puts me at odds with my instincts.

Eros crouches down in front of me, reaching for my hands. He takes them both in his and we lock eyes, saying nothing for a moment. Just looking at each other.

"Callistina," he finally says. "Listen. Something is terribly wrong here."

This is when I realize he's truly afraid of something. I can feel it in the way he grips my hands. I can see it hiding behind those unnaturally green eyes of his. He's afraid. But of what?

"Something is terribly wrong and I think we need to get back to our world as soon as possible."

"But what is wrong? Because I don't *feel* it."

"You didn't feel the danger in Glory Rome, either."

He's right. I can't deny that. That city had a hold on me. Not sure why, but I was wrong about it. The Army of the Gods came after us. The *Army of the Gods*. "What in the hell are we wrapped up in?"

Eros shrugs. He wants to say he doesn't know, but he does. He knows something.

"You know something." I say my fear out loud. And it *is* a fear. Because whatever it is he knows, he's afraid of it. And if he's afraid of it, I should be too. "You know something," I say again. "And I want to know what it is. Tell me and we can go home. Right now. But I want to know."

Eros swallows hard. Like he's steadying himself before giving me his answer. But then he sighs and I know he's not going to tell me. He's going to lie. "I would tell you if I knew, but I don't." He squeezes my hands. "I swear. I have suspicions, I have a gut feeling, I have... reservations, or whatever. But I have no information other than I want to leave and I need you to come with me. Not because of the twin doors. But because I..." He hesitates, exhaling loudly.

But I smile at this part. Because he was about to say something... big. "Because you..." I roll a hand at Eros, encouraging him to continue. "Like me?"

This makes him smile. Grin, actually. All the way up to his eyes. "Yeah. I like you, and we're in this together now, ya know? Partners. Friends. Lovers. And... it's more than that. I..."

"Love me?"

He nods. Slowly. His grin fading. "I feel like I do. And I'm not sure what that means, because I'm not allowed to love. And I'm afraid of this." He points at me. "I'm afraid for you. Because whatever happens next..."

"OK," I say, putting up a hand to let him know he can stop struggling. "I get it. And just so we're clear, you really are my best friend. And I know, coming from me, a person who has no friends, and having known you for a couple of days—"

"Callistina, it's been months at this point."

"Not for me. For me it's been a few weeks of mindless fucking back in Savage Falls and a few days on a hallway road trip. So I understand that 'best friend' really doesn't come with a lot of meaning. But… you're just the one, Eros. You're just my one. And if you say we need to go, then we need to go."

"It's that simple for you, huh?" He's still looking into my eyes. Like he can see into my soul.

I shrug up one shoulder. "If you say it's true, then it is. Because you would not hurt me. And this is what love is really about. It's not about marriage, or rings, or vows. It's about trust. And after all we've been through, I would be a fool to not trust you."

He lets go of my hands and places them on my cheeks as he leans forward to kiss me. I close my eyes and sigh as our lips touch and our mouths open, enjoying this moment. Because it's a long, slow, passionate kiss. And my truth is that he makes me want to climb into his lap and just fall asleep against his chest.

His fear is his truth.

But my truth is, he makes me feel safe.

When we pull back from the kiss we're once again staring into each other's eyes. "OK." He says it low, almost a whisper. "Then let's do this. I just want to go home now."

He stands up, but when I try to get up too, he presses a hand at me. "You rest. I know you feel fine, but

Callistina, you've had a very hard time over the past few months. I've got this. Just finish your stew."

Then he turns and starts messing with some turtle shells that he must've been using for cooking. He empties the fermented acetic acid into the shell and then adds the sharptongue and goldberry, using a crude wooden pestle to mash everything together. Then he sets it on the fire.

"We don't have a bottle," he says, stirring the mixture with a hand-carved wooden spoon. "But we don't need a bottle. The veil here is very thin. I can feel the other worlds pressing against us at every turn."

I don't know what to say to that, but I don't think he requires my input. The god of love has a plan in his head and I'm only an accessory to it at this point.

We are going home.

CHAPTER TWENTY-THREE -
EROS

"*What about your wings?*"

"What?" I'm stirring the turtle shell of magiceuticals, staring down into the pasty mixture, picturing how I want what comes next to play out. This is my intention. A necessary part of effective magic. And my intentions are two-fold.

"Your wings?" Callistina says again.

"What about them?"

"Will you lose them?"

I look over my shoulder at my new, heavy appendages. They weigh a lot more than the bat wings. When I first realized they were back—though slightly more golden than I remember them being—I felt a mixture of horror and relief.

Horror because I have an aversion to feathers. They really do gross me out. I mean, the whole molting thing you do every year—my gods, it's so fucking awful. Itchy, and tender, and a little bit painful. It puts a lot of stress on my body. And I'm thinking that's the reason I feel like shit these days. It's the wings.

But I also felt relief when I saw them there. Because they are the pinnacle of my power. And if one is planning the death of, for instance, a time-travelling oracle who takes pleasure in cutting off appendages in order to milk out some bloodhorn to make potent magic, then one needs one's full power in order to do that.

"Well? Will you?"

"I don't much care if I lose them, Callistina." And this is the truth. Fuck the wings. Wings are just a pain in the ass. You can't wear shirts or leather jackets. It's just all kinds of messed up. "I've lived without them for so long, I just don't much care."

I only need them long enough to get my revenge.

I made two spellings because I really have thought of everything this time. Two spellings.

One to send us home. Together. I have to see Callistina get home or I won't be able to live with myself. I need to know she's safe. I know she looks better and feels better, but after everything she's been through, what I need, for my own peace of mind, is her resting in my foggy little town while I take care of business.

Because the second spelling will take me to Pressia.

I said I would end her. And I will.

She is evil. She is wicked, and vicious, and *bad*.

But most importantly, she hurt someone I love.

And that cannot stand.

*I'M **on the seventh round*** of heating and cooling when Callistina sits down next to me and leans her head on my shoulder. "You look worried."

"I'm not worried." I'm really not. She's just misinterpreting my concentration. "I'm being intentional. I don't want any fuck-ups."

"Was the last try a fuck-up?"

I scoff and turn my head to look down at her. "I would call it one, yes."

"Because I got hurt."

"That, and the fact that Pressia dared to touch you. To bring you into our battle and use you to get to me."

"Why would she do that?"

I scoff again. "She's… bitter. And old. And mean."

"Well, she sounds like a textbook villain then, doesn't she?"

"I guess."

"I'm just not convinced it's her."

"Who else would it be?"

"I'm not sure. But Ire was attacked as well. How does he fit into all this?"

"I don't know."

Callistina leans to the side a little in order to get a better look at me. "Don't you think that's… suspect?"

"Which part?"

"Are you being obtuse on purpose?"

"What are you talking about, Callistina? I just don't know where you're going with this."

"OK. Then I will speak plainly. It's not her."

"It has to be her."

She shrugs. "You're..." She reaches up and swipes a bit of hair off my forehead, sliding her fingertips over my brow, like she's trying to smooth it out.

"I'm what?" I really do want to know what she was gonna say.

"You're in the middle of it. So you have to spin to see everything from all angles. But this is the problem with being in the middle of something. As you spin, you miss things. There is always a blind spot behind you."

"If you can see past my blind spot, why don't you just tell me what's standing behind me?"

"I would, but I'm spinning with you. You're going to do something stupid, I know it. You're not coming with me, are you?"

"Of course I am. I'm gonna get you home no matter what."

She stares into my eyes for a few moments, searching for the truth. But this is the truth. "You promise?"

I smile at her. "I promise."

"And when we get back everything will be perfect."

"I promise." Then I stand up, taking the bowl of magic with me, and offer her my hand so she can stand up too. She takes it, sighing. And I lead her out of the little shelter I made for us and into the clearing. Ire is not far off, munching on some long meadow grass.

I hate leaving him behind, but there's nothing I can

do. He's some kind of tagalong on this journey. Not meant to travel through the doors with us.

"OK," I say, turning Callistina so we're facing each other. "Let's do this."

She stares up at me with those yellow eyes of her, smiling now. "What will we use to replace the bottle?"

"We don't need a fuckin' bottle. I have this." I stretch out one of my wings and pluck out a flight feather. It's long, and golden, and practically aglow with magic. Then I dip it into the thick broth I spent most of the night cooking and swirl it around. Callistina watches, her eyes rolling up as I lift the feather out and paint the magic onto what's left of her antlers.

She chuckles a little.

"There's still magic in there," I say. "That bitch can cut off your antlers and take a little power, but she can't really steal it." I place my other hand over her heart. "Because your power's in here."

She sighs out a little breath. "Who would've thought that the god of love would be a romantic."

"Hold that thought." I put the feather back in the turtle shell and set it down at our feet. Then I take both of her hands in mine and start the spell.

"Forget the hallway and the door
    that leads to places fate and yore
    for we are done and want no more.
    All my power I do implore,
    take us back to the place before.
    The little town of Savage Falls

is just the place we want to call.
We walk, or run, or even crawl
back home to there, the place so small
to live inside its foggy walls."

FOR A MOMENT I think it's not going to work. Callistina too. She's just getting ready to open her mouth and ask me something when everything around us shifts.

There's no explosion. No bright light.

It's just there. The hallway. Like we've been in it this whole time, but it was glamoured from us.

The entrance back to Savage Falls is directly to my left. So close. But before I can take a step and lead Callistina to it, I fall forward. Right back into the ordered list.

I AM RUNNING. Hard. My breath coming out fast, almost in gasps. My legs leap over tree trunks and my feet find purchase in the mud. I've got my bow out, loaded with a bolt. And I'm chasing something up ahead. I can't quite see what it is, just little flashes of something moving through the thick leaves.

Something is running from me.

"Pressia." Her name comes out as a hiss through my

teeth. It's her. I know it's her. I run harder, gritting my teeth as my lungs burn and my legs ache. I'm running up the hill, watching glimpses of a woman weaving her way in and out of the trees.

But slowly, over the course of the long climb up the mountain and through the jungle of underbrush, I get close enough to hear her gasping for breath.

I force myself to go faster, chasing the glimpses of the sand-colored dress flittering through the leaves.

Then a mistake. Hers. A loud thump as a body hits the ground.

She fell! She tripped and fell.

But in the same moment that I'm realizing I've got her, something happens. My head is pounding and my vision goes blurry. Suddenly, I'm on the ground too.

Only... I'm not. I'm still running.

But it's not me, running. It's... someone else. It has to be.

But he looks like me. Bare-chested and with a complicated tree tattoo covering his back as he leaps over a tree trunk and disappears into the bushes, loaded bow in hand.

I scramble to my feet and follow, running hard because he's caught her. He's got her and he's not allowed to get her.

She's mine.

Then from up ahead, a scream.

"Callistina?" It's her. I would know her voice anywhere. She screams again. "Callistina!" I yell again. Then I push harder, ignoring my own gasping and pain in my lungs. "Callistina!"

She screams again, only this time there is a whoosh of a bolt flying through the air. And the next time she screams, it's the sound of something dying.

"Callistina!" I continue running, but then stop short when I come around a large boulder. A large, flat boulder. With Callistina lying face down on it. Antlers growing out of the top of her head, right before my eyes.

And me. Standing behind her. Her hair wrapped around one fist while I saw the still-growing antlers off with the knife in my hand.

"No." This word doesn't come out like a man in denial. It comes out like a man who just found the truth. "No. No. I didn't do this. I wouldn't do this!"

But it is me, standing over her, sawing off her power. Blood is pouring out and he—me—*I'm* catching it inside a skin. Still holding her hair in my fist to somewhat direct the flow of a river of scarlet that is pouring out of the top of her head and flowing down the side of the rock.

That's when I hear the crashing of hooves through the forest. The other me is just as surprised as I am when Ire come into view. In a full-on charge like he's about to take me out.

Eros pulls the bow out, loads it with a bolt, and shoots the beast in the chest.

It knocks him backwards and he goes rolling. Eros has let go of Callistina and is now charging at Ire with the bloody knife.

"No!"

But it's too late for that. Eros cuts off the beast's

wings, then leaves him there, struggling to get to his feet. Which Ire does not manage to do. He simply collapses into the heap I found him in when I first came through the last door.

My attention goes back to Eros—*to me*!. I'm pulling feathers out of the wings I just stole, then I spit a spelling out in between the moaning of the pegásius and the gryphon chimera.

Callistina is her old self now. I think the bolt did it. I was doing some kind of magic and she got away. And Ire… I don't know where he came from. But it was all big magic to get to this one point in time when, from Eros' back—from *my* back—wings sprout!

Giant, golden wings.

The very ones I had when I came through the last door.

He tilts his head up to the sky, laughing. His wings —*my wings*— spreading wide in victory.

And at the same time I watch. Separate from what is happening, but obviously not. I am crouched behind the boulder, as the winged god cleans his knife and sheaths it. Then he stares down at Callistina's lifeless body, his head slumping forward.

When he raises it again, I am him and he is me.

And I have done the unthinkable.

CHAPTER TWENTY-FOUR -
CALLISTINA

There are parts of the trip that are familiar.

Eros and I are standing next to each other, shoulder to shoulder, when everything shifts. The air becomes blurry first. Then it takes on the appearance of water, a distortion of something on the other side.

But then, in the next moment, I'm in the hallway staring at my door. On the other side is movement, a little bit like the first time when we came out on Ire's back. But it's not the smooth rhythm of a walking pegásius, but more like a jarring and jolty runner.

Then, in this same instant, I'm there. In that motion. I am that motion and I am, indeed, running. But something is wrong with my body because I'm shaking all over. Like I'm cold, but it's not cold here. It's hot and humid and I am not shivering.

I'm wearing the dress I put on that morning we left Savage Falls. The sand-colored one that made me look like a pretty peasant. And I have this moment of loss. This feeling of *losing*. Because my gryphon chimera body must be gone and I must be just this stupid, magicless human again.

It only lasts an instant though, because that's not right. I am a chimera. I am me. I can feel the weight of the antlers on top of my head. I can feel the way the boots I'm wearing don't quite fit me because I no longer have feet, but paws. And when I look down at my pumping arms as I *run, run, run*, I see the soft, short golden velvet fur that covers my whole body underneath this dress.

Why am I wearing this dress in this body?

And why am I running? In fact, the urgent pace of my movement is distracting and the effort I'm putting into it is disproportionate to what I'm feeling. Because my legs are pumping hard, working hard. My boots are pounding the ground, the stones, thick, fallen tree trunks as I scramble over them. My breath coming out of my mouth in ragged gasps. My lungs burning.

I am afraid.

I look down again, and the soft velvet fur is gone. My boots fit correctly. There is no weight of antlers on the top of my head. It was left over from the other world? The other door?

An overwhelming feeling of sadness floods through me and I want to be sad about this. I want to wallow in human misery.

But then I hear the footfalls behind me.

And I realize I'm not simply running, I'm being *chased*.

What the hell is happening here?

We have gone back in time, obviously. It fits the pattern, but more obviously, I'm wearing the dress I started out in.

This is when traveling me and other me coalesce into one and I am her.

I want to stop and think. To catch my breath. But there is a voice in my head, so clear, like it's another person running with me, screaming, *Don't. Stop. Don't. Stop. Don't. Stop.* Over and over again, to the rhythm of my feet. Like my life depends on this run.

Which is not a run.

It's an escape.

I go faster, try harder. The muscles in my thighs burning from spent energy. My lungs no longer working right. My vision blurry.

And then I make the mistake of looking over my shoulder and I scream.

Someone, somewhere in the forest, calls, "*Callistina!*"

And it's Eros. I know it's Eros.

But it can't be Eros, because Eros is the monster who's chasing me.

A scream of pure terror bursts out of me. Like a last-ditch wail of a rabbit that's about to be caught in the jaws of a wolf.

"*Callistina!*" Eros screams again. But he's much too far away to stop what happens next, which only takes a matter of moments.

I look over my shoulder.

Mistake, mistake, mistake... This is the new mantra on repeat inside my head.

And it is a mistake. In every way possible. Because I see who is chasing me and it *is* Eros.

But not my Eros. This is a man-god who I do not know. The very one I was sleeping next to for weeks before we walked through the doors, but something else altogether. Because his face is nothing but hate.

Hate is his soulmate, his soulmate is hate.

I trip and fall, but scramble to my feet and keep running. I must run from him. Because if he catches me—

And that's when he catches me. His fist grabbing at this stupid dress. But it rips and I lunge forward, a second chance.

Suddenly he stops and for a moment I have this unreasonable hope—I mean, at this point in my life, there is no reason to hope for anything, so it's all very unreasonable. But I feel the hope in my chest. He's realized this is a mistake. He's not going to hurt me. He can hear himself, somewhere in the distance, calling for me in the woods.

"*Callistina!*"

And he's not going to do it. He's not.

He *won't* do it.

We're best friends! We're more than friends, but even if we weren't, friends is enough.

I love him. He loves me.

And then the ridiculousness of it all hits me in the back like a bolt from his bow and I am flung forward, straight onto a boulder I was just about to leap over.

And it's not ridiculous at all.

THE SAVAGE RAGE OF FALLEN GODS

It was planned this way.

His love is fake.

His friendship is fake.

And I knew that. I have always known that he is fake.

His footsteps come slow now. I'm gasping for breath, face down on the flat, sandstone boulder like a sacrifice. Because that's what I am.

Antlers are growing out of my head.

Fur is pushing out from my skin.

Claws burst from the tips of my fingers and the last thing I remember, I'm digging those claws into the rock as a sharp blade stabs my antlers and bloodhorn pours out of me in rivers.

I am nothing to him but a source of power.

He planned this. From the very beginning. I knew something was wrong when we were on the hillside together. When those man-boys walked through the door and Eros stopped me from following.

"Here's the thing, Callistina. I... might like you."

That's what he told me.

"We are... kind of a team. And I think we should go to this new world together."

That's what he said.

"I want to go with you, Callistina. OK? I want us to go together."

Then he pointed at himself and at me.

I was confused. Then suspicious.

And then he *kissed* me.

He spelled me.

He used me.

He killed me.

Is killing me right now, in this very moment.

A spelling comes to me. In a voice that's soothing, and sweet, and belongs to a very small girl. She is standing next to the boulder like a ghost in a long, sage-green dress that flows down to her feet.

"*A HORN, a hoof, an eye, a bone.*
A god, a girl, away from home.
He takes her magic with his knife.
He takes it all, and ends her life.
She will not wake, she will not wallow
A bitter pill that she must swallow.
The god of love is the god of hate.
He has no soul, he has no mate.
Goodbye, lost god, be gone for good.
You'll never be the man you should."

I watch the little girl with blurry vision as my head jerks back and forth from the effort it takes to cut the antlers clean off.

And then it's over. The antlers are gone. My blood is all over this forest, and this boulder, and this life. The little girl—who can only be Pressia—reaches out to touch my hand. "It's not your fault," she says in a small, sad voice. "It's not your pain. I did my best to explain. He needs to see, he needs to know. I could not tell, I had to show. And so he must live with this, and feel the dark, sad loneliness. What happens next, life goes on.

Adventure over, love is gone. He has two choices before him now. Fix it all or take a bow."

She disappears, but her words linger in my head like an echo in a cave.

And then I simply cease to exist.

CHAPTER TWENTY-FIVE - EROS

watch from the trees. I watch the god as he kills Callistina.

Steals her magic.

Treats her body like he's dressing a deer after a hunt.

I watch as he prepares his spelling.

I watch as the golden wings burst out of his back and spread through the forest like a morning sunrise.

I watch him leave. Just… walk away. Like she was nothing to him.

No one shows up to save Callistina.

Not even me.

She is dead.

I WAKE **up in the woods** just outside the hallway door. The sun is just starting to rise and birds are singing. When I sit up and look downhill, I can just barely make out the sign over the little candle shop.

What. The fuck. Just happened?

Was it a dream?

But the weight of the wings behind me tells me everything I need to know.

I can't even look at them, but I know they are magnificent, and golden, and so full of magic, they glow like the sunrise.

I'm afraid to look around. I'm afraid of what I'll see. I don't even want to stand up. I don't even want to live.

I can't live on if she's gone. I can't.

You killed her, Eros.

It's my own voice inside my head. All me. Not anyone else.

You killed her to steal her magic and get your feathers back.

I did that. I did. There's no way to deny it. No point, either.

"Once you were great, once you were tall." The words come out of my mouth unbidden. "But now you're bait, and now you're small. You steal the love, not set it free. You take the joy, from them, from me. I see you now, I see you then, I see you everywhere you've been. And you will know my name forever, you will know my spell is clever. Not just some words and pretty rhymes, my spells are deep and keep the time. I curse you now, evermore. The magic ends with the last great

344

war. You cannot win, you will not prevail. You will be lost in time and tale. For it is not gods who rule this place—they have no honor, truth, or grace. It is the magic of the spells that keep us safe, and warm, and well. We craft them careful, make the words, and wrap them up in beaks of birds. So go, and live, and rejoice. But know, my enemy, this is not your choice. Goodbye, lost god, be gone for good. Be the man you know you should."

I have failed.

Utterly failed.

She was right about me. I'm a piece of shit. I'm a small, evil, lying, thieving piece of shit.

And I deserve this curse.

"HATE IS MY SOULMATE, *despair is my friend.*
The fog is my solace, the darkness my end.
No love for me, this curse is eternal.
Hell is my home, my existence infernal.

THE ROAD IS LONG, *and lonely, and sad.*
The spaces between drive me wild and mad.
No reward is forthcoming, no prize in the win.
For there is no winning when you're neck-deep in sin.

THE GATE IS TOO NARROW, *too slim, too straight.*
I'll never pass through, it is far too late.

I'll wander all lost and heavy with weight.
Hate is my soulmate, my soulmate is hate."

I GET UP, walk down the hill, enter my foggy little town, walk to the bar, go inside, and grab a bottle of whiskey. I go outside and walk down the street, thinking about Callistina.

Who was my soulmate.

Was. But no longer is.

Because she's dead.

Because I killed her.

And this was my plan from the moment she told me there was a door on my hillside.

I set her up.

I have crossed a line here. A very bright line. I had made peace with what I did to Pie. Accepted that I was being selfish and I had a direct hand in bad things that happened to her as she was growing up.

I even made a promise to her. To try to make up for it.

"I want you to bless Jacqueline," Pie had said. "If she needs help, you will be there. It means, if she's sad, you will make her happy again. It means, if she gets a flat tire in the middle of the night, you will drag your ass out of bed, fly to wherever she is, and fix it. You will bless her. That's what I want. You will make her life a living dream."

I had agreed at the time, but I didn't mean it. I didn't even feel bad about not meaning it because the fog around Savage Falls was still there for me. It's not like I could follow Jacqueline back to wherever she came from. I'm a prisoner. This place is my prison.

I knew the promise was empty. But I had been making empty promises my whole existence. So what is one more to the little girl whose life I stole and who I discarded the moment I had no more use for her?

It's a fucked-up thing to do, and I knew that. But I could accept it.

Things turned out OK for her, didn't they? If I hadn't done what I did, she wouldn't be living out her happily ever after with her monster.

But what I have done to Callistina is a whole other level of low.

I killed her.

I cut off her antlers to steal her magic.

I used her.

And I get it. I use everyone. It should not come as a surprise that I just did what I've always done. But I thought I had grown after what happened with Pie. I thought I was gonna change. I thought there was a second chance for me. I really thought I was going through that door with Callistina so we could start over. I really thought we were gonna be friends.

But all along I was planning to kill her.

I am evil.

I am worthless.

And this is my limit. There is a point in a man's life where he just has to face facts. Reality check, if you will. When all the senseless self-reflection is over and it's no longer useful to deny the truth.

A point when you realize the world is a much better place without you.

And just as I think this, I walk into the fog.

Because this was my limit.

I have crossed my own line.

And I know in my heart that all the worlds that exist are far better places without me.

CHAPTER TWENTY-SIX - CALLISTINA

I **am standing in Vinca.**

Or, actually, the place that *used* to be Vinca. It's utterly destroyed. Large chunks of buildings lie scattered around like a tipped-over toybox filled with building blocks. The air is hazy, but it's not a mist or smoke. It's dust.

Vinca is nothing but leftover dust.

I think I understand the nightmare now. I think it's just... guilt. I feel responsible for the destruction of this beautiful city that I turned ugly.

I was a terrible queen. Possessed with an evil spirit inside me.

The dragon wasn't Madeline, even if it was.

The dragon was me.

And the funny thing is—I loved this city. I loved the people, too. I loved the palace—not because I lived there, but because it was the epitome of human and chimera creativity.

The whole city was, really. The pinnacle of civilization.

Just like Glory Rome.

Why then, after all that struggle and perseverance, do we always end up tearing it down?

Is it because the goal has been realized and the challenge is over?

Maybe. But to me, that sounds a lot like the delusional ramblings of an optimist. Or, more likely, a crazy person.

Which I am.

I can feel the antlers on my head. All twenty-two points of them. I can feel the string that is too tight under my chin. I am wobbling a little atop the wooden blocks. I can smell the mangy coat and the broken broomstick handle is clutched in my hand.

It's not actually a costume, is it?

It's me, pretending to be a queen, for all those years.

The nightmare was a warning, I think. A warning that a change was coming. And I felt it. I had that epiphany the morning I found the man-boys from the Realm of Pittsburgh. I was going to walk through that fucking door and accept my punishment with... determination.

I was going to be human, and I was going to rise to the occasion, and I was going be someone else.

I could feel this new beginning flowing towards me like it was water under a bridge.

"Well, I will say this about you, Callistina. You're a lot more receptive to the truth than Eros could ever hope to be."

I turn, slowly, and find a woman standing behind me. She's pretty and blonde, wearing a light green dress that flows all the way down to her feet. Her eyes are bright, and there's a smile on her face. And in this same moment of recognition, Vinca fades and we are in some other place now. An apothecary, I suppose. Because there are shelves, and shelves, and shelves of books, and jars, and bottles all around me.

I'm not surprised or scared.

I'm just… indifferent.

Pressia smiles at me. I didn't know her back in Vinca, of course. She went missing the same day as Pie. But she had left a mark on the palace that would become my home. She was a very special kind of royal beast. A breeder. Like Pie. Like Pell. And so very, very unlike me.

There were pictures of her everywhere. Photographs and paintings. All under the age of seven, of course, but there is only one person this woman can be and I know she is Pressia.

I reach up to the too-tight string under my chin and pull on it until it comes loose. The antlers tilt, unbalanced, and then just drop over the side of my head and land with a dull thud on the floor.

I slip the coat down my arms and let that drop to the floor too.

Then I slip the blocks off my feet, let out a sigh, and walk over to a couch where I take a seat.

We stare at each other as I do all that. And then, once I'm settled, I say, "He didn't deserve this."

She doesn't ask who I'm referring to. She just tilts her head and smiles. "Didn't he?"

"No. He didn't. He wasn't going to kill me."

"Really?" She laughs this word out. "And here I thought you had it all figured out."

"He wasn't going to kill me. You did it all wrong."

"Did I?"

"I know it was all a spell. I know it wasn't real. Obviously, I am not dead."

She puts her hands together, clapping slowly. It's a very small clap. Dainty and light. "Well, good for you. And where, exactly, did I go wrong?"

I blow out a breath. "You took us backwards. That was your mistake. Because I got to see him as someone else first. And so, by the time we got back to that moment, I knew he wouldn't do it. Had never planned to do it. You lied. You set him up. You made him fail."

"You're wrong." She's no longer smiling, but she's not frowning either. Just determined. "Let me show you the god-man you think you know so well."

The scene around me changes again and this is when I realize that I am currently existing inside her magic. She is powerful.

But power is really nothing more than experience. She's not an oracle, she's a door traveler. In real time not even twenty years have passed. But Pressia doesn't live in real time. She lives in hallways. She steps in and out of them as she pleases. So she has gathered up thousands of years of experience.

We are in a dark room now. But I recognize it. It's inside the palace. A nursery. There are shades over the windows, casting everything in shadow, but sunlight peeks around the edges, so it's not night. It's day.

There is a fancy round crib dressed up in the softest white, cotton sheets. Handmade by the royal weavers. A canopy above with a slowly dancing mobile made of precisely balanced wires with paper stars hanging off them. There are pretty things all over. Toys, and stuffed animals, and a chair where the nursemaid feeds and rocks the baby.

I know the nursery because Lyrica, one of the royal alchemists and Pressia's teacher, used to bring me here. Used to fill my head with dreams of babies.

Of course, there were no babies. Not in the room I knew.

But this is not the room I knew.

Because there *is* a baby in that crib and it is cooing softly. Like it is content, and happy, and every need has been filled.

In this same moment, there is a flash in the center of the room, then a doorway appears and out steps Eros. He looks... good. Shirtless. His wings are golden, his body tanned brown and strong. His hair is lighter than I remember it being, like he's been in the sun a lot.

He lets out a sigh. Then looks over his shoulder. Like he's checking to make sure the door is still there. Then he turns back and looks at the baby as he walks over to the crib. He has pulled a knife out by the time he arrives at the railing and seconds later the cooing has stopped and his knife is covered in blood.

He smiles, looking down at his work. Then turns,

walks back through the door, and it disappears. Like he was never there.

I'm shaking my head the whole time. "Nope. He didn't do that."

"You just saw him do it, Callistina."

"It's magic." I turn and face her. "*Your* magic. It didn't happen, obviously, because you're still *here*."

She looks a little bit surprised that I figured it out so quick, but who else could this baby be but her? It's the same room I knew as a queen.

Her face changes again, this time becoming hard. "It *will* happen. He *will* find a door, he *will* come here, and he *will* do that." She points at the crib. "We just watched it happen. It's not magic, Callistina. I'm not making this up. We came through the fog, not a door. But it is the same thing. What he just did was real. What he just did was his future."

It's starting to make sense, I think. Why she hates him so much. She has been traveling for nearly twenty years now. She has seen many things. Many things she should not know. So I guess she's right. That was Eros.

But there is a flaw in her logic. "You're still wrong."

"OK." She laughs. "Tell me how I'm wrong, my queen."

I narrow my eyes at her, because it's an insult to call me that now. But I put aside my annoyance and tip up my chin. "The future isn't set in stone. It's set in sand. And it can shift."

"No." She shakes her head. "That's not how it works. Trust me, I've watched it all play out. I've checked and double-checked. That's why it took me so long to decide to end him. I needed to make sure that time was truth. Everything that has happened, I have seen. I saw Pie kidnapped. I saw her grow up, and meet Pell, and break the curse, and go back, and make her choice again. I saw you, confused, become princess, become queen, become monster, become prisoner. I saw your punishment in the Bottoms prison and I saw your crazy costume. I saw Tarq, and his wood nymphs, and how he became the Skull King. I saw the destruction of Vinca by the dragon Madeline. I even saw Tomas's unhappy ending." She pauses to stare straight into my eyes. "Eros does this, Callistina. He finds a door, he goes back in time, he comes into this room, and he kills me. It's weeks away from happening. And not only that, but he *will* kill you to get your power. So." She stands up straighter and sucks in a breath. "He *did* deserve this."

I don't know what to say because the truth is, Eros is kind of ruthless. I can actually see him killing baby Pressia. And I can see him killing me to steal my blood-horn. And cutting off Ire's wings.

He's capable of all of it. He is, I know this.

But in the past, though. Not in the present. Not in the near future. That's not who Eros was when we went through the door.

"You set him up."

"I revealed him."

"He didn't kill me. I'm still alive. You worked magic on us. It was a delusion."

"To make you see the truth."

"I don't want to see the truth. I don't want to force

him into a future. I want him to choose. I want him to look me in the eye and do it on his own."

"You want to die?"

I throw up my hands, scoffing. "I'm no better than him. I was a terrible queen. I mean, terrible doesn't even come close to what I was. I was an evil queen. So what I want to know is this. Why didn't you stop *me*?"

She scoffs too. "You, dear girl, are not the problem here—"

"Oh, really?" My laugh is loud. "I'm not the problem? *I'm* not the problem? I'm the entire problem, Pressia. I'm the catalyst for all of it. It is my obsession with Pie's last words that causes the entire chain of events."

"*Wrong.* It is Eros stealing Pie from that room that causes this outcome. And you damn well know he did that. You were *there*."

"Well, then it was Ptah. He gave Pie the rings that Eros wanted to steal."

"*Wrong.* It was Eros who caused Ptah to give Pie the rings."

"How do you figure that?"

She opens her mouth to say something, but then she abruptly stops.

And this is when it all starts to make sense. "It was *you*, wasn't it?"

She tilts her chin up in defiance. "I don't know what you're talking about."

"You took Ptah through the doors and showed him something."

"*Wrong.*"

Her denial doesn't come with an explanation this

time, so I know I'm on the right track. So my mind starts racing, trying to put it all together.

It's actually not that complicated of a puzzle once you get this far.

Fallen gods.

That's what this is about.

The savage rage of fallen gods.

Not Eros, though he has been fallen for a long time now. Not Eros, but the gods in that throne room where I took Pie to receive her gift on her Caretaker Day. Cronus, Zeus, Saturn, and Ptah.

They fell out of favor. All but Saturn, who still has a cult to this day.

"It was *you*." I say this again, only this time I'm certain. "You took Ptah through a door and you showed him what giving Pie a bag of rings would do. You showed him how to change the future."

"I just told you, the future cannot be changed."

"So?" My sneer comes with a shrug. "Like I'd believe anything you'd say."

She shrugs as well, playing it off. And I hesitate here, because I think this is real. I've missed something. What I've deduced is a good portion of what's happening, but not the whole story.

Because Eros is not dead. He has not been defeated. So the plan is still happening.

She has already admitted that whatever we were doing in that hallway was mostly magic. Not the future. Sure, maybe she really did see it all in her travels. But she didn't show me the future. She made me experience it. Backwards.

Why?

Hmm. It's so obvious now.

Love.

She made us live it backwards because of love.

I don't know if I love Eros and he's not able to love, so he says.

But love comes in many forms and friendship is just as powerful.

We were friends. We started to rely on each other. Talk to each other. He wanted to protect me in Glory Rome.

Eros and I *are* friends.

And wouldn't it be *so* devastating to trust him and then be betrayed? Especially in such a selfish and terrible way. That's why we had to live it backwards. Because he didn't kill me. He didn't steal my magic. He didn't and he *won't*.

"You need me," I say. Pressia says nothing, so I keep going. "You need *me* to end him." Still, she says nothing. "You want me to think he's worthless. Evil. A betrayer. But he's not. I will admit," I say—and she is looking at me intently now—"that I don't know the rest of your plan. But I do know the rest of mine."

And then, like I've been planning this moment my entire life, the words just spill out...

"LOVE IS MY SOULMATE, *Eros my friend.*
  The fog is our solace, the sunshine our end.
  No hate for us, this blessing forever.
  Savage Falls is our home, this curse we will sever.

. . .

THE ROAD IS EASY, and crowded, and glad.
  No spaces between to drive us wild and mad.
  The reward is the people, the prize we will win.
  There is nothing but winning
  when you've been cleansed of your sins.

THE GATE WILL BE WIDE, and broad, and great.
  We'll all pass through, it's never too late.
  We will find our place, lifted of weight.
  Love is our soulmate, there is no more hate."

Is that all the magic is? Intentions? And if so, couldn't I just change it all around just by switching the words?

Apparently, yes. Because the scene around me starts fading as soon I start the spelling and by the time I get to the last word, I'm in the fog.

I think I've been here the whole time because I'm wearing the blue prom dress. The whole costume, actually. Antlers, wooden-block shoes, mangy coat that smells like sulfur.

This is the day I gave up. This is the day I wanted to end it.

But then Eros came, and picked me up, and carried me back to the curse.

I sit up, blinking, trying to see past the fog. My head spinning a little from the movement.

"Eros?" I say it too softly, looking around. He came here to find me, so if I never left, is he on his way?

No. He's not. He's somewhere dealing with the idea

that he just brutally killed me. That he cut off the wings of Ire. And he used us to get his own wings back.

The snort of a beast interrupts the utterly still and silent woods off to my right and I startle. I get to my feet and brush off my stupid dress, then adjust my antlers. It's probably someone from town. "Hello?" I say this softly. I'm really not in the mood to interact with the residents of Savage Falls right now, but I might, in fact, be lost in the fog. This might be my only way out.

So I call a little louder. "Hello? Is someone here?"

Another snort. Only this time, I'm not picturing a monster from town. I walk forward. "Hello?" And get another snort. "I'm coming. Just keep snorting and don't move. I'm coming." I follow the snorts for a couple of minutes and then there he is.

I smile. Then chuckle. He's not a pegásius, he's a horse.

But I'm not a gryphon chimera, either. I'm human.

I walk up to Ire and place my hand on the side of his face, looking into his blue eyes. "Is this our punishment, then? Humans, the both of us?"

He makes a noise that I swear is a laugh. A scornful one. A cynical one. And then I wonder what he did to get stuck in Pressia's little scheme. Did he kill people? Pegási are a formidable race of beast. It's probable that his past is checkered. Like mine. Like Eros's.

"Well," I say, sighing out the word. "Now what?"

He bobs his head up and down forcefully, making some growling noises. Then he takes a step to the left, looking back at me. Like he's checking to see if I'll follow.

"I guess I don't have anywhere else to be, so lead the way."

But he doesn't move. He just does that forceful bobbing of his head again. Then he looks back at his ribs and I suddenly understand.

He wants me to get on and I'm not about to turn that offer down. I slip off my wooden blocks—then, because I can't stand the smell of it, I take off the mangy coat too. Untying the antlers from my head seems like the logical next step. And when they drop to the ground, I realize I've done this a lot recently.

Shedding the costume. Trying to get rid of who I was, maybe. But I keep getting sent backwards, so I have to do it over and over again. It feels like a test. Or a punishment. Like I'm Sisyphus, rolling that boulder up a steep hill every day, only to have it roll back down at sunset so I can start again tomorrow.

In that myth, it was a futile effort.

But maybe that's just how it feels? So you give up. And stop doing it altogether. And just accept that this is your life and there's no way to make it better.

I did that already. When I put this costume on I was resigned to my fate.

Taking it off feels like progress, even if I'll probably just wake up in the same place I started and realize it's magic, or a curse, or a hallway, or a dream.

Ire snorts again, reminding me that we've got places to go. So I pat his shoulder, grab his mane, and swing myself up and throw a leg over. Then adjust my ridiculously ugly blue dress and let out a breath.

Which must be the signal for Ire to proceed, because

he starts off though the fog, his hooves making soft thuds that seem to get lost in the mist at his feet, so the sound fades before it goes anywhere.

There is nothing around us and there's no way to tell if we're actually getting anywhere because there are no landmarks to gauge the distance. There is no light, but there is no dark, either. It truly is the worst kind of nothingness and the longer we stay here, wandering forward like lost souls on an endless road, the crazier I start to feel.

Ire starts walking faster, and then he breaks into a trot.

I'm not sure why. There's nothing to indicate that we're actually getting somewhere. But there's no real reason to object, either.

Plus, his gait is smooth, and soothing, and if my punishment is to be on his back, traveling through nothingness, and towards nothingness, and arriving nowhere forever, and ever, and ever for all eternity— well... I could do worse.

At least I'm not alone.

CHAPTER TWENTY-SEVEN - EROS

I am alone.

Singular. Solitary. Apart. Isolated. Separate.

This is how it's always been and this is how it'll always be.

There is no love for me.

There is no soulmate. There is no family. There is no best friend.

But there is a voice in my head.

That's because you killed her, Eros. That's because you're a greedy piece of shit. That's because you're evil. A narcissist. A liar. A cheat. A thief. You are the definition of awful. You're mean, and shallow, and worthless.

The voice is always there, ready to feed me the truth.

And it's right. It's true. I guess they were all right about me. I thought it was kinda cool that I had so much power. That everyone was so afraid of me that I needed to stopped at all costs.

But what if that wasn't it?

What if they wanted to stop me because I'm just truly the Devil?

I can see it, actually.

I can believe it.

So I walk through the fog. Just keep walking. These brand-new wings becoming heavier and heavier with each new step. A reminder of how low I will stoop to get what I want. How far I am willing to sink to get my way.

I stop walking. What's the point? I'm not going anywhere.

This is it. This is *really* it.

This is my end.

Even if I'm stuck here for all eternity, wandering around in the nothingness, it all ends here.

I sit down and think about this. Really let it sink in. Kinda roll it all back in my head starting from the day on the roof of Science and Glory Building One when they pushed me over the edge and the wings came bursting out.

I flew away that day. I was terrified, of course. Because there were nine hundred and ninety-nine other boys there in line before me and not a single one of them grew wings. They were pushed over the edge and they splatted on the ground below.

That sound, bodies hitting the courtyard—it was a thud. Dull and short. Over so quick. But it was such a specific sound that it lingers in my head. Undeniable and real.

But I didn't go splat. I fell for a while. I wasn't able to clock the seconds, or anything. I was screaming, I know that. Of course, this wasn't my first trip over the edge. Because we are gods and we cannot die, so they did all manner of things to us as we grew.

We were all ten years old the first time.

No one grew wings at ten. We all went splat.

But we're gods. Right? Aren't we? So we don't die.

I don't know the process for godmaking. I don't know. I have no clue. All I know is that I will not die. Not jumping off a roof, not wandering in a fog. Somehow, some way I am here forever.

But there did come a day, obviously, when the wings did save me from that indeterminate end. They just flew out of my back. Spreading wide. Glorious golden feathers, like the ones I'm wearing now. And I caught the wind.

I flew forever and ever and ever.

In my head, at least. In reality, I crashed a little way off in the hills just outside Glory Rome. Someone came and collected me and when I got back to Building One, the whole floor—that used to be filled with a thousand boys just like me—was empty.

However they brought us back after we went splat, well, this time they didn't do that.

Because I was the god they were waiting for.

I don't know which one of us came first, but I was one of the Gods of Glory. The initial first group. The Olympians, as they would call us later.

The war started shortly after that with Parting Day. The day we all escaped.

Then came the Forgetting Times. When Glory Rome was torn down to nothing but blocks.

Just like Vinca will be.

It's a cycle. I've seen it turn twice, myself.

But Vinca hasn't been destroyed yet. I don't think anyone understands that. Callistina doesn't, for sure. *Didn't*, I correct myself. *Didn't* understand that.

And she never will, Eros. Because you killed her.

Everyone who saw the destruction of Vinca was seeing what is to come.

It's still there. It's all still there. I don't know the details of how Pell was going back and forth, but it was a magic door, obviously. They almost never take you to the same point in time.

Vinca is still there, but it won't be for long.

It's not my problem anymore.

It's not my time, it's not even my world.

I don't have a world.

I am part of the nothing.

Anyway, the point is—it's once again time to destroy and forget.

A brand-new Forgetting Time.

I'll wake up at some point. Because I can't die. But I'll wake up all confused, and innocent, and clean. And I'll spend my days bewildered and searching for the truth.

And then, one day, I'll find myself much like I am now. With an understanding that I am a greedy piece of shit. An evil narcissist. A liar. A cheat. A thief. The definition of awful. Mean, and shallow, and worthless.

And then I'll start all over.

That's all I have left.

The never-ending end.

I'd like to think that this was the plan all along. That the other me—who killed Callistina to steal her blood-horn and who cut off Ire's wings—he did all that because in order to forget you have to give up your power.

Not the pathetic punishment power of black bat wings.

The *real* power in these golden ones.

I reach around my shoulders, grab the feathers, and start pulling them out by the fistful. Pain shoots through my body like I'm on fire, but I don't stop. I pull them out. Dozens and dozens at a time. I do it quick. Fistful by fistful, I pull them out and drop them into the fog all around me. They start piling up at my feet. And as this is happening, I'm practicing the spelling in my head.

I will do it right.

I will make it last.

I will send myself somewhere dark, and silent, and empty.

Because that is how I feel right now.

And I just want to forget.

But there are thousands of feathers in my wings. Tens of thousands. The big ones are easy, but I have to get every single one of them to do magic this big. I have to pull them out until my wings are bald.

It takes forever.

But that's OK, I just happen to have forever.

I'm plucking the tiny ones that are barely shooting out of the bony edge of the top of my wing when I hear a noise.

I stop pulling on the feathers and lean forward a little.

It sounds like hooves clopping on a dirt road.

And then there he is. The dead beast himself. Smaller. No wings. But I would recognize those blue eyes anywhere.

"Eros?"

Callistina peeks out from behind his thick neck and I drop all the feathers in my hands. "Callistina?"

"Oh, my God." She puts a hand over her mouth. "What are you doing? What have you done?"

"Callistina?" I say again. Then I blink my eyes and shake my head. But she's still here. Off of Ire's back and running towards me. When she's close enough she throws her arms around me, hugging me tight.

I'm not sure what's happening. "I killed you," I manage to say.

She lets go of me, but grabs my shoulders and puts me at arm's length like she's trying to get a proper look. "Why are you pulling out your feathers!"

"Why are you wearing that ugly blue dress?"

We stare at each other for a moment. Unable to move. Like we can't believe this is real. It can't be real. I killed her. She's not here. And if I move, whatever spell is happening or whatever delusion I have cooked up to ease my mind as I find my next ending will stop working. And I won't even have this hallucination to comfort me into the nothing.

But then she laughs. "Oh." And looks down at herself. "I was wearing it when she took me into some spell."

"Who?" I'm shocked. She's real? I'm not hallucinating?

"Pressia!"

"Pressia?" I blink and shake my head again, then look at the almost miniature version of Ire just behind her. When I look back to Callistina I say, "Did you just literally ride in on a white horse and save me?"

She looks over at Ire. "Is he white? Or is he silver?"

I grab her shoulders and shake her. "Callistina, what the hell are you doing here?"

"What do you mean? I was looking for you. Well, that's not entirely true. I figured her out and then I just got put here."

"Who?"

Callistina clicks her tongue at me in annoyance. "Pressia! Who else? She stole me, put me into some kind of spell, and then we went on that trip together."

"Through the doors?" I say.

"Yeah. It wasn't real. It was her and her stupid magic. But you know what? She's wrong about you."

"She is?"

"Yeah. Do you want to know why she's been torturing you for all eternity? It's because she saw you kill her as a baby in the future."

"*What?*"

"Yeah. She traveled through some door and saw you enter her nursery at the Vinca Palace and kill her as a baby."

"Wow. I did that?"

Callistina snorts. "No, you didn't do that. You would *never* do that."

369

Hmmm. I'm kind of impressed with future me.

"I told her that she was wrong. And she's been torturing you, all this time, for something that never happened. *Would never* happen." She says that last part with a lot of emphasis, squeezing my shoulders at the same time.

But again, I'm slightly distracted by future-me's great idea. Kill her in the nursery. I'm a fuckin' genius. Why didn't I think of that earlier? I mean, going back in time is kinda easy, right? How hard would it be to find my way out of this fog and use that door on the hillside to spell my way into Pressia's fuckin' nursery?

"And do you know *why* that would never happen, Eros?" Callistina shakes me a little, so I refocus on her. "It won't ever happen"—she says these words deliberately and carefully—"because if it does, you will *lose me*."

I let out a long breath and fully internalize what's happening here.

In a world without Callistina, I would go into the future and kill baby Pressia. I would not hesitate. I might even smile as I did it.

But I'm not in a world without Callistina. I'm in a world *with* her.

So I take in a new breath and I nod my head as I shrug my shoulders. "You're right. I would *never* do that. Because I would never want to lose you."

And that's the God's. Honest. Truth.

CHAPTER TWENTY-EIGHT -
CALLISTINA

I *know he was thinking about it*. Once that plan of his came out of my mouth, it was done. He *would* do it. I have been thinking about this for a long while as Ire and I trotted through the mist. I have been thinking about Pressia's vision of Eros in her nursery.

An Eros with golden wings walks through a magic door and into Pressia's nursery, kills her, and breaks his curse.

But then I saw him here in the fog, pulling out all his feathers.

If he didn't have feathers, he wouldn't go into the nursery.

And that's how I figured it out.

If he gets those golden wings, then killing Pressia is the only ending there is.

I had kind of resigned myself to this fact as Ire took me through the fog. Come to terms with it. Pressia was right. Eros is kind of a dick. I mean, he's done many bad things.

But with me, on that trip that wasn't real, he did a lot of good things too.

I saw both the god he was and the god he could be.

The man he should be. The one he was meant to be.

And wasn't that part of his curse? *Be the man you know you should?*

I didn't give him an ultimatum. He had already made his choice.

And his choice was me.

I LOOK DOWN *at* the massive pile of golden feathers at our feet. It hurts to look at his mutilated wings, but it gives me a sense of relief as well. I point at the feathers. "What are we going to do with those?"

Eros lets out a breath. "Well. I was gonna use them to forget."

"Forget what?"

"Everything. Just make a clean slate. That's what the Forgetting Time was. Just a clean slate. It takes big, big magic. But golden feathers, they're like..." He sighs. "Like some of the most potent magic ever made."

"I don't think we can leave them here," I say. "They're too powerful."

"Fuck no. And we're not taking them with us, either. We need to use them."

"Use them to do what?"

He looks over at Ire, then down at me. "Well, I think I have enough to put it all back."

"Put what back?"

"You." He smiles. "And Ire too." I'm confused so he explains. "With this many golden feathers, Callistina, I can do pretty much anything. I can give you everything you lost. And Ire, too. Since I was the one who did that to him."

I go to protest here and correct him. Explain a little bit better about how it was just a dream. But he puts up a hand and says, "I would've done it. To him." He nods his head at Ire. "And to you. And I would've killed baby Pressia in that nursery. So I don't want to hear any arguments. I'm going to use every single feather to make the two of you whole again."

I picture myself the way I was. The way I should be. With short, velvety golden fur, and long legs that have hocks and end in paws. Massive golden antlers on my head.

But it's too much. It's a gift that can't be real. So I stop.

"I can do it," Eros says. "Just watch."

And that's what I do. I watch as he sits down and starts sorting his feathers on the ground, putting them into very specific piles. Not by size or color, but some other way that doesn't make sense to me. I could ask him to explain, and he would. I know he would. But I don't want to interrupt him, I just want to do as I'm told. I just want to watch.

There are hundreds of piles all around us by the time he's done. And when he looks at me, his eyes are smiling. "You need a very specific spelling and enough feathers for every single detail." He pans a hand to his piles. "And that's what I've done here."

He stands up and offers me his hand. I take it, stand as well, and he places me in the center of the circle. "Stay right here."

He leaves the circle and walks over to Ire. He has a private conversation with the beast that ends with a snort that must be agreement, because Ire walks towards me, carefully picking his way around the piles of feathers, and stops in the center of the circle right at my shoulder.

Eros follows him, stopping in front of us, looking at us. "Are you ready?"

I don't exactly know what I'm ready for, but I nod yes to encourage him.

Ire gives off a soft snort of affirmation as well.

Then Eros closes his eyes, raises his arms up, pointing his fingers at the nothing sky, and he spells us.

"A god, a queen, a pegásius.
We win, we lose, we can adjust.
But why should we have to live without?
Why should we have to live with doubt?
It doesn't have to be this way.
Stop the game, we don't have to play.
We can go back and be ourselves.
We can live on with the help of spells.

A crown of antlers, like she had.
Soft fur of velvet she was clad.
Fangs, and paws, and leggy hocks
Give her all, turn back the clock.
He's not a horse, nor a steed.
I did this to him, I made him bleed.
Give back the wings and the feathers.
Make him whole, put him together.
I have made the sacrifice.
You cannot say no, you cannot deny.
With this magic we are friends.
Forever more, until the end."

THERE IS a sudden flash of light, blinding and bright. I have to close my eyes because it's so hot, but when it's over, and I open them again, all the feathers are on fire.

And as they burn, I feel the antlers growing back on the top of my head. Every surface of my skin begins to tingle as the soft, golden velvet grows back. And when I look down, the ugly blue dress is burning too. It's not a hot flame, but a cold one. All the threads of the dress begin to move and wiggle and rearrange. And I watch my dress turn into something else.

Chains.

Silver, but not silver.

Godsmetal.

And when it is all done, I can see my paws.

I look up, smiling. And find Eros smiling back at me. He's got wings again. And feathers.

Not golden, but not completely black either. Dark gray at the base but nearly silver near the tip.

I turn and look at Ire, and if a pegásius could smile, he would be smiling.

He is definitely silver, not white. And when his wings spread out, they reach as far as eternity.

I start crying. And Eros pulls me into a hug. "It's OK," he says.

And it is. But I'm crying anyway.

Because this is the happiest moment in my life.

I got what I wanted from the very beginning.

Not antlers, or fur, or hocks, or paws.

I got *them*.

I got *friends*.

EPILOGUE – EROS

We walked out of the fog whole again.

Savage Falls was waiting for us. All the monsters and whatever was left of the humans. No Pressia, though. The bookstore was gone too.

But that's just where the changes started. Because the moment we left the fog, it disappeared. And in its place was a road and a sign on the side of that road that read:

THANK you for visiting Savage Springs. Please come back again.

WE'RE BACK on that road, Callistina and I sitting on Ire's back, his long wings tucked up against his sides and covering our legs. And it feels like we're wrapped up in the softest blanket you could ever imagine.

He's not quite as tall as a house, but he's close. He's magnificent.

But Callistina and I are beautiful enough to stop traffic.

And that's what we do.

We ride down the road and when we get to the highway, we stop and just stand there as cars grind to a halt. Screeching tires as they go off into the ditch.

People start screaming. And running.

Helicopters appear.

People with cameras by the hundreds.

Soldiers too.

And we just stand there. Holding up a sign that reads:

Monsters are real.
Come fall in love with us.
Savage Springs, PA.

END OF BOOK SHIT

elcome to the End of Book Shit, commonly referred to as the EOBS around these parts. This is the part of the book where I get to share my thoughts and feelings about what you just read or listened to. It's never edited and usually very last minute.

MOSTLY I WAS REALLY STRUCK on how many times Callistina took that stupid costume off. I didn't plan that out at all, she just kept doing it. Time and time again. So I was like three quarters of the way through writing it when this dawned on me and all I kept thinking was, Maybe I should take some of those scenes out?

I didn't, obviously. She still takes that costume off five or six times, I think. But the reason I left it in is because in the real world it's very hard to change. We become accustomed to old patterns. They become habits. I mean, have you ever tried to quit smoking? Or to lose weight? Or to go back to college as an adult?

These are big changes and when you make a big change you should expect a lot of failure because change is hard. You have to take that costume off. And then you have to decide again, and again, and again that you still want to take that costume off.

When you quit smoking, you have to replace that old habit with something new. When you diet, it's even harder because you can't just quit food. You have to change everything about what you're eating and how you're eating, and when you're eating. And when you go back to school as an adult you have to relearn how to pay attention, and study, and remember things (probably a lot of useless things that experience tells you don't matter).

The exception to this is, perhaps, is some kind of life-altering experience that shocks you so much that immediate, drastic change is the only way forward.

Like you hear about people having a heart attack or being diagnosed with diabetes or something like that. And this is a crisis moment for them. They either make a drastic change to what they are doing or possibly die.

We're all gonna die, so the threat of death is always there, just hanging out right in front of us. We all know this, but we don't often have to come to terms with it until we're at the very end. A sudden-onset health problem puts death right up in your face and requires a lot of inner reflection.

This is NOT how Callistina experiences her pivotal moment because she lives her life backwards in this book. She sees the end result of Eros's friendship, not the trigger that made him change. It's kind of a weird set up because while he's living life backwards with her, his pivotal moments all happen before he gets to the part where he realizes he's an evil asshole. It's hard to explain—because time travel always is, which is why I hate it so much—but he's actually not living life backwards. He's living forwards. His change comes before he realizes what he did.

He doesn't make a mistake and decide to change. There is no heart attack or diagnosis that gives him the fortitude to turn over a new leaf, so to speak. It's all very gradual and honest and not fueled by guilt.

Which is why his betrayal of Callsitina is so shocking—both to us and himself.

His feelings for Callistina—whether this is love or friendship, it doesn't matter—are genuine by the time he realizes what he's done. Or is about to do, actually. Or planned to do, or didn't plan to do, or whatever it is because it's not very clear if he really would've done that heinous act or not, because again—this is why I hate time travel. Nothing makes sense if you can just go back and forward and change the succession of events, and therefore, the consequences of such events.

This scene with him and Callsitina when he cuts off her antlers to get power is a shock, but it's not the shock that made him change. His change was already complete by the time this act does or doesn't happen.

He's a little bit possessive of Callistina when they go through that first door, but there's no real explanation for it. He just feels the tension in Glory Rome and he understands that this city would hurt her if it got the chance—because this city hurt him.

I think maybe this possessiveness is spurred on by her lack of understanding. She's a child, almost. Enthralled by the big city filled with people she can relate to, even if they are hostile. This is not her world, but it's a lot closer to it than the one she just came from. And that's enough to give her hope. Which is what she was missing back in Savage Falls. It might not be the best way forward, but at least it's better than nothing.

Eros understands this city. He understands that she's in grave danger and that she could be killed at any moment, for any number of reasons, and there would be no legal recourse. This scares him. I think that was his trigger for change. Callistina doesn't have the appropriate level of fear of what's actually going on around her—she's so enamored with her 'new' body, she doesn't care about the threats—so he must be afraid for her.

It's kind of a classic 'bodyguard' trope, almost. But very well hidden inside this dark fantasy about portal magic. I'd like to claim that I set this up this way, but as so often happens, the story comes out and I can only make sense of it after it's over.

By the time they go through the second door he is fully committed to her. She's dying. Except she's not. He knows she's not dying because he's lived the future with her already. Which is another very strange dynamic because it sets up unanswerable questions: Does she survive because he cares for her and nurses her through it? Or would she have survived no matter what?

There is no way to know. There is no way to quantify how important HE is to HER survival. But he did nurse her back and he did take care of her. And this was his hope. But it was only his hope because he made it his hope.

This is why I hate time travel books. All the logical things get mixed up. If he didn't know she would pull through and decided to save her—that's a far more respectable choice than already knowing the outcome and making sure a certain future happens.

I feel like I'm talking in circles, because I am, because time travel is nothing but a loop filled with existential questions that never get answered because what came first? The chicken or the egg?

I think Callistina came first. I think she took her costume off so many times because she was the one who truly learned her lesson and wanted to change. And it was her change that made Eros want to change.

But I don't think Eros has changed. I think he just fell in love. People will do a lot for love, even deny their own evil instincts. Eros never took off a costume. He gave up some feathers to set things right, but he never shed his old self. He just put it away—for now.

AND THIS IS MOST DEFINITELY NOT their happily-ever-after ending. It's just the beginning, actually.

I WILL BE WRITING MORE in this series. Tomas definitely has a book all to himself in the future. We've got a lot of loose ends—Tarq and Nasty Nysta. Plus all the things that will happen now that the world knows that monsters are real and living in PA! Not to mention Jacqueline! And Pie and Pell, of course. Do we like Pressia? I feel like she could be sympathetic, but do I want to make her good or bad? Or both? I'm not sure.

AND WE'VE ONLY BARELY SCRATCHED the surface of all those Damaged Gods.

I WILL CAUTION YOU, though—these PNR books are a side project and I have a lot of other books on my schedule right now. So I probably won't write Tomas's book until spring/summer 2024.

THANK YOU FOR READING, thank you for reviewing, and I'll see you in the next book!

Julie
    JA Huss
    June 29, 2023

ABOUT THE AUTHOR

JA Huss is a New York Times Bestselling author and has been on the USA Today Bestseller's list 21 times. She writes characters with heart, plots with twists, and perfect endings. Her books have sold millions of copies all over the world. Her book, Eighteen, was nominated for a Voice Arts Award and an Audie Award in 2016 and 2017 respectively. Her audiobook, Mr. Perfect, was nominated for a Voice Arts Award in 2017. Her audio-book, Taking Turns, was nominated for an Audie Award in 2018. Her book, Total Exposure, was nominated for a RITA Award in 2019. She lives on a farm in central Colorado with her family.

You can find her at www.jahuss.com